BLUE ON BLUE

D0591706

BLUE ON BLUE

PAUL BENNETT

W RLDWIDE

TORONTO • NEW YORK • LONDON
AMSTERDAM • PARIS • SYDNEY • HAMBURG
STOCKHOLM • ATHENS • TOKYO • MILAN
MADRID • WARSAW • BUDAPEST • AUCKLAND

W**O**RLDWIDE™

Recycling programs
for this product may
not exist in your area.

ISBN-13: 978-1-335-73627-7

Blue on Blue

First published in 2018 by Robert Hale, an imprint of
The Crowood Press Ltd.
Revised text edition published in 2019 by Joffe Books.
This edition published in 2021 with revised text.

Copyright © 2018 by Paul Bennett
Copyright © 2019 by Paul Bennett, revised text edition
Copyright © 2021 by Paul Bennett, revised text edition

This edition published by arrangement with Harlequin Books S.A.

For questions and comments about the quality of this book,
please contact us at CustomerService@Harlequin.com.

Harlequin Enterprises ULC
22 Adelaide St. West, 40th Floor
Toronto, Ontario M5H 4E3, Canada
www.ReaderService.com

Printed in U.S.A.

A NOTE

When it's the police against the police
it's a "Blue on Blue"
and no good ever comes of it.

PROLOGUE

Fifteen years ago

THE CLOCK ON the dashboard blinked red as the digits morphed to 23:30. The driver calculated that, with foot down, just before midnight would be the ETA. There was a chance—a slim one—that maybe everyone would have gone to bed and would be fast asleep at that time. You can but hope.

The driver's head hurt. There was a pounding in the middle of the forehead and a woozy view through the windscreen. Well over the limit. If caught, and at this time of night it was highly unlikely, the driver reckoned to pull some strings, cash in some favours and get out of trouble.

The lightweight boot pressed down hard on the accelerator and the needle moved to seventy miles an hour and the countryside flashed by. A few miles later, the car entered the outskirts of a village. The driver didn't bother slowing down to the 30mph speed limit. A bend to the right came up.

There is that moment when you are driving when you know you have lost it. A seismic chill runs down your spine. The bend was much sharper than he thought. The driver lost it. A yank of the wheel to the right only achieved sending the front wheel across the road to hit the offside kerb. The momentum threw the car across to the other side of the road and couldn't be corrected. The front wheel caught the kerb and mounted it with a thump. The car ran along the kerb, still out of control. Then there were two thuds, one immediately after the other. The driver slew the car to a halt to see what damage had been done.

There were two bodies. A boy and a girl. Both teenagers it looked like. Their hands were intertwined. The boy was dead. His head was crushed. Must have taken the full force from the car's front. The blood was already seeping out of the massive hole that had once been his skull. The driver looked down at the girl. She lay at a grotesque angle. Her spine just had to be broken. She opened her eyes and stared. Green eyes full of questions. 'Why?' they seemed to say. 'Why me? Why now when I had so much to live for? So much that I can no longer experience. You've as good as killed me. Murderer.'

It was a look that would haunt the driver for a lifetime. And so it should.

ONE

I FILLED IN the registration card and handed it to the hotel receptionist. He was aged about thirty, and immaculately dressed in a blue suit. He looked at the card, looked at me and down at the card again. I knew what was coming.

'You're going to ask me a question, aren't you?' I said.

He nodded.

'The answer is yes.'

'Yes?' he said.

'You're going to say "Are you that Nick Shannon? The one that killed his quadriplegic sister and served seven years in prison for murder?"'

He looked surprised. 'Actually,' he said, 'I was going to ask you what newspaper you wanted in the morning.'

You can't win them all. '*The Times*,' I said, turning to go.

'Mr Shannon,' he said. 'If ever I'm in that same position, I hope I would have the courage to do what you did.'

'Thank you,' I said. 'That means a lot.'

He handed me a key card and a piece of paper that meant I could charge things to my room.

'Mr Collins said to meet him in the bar at seven,' he said. 'Your table's booked for 7:30. Enjoy your stay.'

I walked up the stairs to the second floor, opened the door with the card and slipped it in the holder behind the door. The lights and air conditioning came on. I threw my overnight bag on the bed and went to look out the window. I could see the church with its tower and the market square of the town, the last few traders packing up their stalls in preparation to leave. If my memory served me well, there would have been fruit and vegetable stalls, homemade jams and jellies, fifty varieties of bread, beer from microbreweries, rare breed sausages and joints of pork, craft gifts for the tourists and pick-and-mix sweets of garish colours that send kids climbing up the wall. It had been my home town before prison. This was the first time I had come back in all that time. Even a lifetime ago was too soon. Too many memories, the more recent ones bad.

What was Detective Superintendent Collins dragging me back here for? It couldn't be good. He'd just said dinner tonight and a meeting in the morning. It would be a favour of some kind, otherwise he would have told me the details over the phone. He needn't have bothered. I was in his debt—twice he had saved my life—and debts need to be honoured. Everyone should be paid their due.

I turned on the television and navigated through to a news channel. The Home Secretary was on a visit to a local constituency that was due to have a by-election in a fortnight's time because of the unexpected death of its MP. It was the usual routine: tour the streets and shake as many hands, kiss as many babies as possible while trying not to say anything that would upset anyone. Smile and look sympathetic. He was good at it. David Montgomery Yates was perfect for the job. He was photogenic—the ladies always had a soft spot for him like he was their ideal husband—a smooth talker who spoke a lot and said little. He called the interviewer by his first name as if they had known each other since their schooldays. It was so sweet that it was rotting my teeth just listening to him. I walked over to the mini-bar and took out a miniature of vodka and a small can of tonic. There was a glass tumbler on the desk and an ice bucket. It was empty. Thanks, Mr Manager. Good to know you're on the case. I poured the contents of the vodka bottle into the tumbler, added a dash of tonic for the chill it had and drank half of it.

I stripped off, showered and put on clean clothes. It would be wasted on Collins who was the messiest dresser you could meet. His clothes sense always seemed to me as if he had sprayed himself with glue and walked through a wardrobe. Nothing coordinated and everything seemed to get grubby the moment he put them on. Only to be expected. Collins's mission was to catch the bad guys and bring them to justice—even if he had to bend the rules at times—and nothing was permitted to get in the way of that.

I finished the drink before it could get even warmer and walked down to the bar. I was early. Collins was already there as I had known he would be. He was sitting at the long wooden counter on a tall metallic stool with a black leather seat and a whisky on the rocks in front of him. He nodded his head at me and signalled at the young girl behind the bar. He gestured to his glass for a refill and I ordered a vodka, neat with lots of ice to make up for that which I had missed earlier.

I hardly recognized him. He must have had some sort of Damascene moment, a complete transformation. He was wearing a light grey suit devoid of any smears or stains—no cigarette ash, no ketchup spots—recently pressed. His blue-and-yellow striped tie was neatly knotted at the collar of his white shirt. His short ginger hair, streaked with grey, was brushed and shining.

'Good to see you, Nick,' he said.

Bad sign. Whenever he called me by my first name it meant trouble was just around the corner.

'And you,' I said. 'How's the thief business?'

'Too many as usual, but we do our best.'

Collins was head of C squad, one of the three autonomous divisions of the Fraud Squad. His superiors had transferred him there as a place where he could do least harm. Collins hated it. He was an old-fashioned cop with old-fashioned views. Being behind a desk was anathema to him. 'Too much PR and not enough GBH' was his verdict.

The young girl brought the drinks and Collins picked up his whisky and stepped on the thick grey carpet and went to a table by the window that was well out of earshot. The table, like all the rest, was mahogany and tastefully complemented the red velour upholstery of the chairs. It was a room kitted out by an interior designer who had been told not to offend anyone.

Collins sat down and took a large swig from his glass.

'I'm very grateful, Nick,' he said. 'You must have a lot on at the moment what with work and the funeral to arrange. Thanks for coming. And,' he said hesitatingly, 'what can I say? So sorry about Arlene. Life can be a bitch.'

'Don't I know it?' I replied. 'Out with it, Chris. Don't pussyfoot around. It's not your style. What do you want?'

'A favour,' he said.

'I'd guessed that much. Is it work or personal?'

'Both,' he said.

'Then it's going to get complicated.'

'It already is. I have a friend. Name's Sam. Long-time friend. Good cop. We were both at Hendon together doing our training for the Met many, many moons ago. Sam's coming up for retirement and has hit a problem.'

I raised an eyebrow to show interest while I tried to work out what he was going to land on me.

'Sam's been accused of fraud. I want you to investigate and get a not guilty verdict.'

It made sense now. I was a fraud investigator; a forensic accountant was the posher name for what I did for a living. Usually I uncover fraud and bring the perpetrators to justice. Seems like I would be working from the other side for a change.

'Who's my client?' I asked.

'Me,' he said. 'This will be pro bono. That's the favour.'

Norman, my partner, the one who bankrolled the business, was going to love this. He wouldn't understand pro bono if you translated it for him. I wondered how much wriggle-room I had.

'But isn't it a job for the Police Federation?' I said. 'They would usually provide his defence, surely. Isn't that what they do? Look out for the interest of the ordinary police officer? Do what they can for him?'

'It's complicated,' Collins said. 'Some of the money that's missing is Federation funds.'

'Ah!' I said.

'Yes, ah!' he said. 'I told you it was complicated. It's Blue on Blue.'

'It's what?'

'Blue on Blue. The police against the police. That's what we call it. Cop against cop. Nobody likes it. If you're not careful, it blows up in your face.'

'Or in my face.'

'You're a big boy now, Shannon.' What happened to Nick? 'You can take it. Anyway, I thought you'd relish the opportunity to work inside.'

'What? Cops to the left of me, cops to the right and I'm stuck in the middle?'

'This is the Mid Anglia Police we're talking about,' he said. 'Doesn't that ring any bells?'

'Ah…' I said.

'Ah!' he echoed. 'This is the force that covers the area where your sister got mown down by the hit-and-run driver. Whichever way we've approached the case, we've run into a brick wall. We know there was a boot print at the site and we only know that by getting the un-expurgated forensic report—a boot print that someone doesn't want seen. And why? Because it's the type of boot that the police wear. Not any old policeman, mind. A boot that is issued only to Special Branch or a fully-trained Firearms Officer. This is the best chance you'll ever have to dig around. You know it makes sense.'

He gave me a wide smile and took a pull on his drink.

I merely sipped from mine while my brain was work-ing overtime. Collins was right, infuriatingly. He was a Detective Chief Inspector when he had drawn a blank trying to get access to the file on the hit-and-run. When official channels had failed to come up with the goods, he had pulled every favour he could and still couldn't get within a sniff of the truth. Someone wanted the file buried, and buried deep. Here was my chance to find out why.

'I'll do it,' I said, 'though I don't know how I'm going to square it with Norman. Pro bono is not his style.'

'Hell,' Collins said, 'Norman will find a way to make money out of it. He always does. I've always turned a blind eye in the past because he only steals from thieves. He owes me like you do.' He downed his drink. 'Let's go and eat. And give the good news to the innocent.'

'Innocent till proven guilty,' I said.

'For the first time in my career I agree with the sentiment. Just as long as it doesn't become a habit.'

TWO

THE DÉCOR IN the dining room continued the wood and red velour style of the bar, which wasn't to its advantage or that of its clientele. I found myself longing for something beige to liven it up. The room felt cold and underappreciated, as witnessed by the paucity of diners. Still, maybe they were all going to pile in like the French at eight o'clock precisely. It was giving me bad vibes about the food, though.

At a rectangular table for four in a corner sat a woman in her fifties. She stood up as we entered. Just under six foot was my guess at her height. Slim build. She was wearing a black trouser suit over a cream blouse, finished off with a gold necklace and bracelet, elegant and not ostentatious. Her auburn hair was cut in a no-nonsense bob and framed her pretty face. So this was Sam—the reason for Collins's metamorphosis. They hugged each other in greeting and Collins pecked her on the cheek, a little longer than was necessary for the politeness of the greeting, I thought.

'Inspector Samantha Stone,' she said to me. 'But call me Sam. And you must be Nick Shannon. I really can't thank you enough. Chris has told me all about you.'

'And you're still pleased to see me?'

She gave me a puzzled look.

'Ignore him,' said Collins. 'He likes to play the wise

guy. Can be a pain in the butt sometimes. But he's perfect for this job.'

I nodded acknowledgement and we all sat down.
A waitress handed us some leather-bound menus and
asked what we would like to drink. Collins, to my surprise, ordered a mineral water—this really was best
behaviour. Sam had a spritzer and I had a glass of red
wine, my limit for the evening if I was going to stay
focused on the job in hand.

I examined Sam more closely. There were lines
under her eyes, but they were laughter lines. She had
a good sense of humour, I reckoned. Her lipstick was
a pale red and her make-up had been expertly applied.
An eye for fine detail, it said to me. A whiff of scent
told me nothing except she liked the smell of wild flowers. All the signs were encouraging. If you're going to
spend a lot of time with someone defending them, it's
good to like them.

'Let's order and get down to business,' Collins said.
'Nick needs an early night if he's to shine at his nine
o'clock meeting with the Chief Constable.'

'What?' I said.

'That was the other reason for dragging you up here.
The Chief Constable insists on meeting you before permitting you to defend Sam. Without his imprimatur…'
Imprimatur? This was an entirely different man to the
one I was used to. She was having a profound effect
on him. '…you're going to get nowhere. He's covering
his back, of course, but you need his approval to dig
around in the files. I'll tell you more of what to expect
later, but basically sweet-talk him.'

We ordered some food, all of us playing safe with

simple things—steak for Collins, Dover sole for Sam and rack of lamb for me. I sipped some wine and started the interrogation.

'What do you do, Sam?' I asked. 'How did you get access to the money and how much are you supposed to have stolen?'

'I've been a detective for a long while now. Always on the front line, never dodging the responsibilities that go with the job. I like being in the thick of it. I transferred up here from the Met twenty years ago when the area was called Essex Police—before the amalgamation took place. I like it here. It's small towns and villages, countryside, fresh air—a good place to settle down and have a family. The kids have flown the nest now. Husband was a teacher, but he passed away six months ago.'

'I'm sorry to hear that,' I said, understanding her sorrow.

'Nick's partner died almost a fortnight ago,' Collins said, 'so he's not just being polite. He's waiting on the daughter coming over from America before having the funeral.'

'So you won't have had any form of closure yet,' she said. 'You're going to have a hard time. I'm still not used to being on my own again.'

'What Sam hasn't told you about her career,' Collins said, 'is that she's been commended twice. Courage beyond the call of duty in two different armed robberies. Sam was a Firearms Officer. Crack shot. Killed two men.'

'But one of them got me in the right leg with a blast from his shotgun. The doctors had to piece me back together before I could walk again. Still got a limp and can't wear stilettos on my size seven police officer's feet. Small price to pay for being alive, I suppose.'

'The money,' I said. 'Tell me about the money.'

She shook her head. 'I still can't believe it. After the second shooting incident it seemed like I should get out of the firing line. Vacancy came up for treasurer of the Police Federation for the Force. Got myself elected by the Joint Branch Board—eleven people from each rank: constables, sergeants and inspectors. Bit of a formality, really—no one stood against me. I had a good reputation and nobody else felt they could challenge that. Seemed like the right job at the time. Coming up for retirement, spend a couple of years before then doing good for the ordinary copper.'

'And then something went wrong,' I prompted.

'Half a million,' she said. 'Half a million pounds went wrong. The money went missing and some of it finished up in my bank account.'

'How does an operation like the Federation end up with that sort of money?' I asked.

'Easy,' she said. 'The Federation had been frugal in the past. Built up a cash stockpile. Money for a rainy day and to buy larger premises. We don't get funding from the police, just money from subscriptions and commission on purchases by our officers—mobile phones, cars and so on. Every officer pays over twenty pounds a month in subscriptions—new officers about half that. Think of the five thousand or so officers in Mid Anglia. Do the maths.'

'Five thousand times twenty pounds times twelve months equals around £1.2 million a year. What was left after the half million went missing?'

'Not much,' Sam said. 'Pretty much cleared out the current and deposit accounts. I'm not very popular with my colleagues at the moment. If you steal from your fellow officers—or appear to have done so—you don't get any sympathy. If I stepped across the threshold of HQ, it would be like walking around with a target painted on my back. My name stinks. My good reputation is shot.'

'Imagine what it's like for Sam,' Collins said. 'No one talks to her and those that do use four-letter words. It's money supposed to be used for the benefit of the ordinary police officer. It's like stealing the Christmas fund.'

'How much of the half million finished up in your account?' I asked her.

'Just £25,000. Enough to frame me and leave the majority for whoever is doing the framing.'

'Crude, but effective,' I said. 'I'm going to need a lot of details. Can I come and see you after I meet the Chief Constable tomorrow?'

'Sure,' she said with a shrug of her shoulders. 'I'm suspended so I have plenty of time on my hands.'

She took out a notebook, wrote her address on a page, tore it out and passed it to me.

'It's about five miles out of town. Won't take you more than ten minutes from HQ.'

I took a business card from my wallet and handed it across the table to her. 'Phone me any time,' I said. 'I've got some time on my hands, too.'

Our meal arrived and we sat quietly eating for a while, pretending to enjoy overdone and bitty food.

'What's the normal procedure,' I said to Sam, swallowing a mouthful of fatty lamb, 'if an officer is accused of a crime? What would the Federation do?'

'The matter would be investigated by CID like any ordinary crime and the Federation would be there to represent the interests of the accused officer. You would get put on "restricted duties"—filing and the like—if it was a petty crime and suspended like me if gross misconduct. They'd also provide access to a solicitor. My case is awkward. They felt it best to leave me unsupported, effectively washing their hands of me.'

'I'll get a solicitor for you. I know a good man. He'll look after you. We need to make sure the procedures are followed and you get a fair crack of the whip. Get any paperwork you have ready for me when I come tomorrow. Official letters and communications and then all your bank accounts going back to when you were appointed as treasurer. You can trust me—I won't blab and I won't make any judgements. How much time do we have?'

'The first hearing of the case is in a week's time.'

'Good,' I said. 'It gives me some time to start digging around in the files.'

Collins looked at me and raised an eyebrow.

'And to start going through the computerized accounts—they are computerized, I presume?'

'When Mid Anglia was formed, it was given the state of the art technology. This was an experiment that the government didn't want to fail.'

'What was the rationale behind Mid Anglia?' I asked.

Collins gave a snort.

'Do you want the official version or the real reason?' he said.

'Better give me both,' I said.

'Mid Anglia was formed by amalgamating Essex Police and Suffolk Police plus the eastern districts of the Met. It was supposed to be about economies of scale, maximizing budgets and minimizing costs, saving on the backroom staff. More money for bobbies on the beat.'

'And?' I said.

'It was all about the Met,' he said. 'The powers that be had reached the conclusion that the Met was institutionalized racist. They thought it was too big a job to cure if they tackled the whole Met, so they carved it into pieces and spread the problem around in forces like Mid Anglia. Left the Met basically a small force focused on the City of London. Cut its balls off.' He turned to Sam. 'Pardon my French,' he said, 'but Shannon might as well know the whole truth.'

'So it was a case of expediency rather than efficiency,' I said. 'How do the troops feel about that?'

'That we've been lumbered,' Sam said. 'We're the scapegoat when it fails to work, as it surely must. The cultures are too different. It's like mixing oil and water.'

'But which is the oil that will rise to the top?'

The waitress walked up to clear the table and ask us how it had been. We lied, as the British so often do, and ordered coffee with few expectations. We broke off into an uneasy silence until it had arrived and been poured. I added sugar, passed on milk and took a sip. It was OK, would have been excellent at double the strength.

'But the fraud didn't stop at the Federation,' Collins said. 'There are police funds missing, too.'

'Apparently,' she said, 'I am supposed to have raided the main reserve account for another half a million—

all that was in there. How I am supposed to have got access to it no one knows, but everyone assumes I did. Once a thief, twice a thief is the theory.'

'How much did that account have in it?' I asked.

'I don't have an exact figure, but half a million was pretty much the lot. Same pattern, though. Twenty-five thousand pops up in my account. Damning evidence.'

'Two things strike me immediately,' I said. 'Why the round sums? Why not just take the lot rather than a round half a million?'

'And?' Sam said.

'I haven't a clue,' I admitted. 'Not yet, at least.'

'Are you going to be more helpful on the second question?' Collins asked.

I ignored the question since I didn't have an answer.

'Any reason,' I said to Sam, 'and no offence on my part, that they would think you're dumb enough not to spirit the whole lot away rather than putting a minority into your own bank account?'

'Hold on,' said Collins, almost spluttering on his coffee. 'I resent that on Sam's part.'

'It's all right, Chris,' Sam said. 'It is a pretty stupid thing to do. Whoever is behind it must have thought that credence would be given to the deed. I've never been very good with my own personal money, Nick, but that only extends to running out a couple of days before my meagre salary hits the bank. Handling the Federation funds is different, because it's not my money and I can budget more easily.'

'Well?' asked Collins. 'What's your immediate reaction now that you know the facts?'

'Know some of the facts,' I corrected.

Collins gave an inconsequential shrug.

'Bear in mind,' I said, 'that it's always harder to prove a negative—that you haven't done something. The perpetrator had two objectives: steal the money and frame Sam at the same time. Tomorrow, Sam, I want to look at who has a grievance against you, approach the problem from two directions.' I turned my attention to Collins. 'I'll work flat out on this. Try every angle. Just accept that as a fact and don't be on my back all the time wanting progress reports.'

'OK,' he said. 'How do you feel, Sam?'

She thought long and hard about the question and gave an involuntary shudder.

'Do you know what they would do to me in prison?' Sam said. 'Do you know what they would do with a police officer?'

'Yes,' I said. 'I've been there and seen it. You'd be lucky to come out alive, and if you did, you wouldn't be the same person who went in. Have faith, Sam. I won't condemn you to that.'

She stretched across the table and placed her hand on mine.

'I'm not an emotional woman,' she said. 'I've been trained not to be. But this is personal. Someone's out to get me. Stop them, Nick. Or I think I might just fold. There's not much to live for without the job. I joined the police with one aim. Stop bad people doing bad things to good people. There's nothing much to live for without that.'

She stood up, kissed Collins on the cheek and limped out before the tears came. Just.

'Well?' said Collins.

'It's not subtle,' I said, 'but that's often the best method for fraud. Fraud is easy to commit—it's the getting away with it that's the problem. Whoever did this has made life easy for themselves by immediately framing somebody else. Quite clever when you think about it.'

'Well?' he repeated.

'I'll do the best I can,' I said. 'I'll follow the money trail. Sooner or later the money trail has to stop. The money will have to go into an account where the fraudster can spend it. We can only hope that that has some sort of identifier.'

'And the chances of that?'

'Slim. Too many banks willing to hide secret accounts. Do you know what hubris is?'

'Enlighten me.'

'It's the sin of pride. Believing you're better than the gods. We can only rely on the fraudster to get overconfident and slip up somewhere. Then we become their nemesis—their punishment.'

'Amen,' said Collins.

'Amen, brother. Amen to that.'

I SAT THERE for a while after Collins had left, nursing the last of my red wine and thinking over the problem that he had put before me. I hoped I could prove Sam was innocent to repay Collins for his help in the past, but I doubted it. Whoever had embezzled the funds had shown himself or herself to be very clever by appearing to be very dumb. I felt like Holmes facing Moriarty. Intellectually, had I met my match? If so, I had to make the best of this opportunity in terms of digging around in the archives and seeing what evidence I could find on the hit-and-run.

I shook my head, drained my glass and walked out of the dining room. As I did so, someone reading a newspaper in the bar looked over the top of it.

'I thought you were never going to finish,' Walker said.

'What are you doing here?' I said.

'So I could buy you a drink. Vodka, isn't it?' She signalled the girl behind the bar and gestured for me to sit down on one of the chairs.

'You still haven't answered my question.'

She smiled at me. It was impossible to get mad at Walker. She was so beautiful it was disarming. Her skin was the colour of creamy coffee, her eyes black as ebony, her hair long and dark, her lips like cherries, which was appropriate since her first name was Cherry, although it was rarely used since she never slipped from formal.

'Someone has to keep an eye on my superintendent or he will self-destruct. He's skating on thin ice with this case. Three squads in the Fraud Squad so that means a one in three chance of the case landing on Collins's desk. He couldn't take it, so that means it would fall to me. I need to get a heads up on what's going to happen. Where do you fit in, Shannon?'

Walker and I had history and that made our current relationship somewhat awkward. We'd had a brief fling during the time when Arlene was back in the States under pressure from her daughter Mary Jo to finish with me. Walker was at a low point in her life—promotion passing her by—and we just gravitated towards

each other. I took a sip of my vodka to help me come
back to the present.

'I've agreed to get evidence to prove Sam's innocence.'

'So we could be on opposite sides of the fence,' she
said with a certain amount of relish.

'Again.'

'Again,' she echoed.

'Any way we can keep this civilized?'

'I doubt it, but at least we should try.'

'I think the odds favour you,' I said. 'Not seen such
a ham-fisted fraud before. Unless it's a frame up, the
case is iron tight. That's the only line I can take. Try to
prove that someone else did it and is trying to put the
blame on Sam.'

'And how are you going to do that?' she said hopefully.

'I couldn't possibly say,' I said, keeping my counsel.

'Be something sneaky, though,' she said.

'The words pot and kettle leap to mind.'

'I've known you a long time, Shannon. Sneaky is
your trade mark.'

'The words thief, set and catch leap to mind now.'

She shook her head. 'I'll beat you, Shannon. You
can't out-sneaky me. I wouldn't have got where I am
without an element of sneaky.'

'Detective Chief Inspector. And that's not good
enough, is it? If Collins crashes and burns on this one,
out he goes and there's a vacancy for a superintendent.
I bet you'll pull every string you can to get this case.'
She gave me that smile again and I was close to melting.
'How did you know about this meeting by the way?'

'Collins's office is by the water cooler. He tends to leave his door open.'

'And you get very thirsty.'

'On the button, Shannon.'

'If you've got a weakness, Walker, it's that you're too predictable. I won't fail to exploit that if necessary.'

'Then the game is on.'

'Let it roll.'

THREE

IT WAS TYPICAL January weather—a light drizzle, a chill wind and patchy sun doing its best to break through the cloud with little success. Trouble was it was April. I paid the hotel bill and drove outside of Melchester town with the wipers on intermittent and the intention to find somewhere different to stay when I was working here on a more permanent basis. The breakfast had been disappointing—plenty of choice, but only of food cooked two hours earlier and kept warm since then. I was not in the best mood for a meeting with someone who, I guessed, would lord it over me and make me beg for each request I made. Welcome to Mid Anglia.

While the police station and its 'bobbies on the beat' was close to the high street in the town, the headquarters was a couple of miles out on a business park. I spotted the building easily. You couldn't miss it. It was a seven-floor monolith of solar-protected glass, the kind of solid block they looked at in wonder in *2001: A Space Odyssey*. the kind you can see out of, but not into. It made me wonder what they had to hide.

I parked the Beamer in a space marked *Visitor* which made me feel like an alien. My car was a silver M3, but I had asked a very perplexed garage to remove all the signifiers and replace them with a badge from a 318, so that the car looked far less interesting. It was partly for security—an ordinary Beamer is much less of an attraction for car thieves than the eminently saleable M3—and partly due to a personality defect that meant I always wanted something up my sleeve. The 3-litre engine gave the car a top speed of 156mph and a 0-62 speed of 4.3 seconds. Pretty much nothing on the road could touch it. It was a wolf in sheep's clothing. It wasn't ever going to win any fuel consumption prizes, but it made me feel safe and prepared—I could outrun anybody in this and one day that may save my life. Look on the bright side, plan for the dark side—that was one of my many mottos, some much too superstitious to admit.

I gathered my briefcase, slipped on my raincoat and walked to the revolving front door of the building. I entered and stopped dead in my tracks. I couldn't believe my eyes. In the very middle of the downstairs area, there was a round desk of pure white where three young ladies and one man, all dressed smartly, sat at an array of eight terminals between them and with welcoming smiles on their faces. Surrounding this reception area, if you could truly call it that, was a conversation pit: a circular area like a Roman colosseum stepped to various levels and covered in dark grey shaggy-pile carpet. It was the sixties brought back to life on a grand scale. People were dotted around having meetings or simply reading reports. I walked up to one of the attractive young ladies whose tag told me her name was Jacquie and announced my name and destination. She checked my details on one of her screens, looked up at me and gave a knowing smile.

'It's your first time here, isn't it? ' she said. 'It always gets that reaction on someone's first visit. Different, huh?'

'Very,' I said. 'Absolutely remarkable.'

'It's not all totally original,' she said. 'The conversation pit is copied from the DTAC offices in Bangkok, the rest from other buildings around the world. I can give you a booklet to study, if you like. There's a map inside showing all the facilities and where they're located.'

She passed me a glossy booklet and flicked through it, pointing at various features.

'You'll find the staff restaurant on the top floor,' she said, 'together with an outside work area and a putting lawn.'

'Putting lawn?'

'We have an area for table tennis and for pool—that's the snooker thing, not swimming. Now *that* would be crazy.'

'Amazing,' I said, still reeling from the vision around me.

'I'll need to take a print of your right index finger. If you could press on that screen, please.'

'What's this for?' I said, obeying her instruction.

'To enter any floor, to use in the restaurant, to gain entry to certain areas such as meeting rooms, you'll need to swipe a card and confirm it with your fingerprint.'

She ran a card through a slot on the terminal and handed it to me, together with a lanyard in which to put it. 'There are terminals to my right where you can charge your card with money to spend in the restaurant or coffee areas. Lockers—the computer has allocated

you number 404—are to my left. All your possessions
must be locked away. It keeps crime at bay and we
would look pretty stupid if we suffered from theft. Not
a good advertisement for the police, eh? Someone will
be down shortly to collect you. Have a seat and, oh,
have a nice day.'

That wasn't going to be possible, but I liked her
chirpy manner and friendliness and appreciated her
intention to settle me in.

I walked over to the machine that put cash on your
card and charged it up with twenty pounds from my
debit card. I pressed my finger on a pad on locker 404
and put my valuables, together with my raincoat, inside.
Still carrying my briefcase, I drifted across the carpet
and sat down on one of the steps of the conversation
pit. It felt awkward. The desire to create such a relaxed
and informal mood clashed with who I was going to
see and the serious nature of my business. I opened the
brochure and started to read. There wasn't much text
apart from explaining the philosophy that was behind
the futuristic design. This was the office of the future,
cultivating creativity and flexibility where a choice of
working modes could be made by each individual to suit
their own personal style. Pictures there were a plenty. I
couldn't wait to see it all in the flesh.

A woman interrupted my thoughts by saying my
name in a soft Scottish burr, well enunciated—Edinburgh, I reckoned. She was in her fifties, had brown
hair cut short and sensible black low-heeled shoes. A
model of efficiency. Just the sort to have been chosen
by a jealous wife.

'Mr Shannon,' she said again, extending her hand.

'I'm Ms McClellan, the CC's personal assistant. If you would like to follow me, I'll take you to see the Chief Constable. He's a busy man and doesn't like to be kept waiting. He's allocated you half an hour, which is most rare.'

'I'm flattered,' I said.

'You shouldn't be. Needs must. This is all very delicate. I'm to be your chaperone while you are here. Anything you need or want, you go through me. Do I make myself clear?'

'Perfectly,' I said. Stick to the rules that would be laid down and don't make waves. 'So what do we do, ascend on a jet pack?'

She frowned. 'You're going to have to get into the spirit of this building if you're going to fit in here. We have lifts, escalators and rather conventional sets of stairs.'

'I'll take the escalator, if that's OK by you.' I have a problem with lifts, but now isn't the time to go into that. I try to put prison behind me wherever possible, but there are some things that are a constant reminder.

Ms McClellan led me to a set of escalators in the far corner of the room and we worked our way up to the sixth floor. I would have put a bet on the top floor for the big boss, but maybe that had a football pitch alongside the staff restaurant. No, it would be a baseball diamond. Much more trendy.

When we finally stepped off the escalator, another world of wonder lay before my eyes. I'd been to many open-plan offices in the past, but this took the concept to the limit. There were no partitions, no physical separation between the desks, no boundaries set out between the workers or territories claimed. The central space in the floor was taken up by desks in white laminate—not very practical, I would have thought, but then again, who am I to judge? I know what I like and I like what I know.

Working our way outwards there were high tables and bar stools or even higher tables with only space to stand. At the outer edges were glass cubicles designed to be used for meetings or for the most senior officers and which provided some degree of privacy from eavesdropping, but none from onlookers. The Chief Constable's office was in one of these. I didn't envy him.

He was standing alongside a white desk which was devoid of paperwork or any visible computer terminals, only a small trendy tablet. He was grey haired and tall, which is perhaps par for the course for a policeman, and bedecked—there is no other word for it—in a deep black uniform with silver buttons and adorned by badges on the left lapel and a row of cloth medal bars on his left breast. There was a chain coming from his top buttonhole, purely for show, and might have contained a whistle at some time in the past. It was impressive, exactly as intended. And, I guessed, he loved it.

Underneath his brown eyes was a distinct lack of laughter lines; his forehead was ridged from a lifetime of frowns. He was not going to be a bundle of fun, that was for sure. He held out his hand and shook mine vigorously—it was like trying to keep hold of a wet fish. I wanted to rub my hand down my trousers to dry it, but politeness forbade it. Everything told me we would not click, but that wouldn't be the first time. Maybe that said more about me than him.

'Sit down, Shannon,' he said, motioning to a plain white chair in front of his desk. He walked round and sat down opposite me. He pressed a button and a video screen glowed from out of the desktop. He consulted it for a moment and then looked at me. 'Michael Henderson,' he said with long Suffolk vowels—country boy made good—'but I'd rather you called me sir. So, what do you think of us so far?'

It was a challenge to see how I would react and whether I could suppress my honesty. I needed to choose my words well as this would set the tone for the meeting.

'Spectacular,' I said. 'I have truly never seen anything like these offices.'

I hoped he wouldn't ask for too many details at this stage.

'Good,' he said. 'I'd thought you would say that. Coffee?'

'That would be welcome,' I said.

Ms McClellan, who was still standing in the doorway, turned around and set off on her errand. Sexual stereotyping not quite eradicated, I thought, no matter how futuristic the offices.

Now I was assured of a coffee, I could open up a little more.

'Although,' I said, 'I'm not sure that the taxpayer would approve of some of the expenditure. How do you justify a putting green and games area?'

'You need some background, Shannon. Background on the Mid Anglia force and on this building, although they are interlinked.'

I took out a notepad from my briefcase and sat there, pen poised, for the words of wisdom.

'Mid Anglia is the force of the future. We are a test-bed for everything that is to come. In the past, when we were Essex, we were used for the trial of Number Plate Readers and for the Taser. This is the big one. Now we cast off the shackles of the past and stride confidently through the twenty-first century like a golden arrow to point other forces along the path to a new dawn of creative policing.'

God, he was pompous. Everything he said needed to be decoded and wasn't worth it when you'd done so. And as for creative policing, I thought that only occurred when CID made up confessions.

'Still seems a lot of money,' I said, not to be browbeaten.

He gave a long sigh. Must have heard the same comment many times before.

'What you have to understand, Shannon,' he said, 'is that Mid Anglia is an experiment too big to fail. The government has decided this is the way to go and will pour resources into it so it shines like a beacon for what is best for all other forces. There is no turning back from here. Everything we do here will pay off, because the opposite is unthinkable.'

Ms McClellan entered with a tray containing a stainless steel thermos of coffee, two china cups, a jug of cream, sugar and a plate of chocolate digestives for the self-indulgent—not exactly cutting edge, but maybe it was part of the perks of the job, being allowed a little touch of individuality. She poured two cups and left us to make them to our taste. I added sugar, but no cream.

I would have preferred espresso, but that didn't seem an option.

Henderson took a sip of his creamy coffee and gave a little self-satisfied sigh. He was a bad judge of coffee. Too little taste, which in this blend was a distinct advantage, I suppose.

'Stone,' he said, getting to the point in hand. 'Shame. She was what the old brigade called "a good copper".'

'You're talking of her in the past tense,' I said.

'There doesn't seem much chance she's innocent. Open and shut case. You can dig around all you want, but it won't make any difference. So close to retirement, too. What a way to end a career.'

'Let's talk about me digging around as much as I want.'

'I meant what I said. Ask Ms McClellan anything and she'll set it up.'

'I'd like to broaden the scope of my investigations,' I said. 'I'm doing this defence of Sam pro bono at the moment, but I have a deal for you: one that may benefit both of us. Let me look at all your systems and pay me ten per cent of any fraud I find. Plus, of course, the same ten per cent of the money recovered from the half a million stolen. Call it a finder's fee. How confident are you that I will give you a clean bill of health and get your money back?'

It was a direct challenge. Could he lose face by turning my offer down? I didn't think so.

'Like I said, dig around as much as you like—you'll find that we're as clean as a whistle. Apart from Stone, that is. Still, one rotten apple is a danger to all; it has to be disposed of before it can contaminate the rest of the barrel. Now,' he said. 'How long do you think you will be here? You are obviously going to disrupt our normal efficient running—do I need to say as little as possible and for as short a time as possible?'

'You'll hardly notice I'm here,' I said. Especially if I could hide myself away somewhere and dig around in any old files on the hit-and-run. But where could one hide away when all around is glass?

'Right,' he said, not caring whether I had finished my coffee or not. He looked at his watch. The audience was over. But then he didn't know me.

'Why do you think she did it?' I asked.

'What?' he said.

'Why do you think Sam Stone stole that much money? She didn't seem the sort of person who would need a lavish lifestyle. And then she must have known that she could be found out. If she stole the money, then why did she stick around? It doesn't make sense.'

'The criminal mind is a strange beast,' he said. 'Trust me on that one. Years of experience have taught me that criminals don't act logically. If they did, then crimes would go undetected and no one would be sent to prison. Now…'

'But she's had years of experience, too,' I persisted. 'As you said yourself, she's coming up for retirement and, I imagine, would be due a handsome police pension. She had no need to steal the money at this time. If she fancied living somewhere sunny and far away, why didn't she put everything into a new account and then take flight? Why put two tranches of £25,000 in the first place people would look—her current bank account? My guess is that she's been framed.'

'Well, you would say that, wouldn't you? It's your job to say that. But the evidence is overwhelming. There's nothing you can say to change my mind. She did it. She must be made an example of. Justice not only must be done, but must be seen to be done. Punishment, as harsh as is permitted, must be meted out. Now…'

'Did you like her?' I asked.

'I don't see that that is relevant,' he said testily. 'I have thousands of people—police and civilian staff—under me. I can't be expected to like all of them. My relationship with Ms Stone has no relevance.'

'So you didn't like her,' I pressed.

'If you must know,' he said, 'she was a prime example of the old-style copper. Police like Stone are, luckily, a dying breed. Look around you. The world has moved on. We're computerized to the maximum. Everyone here has an especially-customized tablet—we don't use notebooks anymore—and we don't go around calling the boss "Guv", shouting "Go, go, go", having car chases or beating up suspects.'

'Is that what you thought Stone was like? What was her disciplinary record?'

'I really don't see why this is relevant,' he said.

I felt I had him on the rack. He was squirming.

'Just trying to get to know her more. How other people regarded her. Obviously, your opinion is the one that matters the most. Was she disciplined for any offences or acts of misconduct?'

'Nothing on her record.'

'That sounds like there's a but to come.'

'It was just her attitude.' His voice had moved up a pitch. I had finally touched a nerve. 'She was verging on the insubordinate at times. Nothing that you could put your finger on.'

'So you didn't like her.'

'No, I didn't like her,' he shouted. 'Satisfied now?'

'Guess it's time to see Ms McClellan,' I said.

'Guess it is,' he replied with a barely suppressed sigh.

I backed out of the room so I didn't have to shake hands with him again.

'Many thanks,' I said. 'It's been most illuminating.'

I quietly closed the glass door behind me before he could get up and slam it shut.

Ms McClellan was nowhere to be seen, providing me with a perfect excuse to start snooping. I roved into the centre of the floor and looked over people's shoulders while they worked. Yes, there were tablets around, but people were also making notes on scraps of paper. No one was willing to be seen as a Luddite, so they wrote like they were taking an exam at school, arms covering the movements of their pen hands. It would be interesting to see how many of the staff shared Henderson's view on the future of the force. Time would tell.

'Can I help you, Mr Shannon?' came a Scottish trill behind me.

I turned around and there she was.

'I think it's time you started to call me Nick,' I said to the redoubtable Ms McClellan. 'I'm going to be here a while and, seeing as you will be my chaperone, we're going to be working pretty closely together. I'm bound to get in the way and wind you up with endless questions—I always do. There's nothing I can do about that. But my intentions are good—they always are. There's nothing I can do about that either. Morals drummed into me from an early age. You'll find, hopefully, that I'm not a bad guy. Let's be friends. Now call me Nick.'

I extended my hand in peace. And she took it.

'Morag,' she said. 'Please call me Morag.'

'Well, Morag. Is there anywhere a person can get an espresso?'

'Follow me,' she said. 'Lift or stairs?'

'Stairs.'

She led me to the stairs and we walked up a flight to the next floor. As we stepped through the door, a whole range of stimuli attacked my senses. The lights were too bright. OK, it was a restaurant and they wanted to maximize the capacity so it was an eat-up-and-move-on environment, but this wouldn't help someone to relax during what I suspected was a limited break. Then it was the smell—or rather a confused range of aromas. I could detect curry certainly—chicken tikka masala, if I wasn't mistaken—and the warm vinegar smell of sweet and sour, probably pork, but overlaid was the whiff of today's fish special—God knows what it was. On top of all that, there was sound being piped through speakers arranged all around the room. It was music of some sort—second-rate songs sung by third-rate musicians. The place was nearly empty and I didn't blame those that opted not to bother. I wanted to turn around and leave, but I had got this far and there was the pipe of peace to be smoked with Morag.

The restaurant was arranged in sections and it all started to fit into place. There were several serving stations with themed menus. The Indian, Chinese and fish that I could smell, plus a sandwich/wrap/ciabatta stall with a range of fillings in a chilled display case. We headed to an area near the till where a large woman in a black apron was acting as barista. I asked for a double espresso and Morag chose a cappuccino with cream and dusted chocolate. 'My weakness,' she admitted as we waited for our order to appear. When it arrived, I asked Morag to show me how to use the system—it turned out to be remarkably smooth: swipe the card, put your finger on some sort of reader device. We took our coffees to a white plastic, window table where we could look out at the people down below and feel superior.

'Let me first make it clear, Mr Shannon—er, Nick—that just because we are sharing a coffee doesn't mean I will compromise my loyalty to the CC.'

'Understood, Morag. The thought never crossed my mind.'

'He's not as bad as he seems,' she said. 'Did he tell you to call him sir?'

I nodded.

'He really is a sir. He was knighted two years ago. I know he comes across as a bit pompous, but he's not so bad once you get to know him.'

'I'll take your word for that,' I said. 'So tell me about Morag McClellan.'

'Not much to tell. I live on my own—my husband died five years ago—with two cats as company. Pretty boring really.'

'Well, accountants aren't exactly famous for being riveting company. But I specialize in fraud and you'd be surprised by some of the stories I could tell you.'

'Ah, fraud,' she said. She skimmed a layer of cream from her coffee and looked at me while she spooned it into her mouth. 'I liked Sam a lot. I hope you manage to find some way of getting her off the hook.'

'Together, Morag, who knows. But like you, I hope so too. She seems like a good person.'

'She was.'

'You're doing it, too. You talk about her as if she is in the past and dead and gone. I believe someone has framed her and I'm going to find out and clear her name.'

'I'll help as much as I can. When can you start?'

'Not till Monday. I have a lot to sort out over the next few days.'

'I'll have everything ready for you.'

'Thank you, Morag,' I said, finishing my espresso. 'See you Monday?'

I SHOOK HER hand and headed for the escalator so as to get a second look at the other floors. They hadn't improved. Everything looked so manufactured that it made the employees seem like robots working away unthinking on repetitive tasks. It was a production line. I wondered how these people switched off when they got home in the evenings. Kick the cat and stroke the wife or vice versa?

Outside the wind was swirling and, with a vortex created by the height of the building, it blew me back to my car.

I climbed in, took out Sam's piece of paper and pro-grammed her address into the sat nav. It was a part of Melchester, the county town of the new Mid Anglia region, that hadn't existed when I had lived here. I drove through a large sprawling housing estate and its associated infrastructure—school, playground, doctor's surgery, small parade of shops and a post office. Sam's house was a two-storey detached in a nineties style compatible with the rest of the development. Understated might be the best word to describe it, always assuming it was better inside than out. I parked the Beamer on the driveway behind an ageing Fiesta and walked up the path to her front door. I rang the bell and waited. Maybe I should have phoned first, but she had said anytime.

The door opened and Sam stood there in jeans and a sweatshirt. Her hair was swept back and tied with a frilly black band. It looked as if I had interrupted some menial task like assembling flat-packed furniture or making marmalade, neither of which I had ever mastered.

'Nick,' she said. 'I'd forgotten you were going to drop in. Excuse my state. I've just been rummaging around in the loft.'

'I can come back another time, if it's inconvenient,' I said.

'No, no. I'm just about finished. Come in.'

She led me into a narrow hall with four doors leading off it—dining room, lounge, kitchen and a small room that looked like it was being used as a study. We went through to the kitchen and she motioned for me to sit down on one of four chairs set round an oblong pine table only really big enough for two. The kitchen, with its light wooden cupboards a little scuffed and stained laminate worktops, looked weathered, like it had seen better days, and I guessed it probably was the original fitment from when the house had been built. It was tired and needed a lot of love.

'I deserve a large white wine,' she said. 'Will you join me?'

'Make it a small glass for me—I still have to drive back to London.' I could have pointed out that it was still early in the day to be hitting the bottle, but didn't want to be a killjoy.

She went to a cupboard, took out two glasses, got a bottle from the fridge and poured wine into them. She handed one to me, took a sip and sighed.

'Marvellous,' she said.

'A hard day?' I asked.

'Spent most of the morning in the loft preparing to clear out as much as I can—whatever happens in this case I'll have to downsize. Can't justify living in this house when I'm so short of funds. So you could say it wasn't exactly fulfilling.'

'Couldn't be as bad as listening to the Chief Constable droning on about Mid Anglia being the beacon for the future or some other blown up simile or metaphor,' I said. 'He doesn't like you much, does he?'

'The feeling's mutual. It's a feud that's been going on for many a year now.'

'How did it start?'

'Once, just once, and many years ago, I got promoted ahead of him. He's hated me for that, not that he hasn't had a meteoric rise since then. Shot up the ladder. Must have friends in high places is all I can think.'

'Anybody else who has a grudge and would want to frame you?'

'Not that I can think of. Of course it could be some

villain I put away—there's been plenty of those over the years—but to do something as complex as moving money around to set me up doesn't seem like their style. More likely they'd put a bullet in each of my kneecaps.'

'Anyone in the force?'

'I was an old-school copper, I guess the CC told you that.' I nodded. 'I didn't always play by the rule book. That got under people's skin. I was getting results when they couldn't. The police is as bad for jealousy as any other profession.'

I sipped my wine. It was the cheapest Chardonnay I had tasted since my student days and that was a long time ago. This woman was living on the edge.

'Don't take offence by this,' I said, 'but I need every bit of financial data you have. The prosecution will almost certainly sequester it to prove you were short of money and had a motive. I need to know what evidence I'll be up against.'

'I dug them out earlier this morning. Last three years of bank statements and credit card bills, plus a few hire purchase agreements and the mortgage.'

'Don't take offence at this either, but would I be right in thinking you're not rolling in money?'

'I live from hand to mouth. My husband died six months ago and left me with no inheritance, just a fistful of gambling debts. I struggle, Nick.'

I changed the subject. 'Any other background—for or against—that you can give me?'

'I'm a Marmite person—people either love me or hate me. You'd best look at the latter.'

'That's why we're having this conversation. In your

role as treasurer of the Federation, how did you transfer money?'

'Simple online banking. I'd log on and settle the bills at the end of each day—I don't think it's fair that people should have to wait to be paid for the work they'd done. I see it as a moral issue. Just before paying I'd transfer the money from the interest-bearing deposit account into the current account. Very easy. I'd use the app on my tablet—I could do it anywhere, anytime if necessary.'

'Anyone have access to the login details or passwords on that tablet?'

'It doesn't work that way. It functions by fingerprint and that provides access to the system and the cloud where everything is stored. You'll need one of those if you are to look at the accounts and any other files.'

'Do you still have it—the tablet?'

'No. They took it from me when I was suspended. But it's a lookalike, a pretty basic copy of the iPad—bought for price not quality. Made in China. I guess we got a hefty discount for the quantity we ordered.'

'So without your fingerprint it won't function?'

'That's how it works, yes.'

'Anyone else have access to the accounts?'

'My secretary as a backup in case I'm away and they need funds urgently.'

'What about the other money? The second fraud that cleaned out the police funds? What access do you have to that?'

'None at all. I have no involvement with the force apart from defending its officers when necessary.'

'OK, that's fine for now, but I may want to come back when I've started to dig around.' Then a thought occurred to me. 'This is left field,' I said. 'Are all the case records in the cloud, too?'

'Some are,' she said. 'They've been working on putting everything on the system, but there's a backlog. The oldest files probably haven't been transferred yet.'

'Where would I go to access them?'

'They'd still be in the bowels of the police station in town.'

'Who would be the best person to see, if I wanted to take a look at one?'

She took a gulp of wine and thought for a moment. 'Curly,' she said.

'Curly?'

'It's an old joke. He's as bald as a coot. He's the longest-serving officer. He might even remember the case.'

'Does he owe you any favours?'

She shook her head. 'You're on your own on this one, but I wish you good luck.'

I drained the wine glass, congratulated myself for only having a small one, and then got up from the table.

'I'll get all the records for you,' she said, walking out of the room.

She came back with three carrier bags filled with paper. It would be a slog going through them, but most of my work was done on the fine detail.

'I really appreciate what you're doing for me. Someday I'd like to repay you.'

'That's OK. It's one less favour that I owe Collins.'

'And would help your own digging around. It's about your sister, isn't it?'

I nodded.

'I need closure,' I said. 'This is going to be my last chance to get it.'

'You know, I get a funny feeling you're going to get it. Chris said you were stubborn. You're not the kind of guy to give up without a fight.'

She raised herself up on her toes and kissed me on the cheek.

'I'm glad you're on my side,' she said. 'Come back soon and tell me how you're getting on.'

I walked out the door and over to my car. Dumped all the documents in the boot. I was glad I was on her side, too. She was a good woman. I liked her a lot. I just hoped that everything would work out fine in the end. She didn't deserve this. Whoever framed her was in for a shock. I would move the earth for her and see justice done. Not a bad motto.

I HAD A choice between two routes to take me back to my home/office in Docklands—the dual carriageway or the local road. I chose the latter: I was in no rush and I had something to do. I hadn't driven down these country roads for many a year and today it felt fitting.

I stopped off at a garage and filled up with petrol. I bought some essentials and slowly meandered down the narrow road. When I got to the spot I pulled over and turned off the engine. I sat in silence for a while and let the memories flood back. With tears in my eyes, I got out of the car. I placed the bunch of flowers I had bought on the pavement resting up against a tree on the very spot where the damned deed had been done.

'Hi, Sis,' I said. 'Hope you are listening. You're still in my heart and you know you always will be. Maybe, if things work out, now is the time for justice. A life for a life would be good, but we can settle for a long spell in prison. Once they find out what they did—whether it be male or female, young or old—they will go through hell. All day and every day. Just like you would have suffered if you had lived. Sweet revenge, served very cold. Amen to that.'

FOUR

By the time I arrived home, my brain was buzzing with all that there was to do in preparation for the funeral. Death was looking over my shoulder with a presence I could nearly touch.

Our home and office was in Docklands, an old warehouse that Norman had acquired through nefarious means as a result of the insurance fraud we had uncovered. It was five storeys high and still had the original cranes on the higher floors for lifting up and then storing heavy loads. The formal offices were on the ground floor and an informal get-together lounging area on the second floor. Norman's accommodation was on the third floor. The fourth floor we had kept empty as a kind of firebreak between Norman and the fifth-floor accommodation for Arlene and myself. It was a magnificent building with many of the original features being retained: clients were always impressed, which got us off to a good start.

Time to tell you about Norman, since he has played such a pivotal role in my life. He was my cellmate in Chelmsford, a Category 3 prison, after I had spent the months of the trial among the hard cases of Brixton—Category 1, and then some. It was Norman who had nursed me through the worst of my claustrophobia—not a good thing to suffer from in a place where doors are banging shut all the time—and who had encouraged me to study accountancy while in prison to learn a lucrative future trade during those long years. I never worked out whether it was a plan for the future on his part or he was just occupying my time so that my mind didn't atrophy on the one hand or dwell on painful matters on the other.

Norman was an embezzler. The little nobody who sits in a corner of the accounts department slaving away in all-seeming innocence. He had stolen a million pounds from his employers, hidden the money away where it couldn't be found and then given himself up. He didn't want to be looking over his shoulder all the time, so he served his time and enjoyed the fruits of his ill-gotten gains when he had finished his sentence. I might have learnt the theory of accountancy from the textbooks, but Norman had shown me the practice— how the figures could be made to lie, all the scams and tricks of the trade. He was now in his sixties, but as sharp as ever. If there was a fast buck to be made, Norman would finish up with it. No one else would stand a chance. He always seemed to come up trumps. There was no one craftier or more numerically creative than Norman. He was a dear friend, too.

He was sitting at the reception desk when I got home. That had been Arlene's role when she was alive and it seemed strange to see him there instead of her. That was something we would have to sort out as quickly as possible, preferably before Monday when Norman would be here holding the fort on his own.

'We're going to have to make getting someone new a priority,' he said.

'Let's get the next few days over and we'll contact a recruitment agency to get us a replacement.' Immediately, I regretted what I had said. No one could replace Arlene. 'Someone new, I mean.'

'I need some coffee,' I said to him with a sigh. 'I've only had one half-decent cup in the last two days and my system needs a heavy dose of caffeine.'

'Mine needs a good old-fashioned G and T, but I'll postpone that to keep you company.'

We walked through to a small back room with three Chesterfields and a coffee table. It overlooked the Thames and had an inner peace about it—it was a great place to unwind. You felt your cares drift away with the slow-running movement of the river. I turned on the espresso machine to heat up. The huge machine occupied a good part of the room and was pure indulgence, but business had been good for several years now. We—although I did the legwork, Norman was always there with advice and a new slant on the seemingly ordinary—had built up a fine reputation from word of mouth from satisfied clients which freed us from the need to tout for work.

I busied myself in grinding the beans, filling the holders and slotting them into the machine. I pressed the buttons and watched the cups filling up. Norman was an Americano man so I had got out a bigger cup for him. It was part of our morning or after dinner ritual.

'You've done it again, Nick,' he said.

Mystified, I looked at him. Followed his eyes to the worktop where I stood. I had made three coffees.

FIVE

I MUST HAVE spent most of the next couple of days final-
izing arrangements for the funeral, protected in my own
small way by the organization and bureaucracy of of-
ficially letting someone depart from this world. There
were the complications of managing Arlene's dual citi-
zenship—repeating some of the procedures for the benefit of US records and legislation, but it helped to lose
myself in the work. It kept my mind off the weight of
emotions compressing my spirit into the ground like
excess gravity. Still, when the day of the funeral came
round, I couldn't think of what I'd been doing for the
past few days.

It was a bright day, but I could see from the clear-
ness of the air and the breath of the walkers striding past
that it was a cold one, too. This was Arlene's favourite
weather, a reminder of fresh spring days in America,
and for the first time I thought of her as she lay in the
hospital just a few weeks ago, hardly any time left to
her. She was smiling every time I saw her, in a way
where I could tell she wasn't just putting it on to try
and keep my spirits up.

Her room in the hospital was quiet and calm, like the
way she was treating her illness, and it had a large window that she insisted on keeping open as much of the
time as possible. Whenever she was asleep, either the

nursing staff or I would close it to keep the chill out, but she'd insist on having it opened again when she woke. Even to the end she kept her strong will (or 'sassiness' as she would have called it) and I had to admit it did so much to help what I was feeling, too.

In our bedroom now, I threw the window open and relished the same air that would have made her nose and cheeks cherry pink as we walked by the river in the London docklands. She had told me to carry on as normal, or in her words, 'Don't you dare go moping, y'hear me, sweetheart?' and, on the whole, I'd done OK.

I got dressed into the black pin-striped suit that I normally only wore for client meetings and slipped on the white shirt and black tie. I vowed to wear the same outfit each year on the anniversary of her death and only then. Till death do us part.

I was sitting in the kitchen nursing a cup of strong sweet tea when the buzzer sounded. I looked at the CCTV screen and saw it was Arthur, with Norman just about fitting behind him in the corner of the screen. It could be no one else but Arthur. Arthur filled a screen like no one else. He was six feet five inches tall and built like a bear, and, like a bear, he could be both dangerous, and sweet and cuddly. In fact, his nickname when he was a professional wrestler was 'Dangerous'. Arthur 'Dangerous' Duggan. And it was fitting, for his opponents at least.

Arthur would readily admit that he wasn't the sharpest knife in the box. For one thing he takes a long time to make a contribution to a conversation, but when he does it's well worth the wait. Alas, his slowness of thought carried with it the disadvantage of not being able to come up with the rehearsed manoeuvres in the ring, resulting in a lot of injuries for his unfortunate opponent. In the end, no one would fight him and so he had to find another profession. He didn't make a good choice.

He became a debt collector—muscle to persuade people to pay up. The trouble was that there were no debts to collect, only protection money. That's how he landed up in Brixton—demanding money with menace. There he became my cell-mate while I was on remand. Arthur taught me how to acclimatize to prison life and how to defend myself. His lessons worked well until the day of my transfer to Chelmsford. That's when I learnt that in prison you should never make an enemy of someone with money. Money buys everything in prison, even favours from the warders. The bent screws, to use the jargon, had exacted revenge on me. I had blinded that man with money in defence of my virtue—to put it in the weakest terms so as not to cause you to lose your lunch. In return, the two bribed warders had sliced off two fingers on my left hand by sticking them in the frame of the steel door to my cell and slamming it shut. I never really recovered psychologically, I freely admit—closed doors still make me sweat with fear. Maybe I should do something about it, but now was definitely not the time.

I moved slowly to the door and went outside where they were waiting with the car. If you could choose two men with whom to face the world, then these were they.

This was it. Part of me was glad the day was finally here—while the grief and memory would continue to be a big part of my life, at least after today a line would be drawn under the physical experience of death.

Norman, Arthur and I sat squashed together in the back of the car, or rather Arthur sat in the middle squashing us both. Past a short exchange of 'Mornings' they clearly both understood that there was no call for conversation and seemed lost in their own thoughts anyway.

The journey out of East London was surprisingly quick. The early hour meant the usual layer of traffic had not yet formed and my preoccupied mind added to the feeling that time was passing quicker than usual.

When we arrived at the crematorium and stepped out of the car, the sun shone brightly on our black, heat-seeking attire and troubled minds. A small group of people were hovering in the ante-chamber—easily recognizable from behind were Collins's now ginger and grey-haired head and the roundness of Toddy, an old friend from Chelmsford Prison. There was very little that could be said between us, but the handshakes and somewhat awkward hugs did a lot to ease the difficulty of the situation and create a sense of solidarity between us. There was a notable absence in the group: Mary Jo.

We were directed to enter the chapel and we each took our seats, clustering in the first few rows. As the minister began to speak, the doors opened again and I turned around to see Mary Jo hurrying in, walking briskly towards us in what looked to be uncomfortable heels and a distressed expression. She sat down next to me and apologized for her late entrance.

'I'm so sorry, Nick, my plane only just made it in time.'
Her face was blotchy even with the layer of make-up

applied, but any previous tears had abated for now. It was probably an uncomfortable flight for whoever was sitting next to her from San Francisco, though. Mary Jo had that effect on people. I nodded my acknowledgement before my gaze returned to the front of the chapel and the coffin that lay there.

Time was, Mary Jo would only have glared at me in the place of any exchange of words, but over time the frostiness between us had thawed.

Mary Jo was Arlene's daughter, now in her early thirties, but I had been introduced to her when she was a spoilt young college student and she had the attitude to match. She hadn't taken kindly to this British stranger who was suddenly part of her mother's life and it had taken many years of work to turn the situation around.

Mary Jo had only been able to come to visit Arlene in the hospital once before she died. She now lived in San Francisco with her Silicon Valley entrepreneur husband and their three-year-old daughter, Ella. We had attended their wedding in sunny Sausalito four years ago and a year later when Ella was born, Arlene had spent a long time out there with them, about as much as Mary Jo could stand apparently. Ella had been able to spend many happy hours with Arlene, but not nearly long enough.

The minister's words slipped through my consciousness with very little impact until it was time for the readings. I clutched the piece of paper in my hand and made my way up to the lectern. It seemed to take an age to walk to the front, as if time was slowing down in an effort to prevent me ever getting there and acknowledging the fact Arlene was gone.

'Arlene and I have been together for eight years and I can only think that my life truly began when I first met her. Who would have thought that a chance encounter outside a London hotel would have led to so much happiness? She supported me after the most difficult times of my life with her determined and resilient character and enabled me to start over with a renewed outlook on life. My life, and the world, will be a darker place without her.'

I simply felt numb when I sat down, reality finally settling in. Mary Jo got up to speak and managed to remain remarkably composed.

'My mom was always a bigger part of my life than most kids' moms were. She was my mom and dad, my brothers and sisters; and we were the best family I knew. She was such a strong person and I'm sure a lot of you here would agree that a lot of her attitude is also in me.'

She looked especially at me when saying that and I gave a knowing smile.

'She became a new person, an even happier person when she met Nick, though, and, while we had our teething troubles, I am so grateful for the difference he made to my mother's life. Now, when I think of my own family, and my daughter Ella, I want to be as good a mom to her as Mom was to me. I hate that Ella won't have her grandmother there to see her grow up, but I'll make sure she never forgets her.'

She finished her reading with a short poem from a book that Arlene had apparently read to her as a child. It wasn't a sad poem, and I was glad about that—Arlene would have hated this being an entirely mournful event.

I felt that Mary Jo had done a much better job of expressing her sentiment than I had done, but I knew everything I wanted to convey was in this final gesture. The minister finished the service and as the coffin was conveyed through the doors to the back room of the chapel, the song I had chosen began to play. It was 'Till There Was You' beautifully sung by Etta Jones and I knew that anything I had failed to mention was being expressed now. I also knew I would never stop thinking about her.

THE WAKE WAS back at our building, a space big enough to cope with all the guests. We had caterers circulating with wine and soft drinks and various canapés and finger food. It was interesting that there was a magnetic attraction of the room with the sofas looking out over the Thames as it flowed lazily downstream as if carrying our memories with it.

I managed to get Mary Jo alone and thought I might prepare the ground in case I needed her help.

'Can you still do that trick to hack into computers?' I asked her.

'Only UNIX computers. The rest have put in firewalls I can't get through. Life's more sophisticated now. I'd have to change husbands if I wanted to learn more.'

All Mary Jo's knowledge of computers had come through boyfriends and, latterly, her husband.

'I may need your help on a job,' I said. 'How long are you in town for?'

'A couple of weeks to sort out Mom's affairs, but I can hack remotely. I don't need to be here to do a job for you.'

'I'll bear that in mind.' The ground prepared, it was

time to switch away from thinking about proving Sam innocent and say a final goodbye to Arlene. After today it was time for a new leaf. 'How's Ella taken it?'

'She doesn't understand. Too young. Keeps asking where Granny is. We tell her that Granny's with the angels. She just about gets that. When she's older we can explain things more, but that's all we can do till then.' She sipped some white wine—a rather nice Chardonnay chosen by Norman—and said, 'How's business? Still doing well?'

'I'm about to start working on a case for Collins. Pro bono. Norman's still recovering from the shock.'

'It was good to see Norman and Arthur again today. It's reassuring to know that you have such supportive friends you can turn to when you're feeling low. Who's the dazzler?' she said, pointing with her wine glass.

I hadn't noticed her before. Strange. 'That's Walker, Collins's deputy. An old sparring partner of mine. She's much harder than she looks.'

'Jeez, but didn't she hit the jackpot when the Lord handed out beauty. I think I might stride over and see if she has any tips for an ordinary mortal.'

'No one could call you ordinary, Mary Jo.'

'I'll take that as a compliment.'

'And so you should.'

She kissed me on the cheek and walked over to where Walker was standing talking to Collins. He seemed grateful for the interruption and came across to me.

'Good turn out,' he said.

'Arlene made a good impression on everyone she met.'

'At least you know you can bury yourself in work

for a while. Be a good way to create a transition towards normality, although I appreciate nothing will be the same again. Hell, I'm awful at these things. I better get back to the office. See what mess everyone has got into in my absence. I'm not much of a listener, but I'll share a beer anytime you need to talk.'

He shook my hand, gave me a hug and walked quickly to the door. Walker registered the fact and checked her watch. Shrugged her shoulders. Looked across the room at me and continued her conversation with Mary Jo. Something was too important for her to rush back.

I circulated and gradually people started to drift away. They had made their farewells and it was time for me to do the same. History told me I had no chance.

WHEN EVERYBODY HAD left I sat down on the sofa. The sun was setting over the river in its own sad, beautiful way.

Both my skin and muscles were itchy, one from the saltiness of tears and the other, I supposed because it was restless and didn't know what else to do. Arthur plonked himself down next to me and I bounced into the air a few inches as the sofa adjusted to his bulk. Before he spoke, I thought to myself that there was nothing he could say to make me feel any different at that moment in time.

'I think I know what we need to do right now. I guarantee it'll help how you're feeling. We're going for a run.'

Obviously, I was wrong, this was a whole new level of negative feelings.

'I really don't feel up to it, Arthur.'

'Great. See you outside in five.'

My mind was too exhausted to protest and my body too restless, so I went upstairs and changed.

For a man in his fifties, Arthur was still fit and able to push himself to levels that would have made a much younger man proud.

At least the day was doing everything it could to provide a beautiful setting for my torture. The sunset illuminated our path along the canal, and the chilly breeze which hadn't abated all day kept pushing me along.

We jogged a little way along to Island Gardens tube station, past the foot tunnel to Greenwich and the Cutty Sark, along the Thames path and back and finished up at the three acres of parkland on the banks of the river. I was expecting Arthur to talk the whole time, to try and engage me in motivating chat as I puffed along, but he maintained a concentrated silence. It was the perfect opportunity to let my mind tick along without my paying attention and I found each mile a relief as my mind emptied.

Arriving back home, the sky had turned red. As we walked in the front door, Arthur simply gave me a smirk which said exactly what he was thinking—'I told you you'd feel better'.

SIX

'WHICH ONE OF YOU is the boss?' she asked.

'I am,' Norman and I said simultaneously.

'Good to have that cleared up,' she said.

She had come to be interviewed for the job of receptionist and general aide-de-camp. We must have seen a dozen people so far, all of whom simply regurgitated the material on our website and didn't seem to possess the ability for independent thought. It had been a wearing process and we were getting jaded.

Her name was Anji and she had walked in like she already had the job. She was wearing a black cropped T-shirt, black-and-white polka dot skating skirt and tall black biker boots that came just above the knee. There was a lot of tanned leg on show and I was finding it difficult to know where to look. I focussed on her eyes and hoped I wouldn't be drawn into them like a man being swallowed by a maelstrom.

'It depends what you mean by boss,' Norman said, drawing the attention away from me while I was still working on a strategy on the leg front. 'Shannon runs the show, but it is my money backing him. We're partners would be the best description.'

'So who should I work on?'

We were sitting in the lounge area on the ground floor. Norman and I were opposite each other and we had placed her with a magnificent view of the river overlooking Greenwich to see whether it affected her concentration. It seemed like a ploy worth trying.

'Let's start again,' I said. 'Tell us a bit about your-self.'

'I'm twenty-two, have a degree in economics from Exeter, upper second, and since graduation I have found it difficult to find work—it's a tough world out there. I've had offers, but they all had strings attached and they weren't the kind I wanted pulled so I spent some time in the entertainment industry.'

'In what field?' Norman said.

'Pole dancer,' she said.

I was knocked back in my seat, not that I couldn't understand it. She was a stunner. Tall, athletic build, long blonde hair, deep blue eyes. Not forgetting those long tanned legs.

'So why us?' I asked.

She looked me straight in the eye. 'I thought if any-one would give me a job, it would be you. You having been in prison and such. I thought you wouldn't be judgemental and might give me a chance.'

'You've done your research well,' Norman said. 'It's a trait that will be of great help here.'

I could see that, for whatever reason, he had made up his mind already.

'Where are you from, what's your background?' I probed. 'More importantly, where do you want to be heading? And why us?'

'I've had more interviews than I care to recall,' she said. 'The accepted methodology is to ask one ques-tion at a time.'

'Thanks for pointing that out,' I said. 'Here, we work differently to other businesses. The conventional doesn't apply here. Humour me.'

'I'm the only daughter of a Jesuit priest who gave up the church to marry. Educated in a convent in my home town of Canterbury. I like music and reading and play a good game of poker.'

It was a good story. If she'd been educated in a convent, then she had staying power and a lot of patience. I made a bet with myself that she'd been a rebel and had driven the nuns perpetually up the wall to the extent that their vow of forbearance had been tested.

'And how much of that is true?' I asked.

'You're the fraud detective, you tell me.'

Norman smiled and I fought back the impulse myself.

'Excuse me for a moment,' she said, picking up a voluminous bag and heading for the door.

'Straight in front of you,' Norman said.

'Well?' I said, after she had left the room.

'Well, indeed,' he said. 'I like her. She'd bring a breath of fresh air to the place. Maybe we've got a bit set in our ways. And by that, I hasten to add, I don't mean any criticism of the past regime. You understand that, Nick?'

I nodded. He was on thin ice, but negotiating the journey with the lightness of touch of a Shaolin monk.

'Let's just see how she does when she returns.'

He shrugged. 'As you wish.'

The door opened and in she came. Except it could have been a different person. Her hair had been pinned back and she was wearing glasses. She'd changed out of the T-shirt and skating skirt into a white blouse, on-the-knee black skirt and black patent low-heel shoes. She sat down and smiled at us.

'I preferred the feisty look,' I said.

'Me, too,' she said. 'Good for you to know, though, that you can choose your package according to circum-stances.'

'Three month trial,' I said. 'We'll pay you two grand a month, but you have to be prepared for a very loose job spec, some of it pretty mundane.'

'When do I start?'

'Now. Get to know the coffee machine—most prized piece of modern equipment we have.'

She gave a huge smile and came over to where I sat. She bent down and kissed me on the cheek. Then she shook hands with Norman and exited the room.

Boy, were things going to change around here and I wasn't completely sure I was prepared for it.

SEVEN

I PARKED THE BEAMER in a space marked for visitors like a good boy. The CC's spot was nearest to the doors to the building. Rank has its privileges. My friendly receptionist called through to Morag, who came down to meet me. I probably would have found her eventually, but it was quicker this way. The trouble with flexible working space was that anyone could be anywhere.

'Let's sit and plan the day,' she said, leading me to the upper tier of the conversation pit.

I still felt somehow awkward sitting down in plain view of everyone, but it was going to be something I had to get used to as it was the reigning philosophy here. There were little scattered groups of people whose main aim seemed to be to sit as far away from anybody else as possible.

'Before we start I need to ask you a question,' I said. 'Is your remit chaperone or spy?'

She blushed.

'OK,' I said. 'I'm just going to have to earn your trust.'

'Don't think badly of me,' she said. 'This case is important to us. You must remember that we are the flagship force. We lead the way. If anything goes wrong here, we spoil things for the other forces in the country. It's not just about Sam. On a personal level I hope you find the evidence to prove she's innocent, but that would mean something even more wrong is going on here. I don't know what to think or where I stand.'

'I understand,' I said, 'but maybe I can make things better for everyone and every force. Set an even better example.'

'We must hope so,' she said. 'Now what's the plan for today? What's your starting point in your search for the holy grail?'

'I need to talk to the person who heads up the finance function, find out how it's run and get his permission to talk to his staff. Then we work on from there. Not much of a plan, but it will develop as we go along.'

She took out her phone and made the call. I could tell from this end of the conversation that the recipient was not pleased, but the instruction of the CC for full cooperation won the day. We were to meet in half an hour.

'I have a present for you that will occupy that time,' Morag said.

'I'm intrigued.'

'So you should be,' she said. 'It's going to change the way you work forever.'

Morag dug in her bag, pulled out a tablet computer and handed to me.

'You're going to need this for almost everything you do.'

It was about the size of an iPad Air with an unusual silver body. From the case she pulled out a separate keyboard.

'This will give you access to our own personal cloud. All our records are stored there including all the finance operations. Now we need to set it up.'

She pressed a button and the screen came to life.

She swiped it and went through some basic questions
and answers—language, time, date, that sort of thing
that computers need to know in order to function. She
turned to me.

'Choose a four-digit code,' she said, passing the tablet to me.

I inputted four digits, shamefully the ones I use for
everything.

'Now put your index finger on the button so the machine can read your fingerprint.'

I did as she said and the computer read my fingerprint. It wasn't ground-breaking technology, but it
would suffice.

'Now you can log in by inputting the digits or by
pressing your index finger on the button. If you then
press this icon, you have access to the cloud. There are
several levels of security so that users only have access
to the data needed for their job. I have set you up with
level four. That's all you should need.'

'And if I decide I need higher access?'

'Then you talk to the CC, who will need a good explanation.'

'And who will probably still say no.'

'I suspect so, but at least you won't be able to blame
me for not arguing your case well enough.'

'And how have the staff taken to it?'

'We've had a few teething problems—there has been
a higher failure rate than we were promised, but the
Chinese manufacturers send us replacements so we're
not suffering financially. The staff adapt after a while.'

'And do they adapt as productively as they were on
the old system?'

'It's true we've had to take on additional staff.'

'For a system that was introduced to cut overheads?'

'Well, let's see how you think when you've finished here. I hope you will then see our point of view.'

I had a nagging feeling that things weren't right. That the system was failing in its high expectations. That there was a lot of covering up going on. But was it my concern? Why should I worry if the taxpayers' money was being wasted? Because I was a taxpayer myself, I suppose. And because I just couldn't help sticking my nose into other people's business.

'Let's go,' I said. 'Can't keep the man waiting. What's he called?'

'His title is Finance Director and his name is Edward Tennyson. His friends call him Ted.'

'So I should call him Edward.'

'That would be wise,' Morag said. 'Maybe when you get to know him you can be less formal.'

'I doubt it,' I said. 'Normally on a case like this first impressions are as good as it gets.'

We headed down a floor and knocked on the door of another fishbowl just like that of the CC. The inside was very different. Whereas the CC was an anal retentive with his fussy predilection for neatness and tidiness and everything in its place, tallest on the left, shortest on the right, this occupant was an anal expulsive. I'd seen pigsties that were in better shape than this office. There was a single desk of black wood with a chair behind and two on the other side for visitors. The desk and both chairs were merely receptacles for paper. Masses of paper. A filing cabinet had paper on the top, too. Even the floor was littered. I hovered in the doorway, wondering what was the best route to get near enough to shake hands. We tiptoed inside and Tennyson leapt round the desk and moved the piles of paper from the chairs, more fearful of the damage we would do to his filing system than out of politeness. Again, covered in paper, sitting in one corner was a safe. Ah, that's why he qualified for an office all on his own.

'Tennyson,' he said, extending his hand. 'And you must be…?'

'Shannon,' I offered, 'but do call me Nick.'

'Take a pew, Nick,' he said, 'and you, too, Morag. Good to see you again.'

He went behind his desk and sat down. Which was fine by me as it meant I only had to see the top half of him. He was short and very rotund. His trousers were low slung and I knew that if he bent over there would be sight of a builder's bottom. His hair was thinning and he had mistakenly tried to camouflage it with a comb over that only served to attract attention rather than distract. Julius Caesar distrusted those with a lean and hungry look: he would have felt secure with this man. To crown this unappealing image were the clothes he wore. With his ill-fitting suit and grubby shirt he made Collins look immaculate. To cap it all he had a nose with flared nostrils that looked like a snout. couldn't get the image of a pig from out of my fertile imagination.

'Good to see you both,' he said again. 'You have my full attention. What can I do for you?'

'Mr Shannon,' Morag said, 'is here to investigate the missing money and also to cast his eyes over our systems. The CC said he should be given every co-operation.'

'Quite so. Quite so. So how can I help?'

'I'd like you to explain how the finance system operates and then allow me to spend some time with your staff. But first, I notice the safe. What do you keep in it?'

'Cash,' he said, 'but the kind of cash you won't have encountered before.'

I raised an eyebrow to encourage him.

'The reptile fund,' he said with a smile.

He was going to make me work for it.

'Give in,' I said. 'What's the reptile fund?'

'All police operations work on the acquisition of information before a crime is committed. That way you can stop the crime rather than working infinitely harder to catch the criminals after the event. Most front-line police officers have their informers—"snouts" is the vernacular for them.'

'And you have to pay for that information. What's the going rate for a snout?'

'It varies widely. Maybe fifty or a hundred pounds for a low-level piece of information that may even prove worthless, £500 maybe for something really juicy.'

'And snouts don't take cheques,' I said. 'The safe contains cash.'

'A goodly amount. You never know when you might need a big sum.'

'Don't tell me,' I said, 'and snouts don't give receipts. How does the system operate?'

'The police officer needs some cash. He gets the payment sanctioned by his superior officer—gets a chitty signed. He comes to me, presents the chitty. I pass over the cash, the officer signs a receipt. All done and dusted.'

'And open to abuse.'

'As are all cash payments,' he replied. 'We keep maximum control from our end and have to trust the officer. Where would the world be if you can't trust a policeman?'

'At some stage I'd like to go through the receipts to get a better idea of the sums involved.'

He nodded his agreement. Could hardly say no without raising suspicions. My hopes were raised: where there's cash there's a fiddle.

'Who looks after the bank account?'

'One of my staff looks after inputting and I have overall control.'

'I'd like to look at that in detail,' I said.

'I have no objections to that and nothing to hide. Everything here is tickety boo.'

'Except the missing money.'

'Except that, I suppose.'

'How about the day-to-day operations?' I asked. 'How does that work?'

'You'll love this,' he said.

I very much doubted it from the smile on his face.

'That's Milly-Molly-Mandy,' he said with a grin.

I shook my head, wondering if he was being deliberately opaque.

'The three witches,' he said, almost shaking with laughter. 'Hubble bubble, toil and trouble.'

I could sense Morag getting irritated at his attitude and her powerlessness to do anything to intervene. I felt that irritation, too.

'I have three wonderful ladies who look after the accounts. Some call them the three witches like in the

Scottish play. Others, more charitably, call them Milly-
Molly-Mandy. It's from a children's story from way be-
fore your time. You'll see why when you meet them.
One girl, three names.'

'So what's the system for purchases?' I asked, dread-
ing a convoluted answer.

'Invoices come in, are authorized, scanned, inputted, filed and recycled.'

'We try to be as green as possible,' Morag said. 'The
CC is very hot on our environmental responsibilities.'

'So you don't keep paper records?' I said.

'Once they're scanned and filed on the system they
are disposed of.'

I hated having to rely on computer control. There was
something about having a paper record in your hands,
you get a strange feeling when things are amiss. Call
it intuition, gut feeling even, but it had proved useful
in the past.

'Who handles the actual ordering and authorizing?'

'That would be procurement,' he said.

Why couldn't it be called purchasing? When faced
with two options for a name, one that's self-evident
and one that's cloaked in a cloud of obfuscation, why
choose the latter?

'You'll be impressed with our buying,' he said. 'Since
the three forces came together as Mid Anglia, we have
made huge savings through the greater bulk of our orders. See Terry in procurement—he's got some graphs
that prove it.'

He looked pointedly at his watch.

'Why don't you introduce me to Milly-Molly-Mandy

and I'll come back to you if there's any further questions I need answering.'

'Quite so,' he said, getting up from his chair. 'Quite so.'

We wove our way back though the Augean stables of paper and followed him into the main open-plan office. In a corner by a window sat three indistinguishable ladies in their late fifties or early sixties—civilian staff, I assumed. They all had silver-grey hair, powdered faces with rouged cheeks, and were wearing twin sets of subtly different—so subtle that the difference was lost on me—shades of pink. Fake pearl necklaces seemed to be the order of the day, too. Tennyson introduced me.

'I'm Milly.'

'I'm Molly.'

'I'm Mandy.'

'Pleased to meet you,' I said, trying hard to pick out a distinctive feature to sort them out. Some mnemonic perhaps. Nothing came to mind.

'I'll leave you in their capable hands,' Tennyson said, beating a hasty retreat.

'Have a wine gum,' said Milly—or was it Molly or Mandy?

'Have a caramel toffee,' said Molly—or was it Milly or Mandy?

'Have a liquorice allsort,' said—well, you get the picture.

'I want to spend some time with each of you young ladies,' I said, knowing that Morag would be marking the white lie as a deficit in the trust account, 'but for now, who handles the bank account?'

'That would be me,' Liquorice Allsort said.

'Let's go through the last month,' I said, sitting down

in a free chair at someone's side. 'First, ladies, in a mobile or should I say fluid seating arrangement, how do you finish up all sitting together?'

'We leave our cardigans over the back of our chairs overnight, silly. Think of it like the Germans and swimming pool loungers.'

Wherever there was a system, someone would find a way around it.

'How does the bank account operate?' I asked.

'There are two accounts, current and deposit. There's an automatic sweep in place each close of business so that we have as much on interest-bearing deposit as possible, although the interest rate is so meagre at the moment it doesn't make much difference. Any other transfers are made by Mr Tennyson. They also need the CC's authorization. Quite simple really. All standard payments are automatically taken once approved and input according to the payment terms we have agreed with each supplier.'

'Can you show me the latest records—the large amount that was paid out?'

She pulled her tablet next to me and tapped some options.

'Damn things,' Caramel said. 'Why we had to change to these things I don't know. Even the computers we had when we were Essex were better than this—paper and ledgers were always my favourite, though.'

A long list of names and numbers, spreadsheet fashion, filled the screen. She pointed to two of the figures. 'There you go,' she said.

There were the transactions I sought: one for £25,000

and the second to bring the total to half a million. There were dates on the left and transaction codes on the right.

'I'm going to need to get an appointment with the bank. Morag, could you get me fixed up with a letter of authorization? I don't suppose the Federation uses the same bank.'

'I'll check,' she said, getting up. 'Now don't do anything while I'm gone. I shouldn't be long, but I'll need to get the CC to sign the letter and he might not be free.'

I nodded at her and she moved towards the CC's office.

'Why don't one of you show me the purchases system?' I asked.

'That would be me,' said Caramel. 'Come and drag your chair over, young man.'

It was the first time I had been called young man for a while, but I suppose it's all relative.

'This is today's batch,' she said. 'Are you sure you don't want a caramel?'

I took one to get on her sweet side, no pun intended. Morag would have approved. It would keep my mouth shut for a while.

'I take an invoice—it's already been signed by the person who placed the order—check the order number and that the amount matches the purchase order, open the scanner app thing, take a scan and file it and then enter all the details into the finance files—purchases in this case—so that there is an automatic analysis for cost centre.'

I watched her go through the procedure on a dozen or so invoices while I sucked my caramel. It seemed a little cumbersome to me—the system, not the caramel—and I reckoned it doubled the time it would have taken on a normal computer.

Morag returned clutching the authorization letter. She passed it to me and pulled a chair up beside me.

'May I look at some, please?' I said.

Caramel passed the pile to me and I riffled through some. There were a lot of purchases common to most large organizations—stationery, office equipment and mundane items of daily life—and then some specific to the force such as uniforms, telecommunications equipment, recording machines and blank DVDs to be used when interviewing suspects. I was most interested in the bulk purchases of equipment—that was where the fiddles were most likely.

'Can I keep these?' I said, taking three from the pile. 'Just for reference.'

'Of course,' she said. 'It's only going for recycling from here.'

'I'll come back and badger you more when I've been to the bank. I'm very impressed. Many thanks, ladies.'

I got up, still chewing the caramel which seemed to be lasting a lifetime, and sweeping up my three invoices.

'Time to prepare for the appointment with the bank,' I said. 'You are coming, I presume?'

'Wouldn't miss it for the world,' Morag said.

'Not to mention the fact that it's CC's orders.'

She blushed again. She'd make a lousy poker player.

We sat back down in the pit.

'You look smug,' said Morag.

'For that I apologize. Most of my work is dull, so it's good when you hit the target straightaway.'

'It's these invoices, isn't it?'

'You betcha. But not exactly.'

'Don't make me drag it out of you. What is different about these three invoices? They are different, aren't they?'

'One is different, the other two are a blind. I only picked those out to disguise the fact that I was interested in this one. You can't be too careful.'

'Not with those sweet little old ladies, surely?'

'Many a fraud has been committed by sweet little old ladies.'

'Get to it, Nick. What have you found?'

'Take a close look at this one,' I said, pushing the invoice nearer to her, 'and compare it to the other two. Think laterally.'

She stared for a while, her eyes flashing every now and again at the three sheets of paper.

'I give in,' she said. 'Put me out of my misery.'

'It has no crease,' I said.

'So what?'

'These two have been through the post, folded up inside an envelope. This one hasn't been through the post. It's been printed out in this building and slipped into the pile. Someone is generating false invoices for goods or services that have never been received. *Voila*!'

She clapped her hands. 'You're good at this, aren't you? I'm going to enjoy working with you. A whole new education. What next?'

'This had a large element of luck about it, but you have to know what you're looking for. You have to try to put yourself in the fraudster's position and get inside his or her mind. People can be very ingenious when it suits them.'

'So where do you go from here?'

'I'll get my PA'—if the CC could have a PA, then why not me?—'to dig out the information on the company and check out the directors and ownership. Presumably one of them will be the person who authorized the payment of this invoice. Meanwhile we search the purchases file and find out how much money is involved. Until we have all the facts, we don't tell the CC. Agreed?'

'I can go along with that. It seems prudent not to accuse anyone without knowing the full facts.'

'I've got a couple of phone calls to make. In private. No offence meant.'

'None taken.'

'Give me a few minutes and I'll drive us to the bank.'

'I'm looking forward to it. This is exciting.'

I could sense the dynamic of our relationship subtly changing. Shame that once I'd gained her trust, I would have to abuse that trust by getting some space between us so as to dig around in the records to investigate the hit-and-run. I liked her. I hoped at the end of things she would still like me. Omelettes and eggs, Shannon. Omelettes and eggs.

WHEN I PHONED Norman he was over the moon. We'd make some money out of this assignment after all. He said he would teach Anji what to do to research the company and make that her first test. Pull this off and she could be a real asset. She was a bright girl, although unconventional. She'd do fine.

Morag sat in the passenger seat of the Beamer and was quiet. I accelerated away from the headquarters and she was forced back in her seat by the forward momentum.

'Wow,' she said. 'This is fun.'

'It needs to be. If my experience of banks is anything to go on, we're due to be bored rigid. You need to manage your expectations. Time to see another aspect of the work.'

I found a parking space on the main square and sat for a minute or so looking up at the building that was the bank. It was a grand old edifice of York stone that had been recently sandblasted so that its creamy colour glowed in the sun. On either side of it there was the omnipresent coffee house and a store selling everything for a pound.

'Sad, isn't it,' said Morag. 'A beautiful jewel for an ugly lady.'

'Do you remember the time when banks had a manager? Someone in charge of the whole operation? Someone who took an interest in you as a person and not just a number and an income stream? We're due to meet a corporate manager called Mickey Dunn. Doesn't exactly fill you with confidence, does it? How much better it would be to be a little more formal. You don't have to go as far as to say esquire, but Michael would sound a whole lot different. Seven years in prison and I come out to a world that has changed for the worse in many ways.'

'You can't hold back progress,' Morag said. 'Time marches on with no regard for those it leaves in its wake.'

'Let's go and see whether the omens are right or if I have misjudged the situation.'

We walked through the impressive oak doors into a

world of glass and brushed steel. A man in a shirt and tie but no jacket who was behind a reception desk showed us into a cubicle. Another cubicle. Was the world full of cubicles like fish tanks for everyone to stare at the specimens inside?

A man in his late twenties stood up as we entered and we shook hands with the said Mickey Dunn. He was a few inches short of six foot and was wearing a dark grey suit and no tie. Hell, Shannon. Don't judge him yet. Maybe it's to relax us. Give him the benefit of the doubt.

We sat down in two modern chairs of bent steel and black faux leather providing little comfort and Morag gave him the letter of authorization. He managed to read it without his lips moving.

'How can I help?' he said.

I passed him my notebook. 'We can get on to the Federation accounts later—they are at this branch, too, I understand, but for the moment these two transactions were made a little over a week ago. I need to know their destination.'

He gave us a smile, which was encouraging, and tapped away on his laptop inputting the first transaction code.

'The smaller sum was paid into the account of a Samantha Stone.' He tapped away again with hopefully more revealing results. 'The larger sum was to a company named Melchester Blue.'

'Limited? Partnership?'

'It has limited in the account name.'

Seemed like time to increase Anji's workload.

'What else can you tell us?' I asked.

'Bad news, I suspect. The bank account it went to

was in Liechtenstein so there the trail ends. With their secrecy laws you won't get any joy on further information. Dead end, I'm afraid.'

It wasn't looking encouraging.

'And the Federation account. Same amounts. Same payees?'

He tapped away again. 'Exactly. Samantha Stone and Melchester Blue.'

I wondered if the Blue in the name was someone laughing at us. A little joke at our expense.

'And you can't reverse the transactions?'

''Fraid not, Nick,' he said, proving my point on formality. 'Far too late and nothing for us to work on. Once it's done, it's done.'

He got up and extended his hand. The meeting was over, it seemed.

'Good luck,' he said. 'You could always try the Fraud Squad.'

'I am the Fraud Squad,' I said. 'We've reached the bottom of the food chain.'

'Bad luck then,' he said. 'My little joke.'

'Very,' I said.

And we left.

MORAG DECIDED SHE could leave me alone for a while and went to cater for the CC's whims and I settled down to tracking the phantom invoices. I started on the purchase ledger and got the dates and amounts for the current year and the one preceding. Before that it was Essex and not Mid Anglia and so beyond my remit. Then I went through the scanned invoices and looked at them in detail. Each invoice was the same. One thousand pounds for 'general consultancy'. Small beer, yes, but once every month it all adds up. It would only net us a little less than two grand, but it was a start.

While I was going through the scanned files, I worked back, taking an overview of purchases—what the item was, when and what amounts. Nothing leapt out at me at this stage, but I thought I might dig deeper over a lonely meal that night. At five o'clock the place started to clear and Morag returned to shepherd me off the premises.

'A good day's work would you say?' she asked.

'Not bad for day one. We'll assemble the facts on the phantom invoices tomorrow and then see the CC. Leave it up to him as to what action to take.'

'You'll be staying at the Metropole, I assume.'

'I've tried that and didn't like their brand of antiseptic. I asked my PA to find a place with character and she's booked me into the Green Dragon.'

'The food there is supposed to be excellent.'

I had an idea that I hoped I wouldn't regret.

'Why not join me,' I said. 'It gets lonely eating by yourself.'

She thought for a moment.

'The CC doesn't have to know.'

'I'd love to,' she said. 'It's been a long while since I last ate out. I'd be delighted to accept your offer.'

'Then meet me there at eight o'clock. Get a cab so you can enjoy some wine. My treat.'

'See you then,' she said and she walked to her car. I might be wrong, but I thought I could see a spring in her step.

Nick Shannon! You old smoothy, you.

EIGHT

I SHOWERED AND put on a pair of sand-coloured chinos with a light blue shirt and dark blue bomber jacket. The shower had worked efficiently, the room neat and tidy, the views over the green countryside breath-taking. Anji had made a good choice.

I went downstairs and found a saloon and a public bar, the latter was full as if it were some special occasion. The former was bustling and in the restaurant most of the tables were already occupied. Without a reservation, I wouldn't have got a table for dinner.

The place may have been crowded, but the noise was jolly. People enjoying themselves after a hard day's work. The clientele was mixed: the odd businessman like me trying to soak in the atmosphere and relax over a paperback; a few young men with sports jackets who looked like landed gentry, tapping away on a tablet or their phone.

Morag entered and looked around. I waved a hand and went over to meet her. She looked like she had spent a lot of time getting ready for the evening; her makeup was heavier than during the day and she wore a dark blue dress and mid height black shoes. She gave me a wide smile that would have melted a few hearts in her younger days. I put my arm around her and led her to our table. I pulled her chair out, sat her down, pushed the chair in and took the seat opposite her. A waitress came and handed us menus and took our drinks order. I had a vodka and freshly squeezed orange juice, Morag a dry sherry and I asked for a half bottle of Australian Merlot to be opened to breathe. Morag said she liked Chardonnay so I said to have a half bottle chilling.

'We may be the talk of the office tomorrow,' Morag said.

'Why do you say that?'

'The two men at the next table are Mid Anglia people. I can tell by the tablets on the table. Only Mid Anglia has that distinctive silver colour.'

'Do you recognize them?'

'No, but we employ a lot of people.'

'Well, if you don't recognize them, then they may not recognize you. Relax. What do you fancy to eat?'

'The monkfish sounds good. I haven't had one for a long while. Too fiddly to cook just for myself. Too prone to stick and break up, too.'

The waitress came back with our drinks and took our food order. sat back in my chair and toasted her. We clinked glasses.

'So tell me more about yourself you haven't already divulged.'

'Born and educated in Edinburgh. After school, to secretarial college. Met a man who swept me off my feet. We got married and then a few years later he got relocated to Essex. We moved south and I got secretarial job with the police. Been working here now for twenty years. I deserve a medal.' She giggled.

She had gone into schoolgirl persona. The meal and setting were bringing her out of herself.

'Always been looking after the CC?'

'Gosh, no. Pretty lowly job typing for most of it and then gradually moved up the organization. Been with the CC now for five years. Rose with my husband as he moved up the ladder. Meteoric rise, too.'

'Good at his job then, I presume.'

'Standing on the shoulders of giants.'

I sipped the vodka and raised an eyebrow.

'He's friends with the Home Secretary.'

'David Yates?'

'David Montgomery Yates, if you don't mind. He's always quick to remind everyone of that. He likes to tell the Churchill story. You know the one? Before Al-amein we never had a victory: after Alamein we never had a defeat.'

'I get the picture. Promoted above his station?'

'You won't get me to comment on that. It will take more than a dry sherry to get me to be indiscreet.'

'I respect that. I shouldn't have asked. Fill in the gaps You said your husband died five years ago. Children?'

'We couldn't have children so I'm all on my own. Live like a typical spinster. Got two cats that I dote on and spend the evenings knitting and watching the TV. I like to listen to classical music and that's about it. Now it's your turn. Tell me about the real Nick Shannon.'

'You mean those bits of the story you haven't read about in the papers or seen on the TV news?'

She nodded and took a sip of her sherry. There was a silence I needed to fill.

'The ten-year sentence was my own fault. I've Irish blood in me and it took over. I kept shouting at the judge, trying to get my point of view across. That it wasn't a crime or it shouldn't be a crime—either way he didn't listen. He gave me one year for each outburst—ten years in total of which I served seven. I managed to keep my nose clean due to a lot of help from two good friends. Without them I wouldn't be what I am today.'

'Tell me about them. They're obviously important to you.'

'Arthur was my cell mate in Brixton while I was on remand. He taught me how to survive among the inmates. I didn't know I had to watch out for the warders, too. That's how I lost the two fingers on my left hand. Cut off in a door frame. I can't cope with closed spaces after that.'

'So that's why you don't use the lift. Maybe you should get some help with it. Psychoanalyst or something.'

'I cope,' I said. 'I don't like the idea of someone poking into my brain.'

'OK. I can buy that. What about the other friend?'

'Norman,' I said. 'He was my cell mate in Chelmsford where I served my sentence after Brixton. He was an embezzler. A wilier old fox than Norman you couldn't meet. He cajoled me into doing a correspondence course and I qualified as an accountant. The books taught me accountancy, Norman taught me the tricks of the trade.'

'And now? Is there a Mrs Shannon back home?'

'There was, but no more. That's where my story will end today.'

The starters arrived at an opportune moment. The waitress poured wine into our glasses and we concentrated on the food for a while. Morag's goat's cheese salad looked good for those who like warm cheese, which she did. My pâté was gamey—supposed to come from rare-breed boars. I refilled our glasses and we settled back deep in thought while the plates were cleared, each wondering where the conversation should go next. She cracked first.

'What's your view of us from what you've seen so far?'

'I think you've got problems. You're in too deep with all this creativity while carrying the burden of expectation. People will find a way round the system. They always do. You saw how Milly-Molly-Mandy had beaten the flexible seating plan. Then there's whoever it was who came up with the phoney invoice scam. Where there is one fraud, there are usually others. It's part of the ruling culture. The CC is going to regret his deal of a ten per cent bonus. I think it's going to cost him a lot of money.'

'So what's your plan for tomorrow?'

'Spend more time on the purchasing side. There's no need for you to stick with me all the time. It's going to be a drag for you.'

'I must admit that I'm getting behind with the CC's work. Wouldn't mind a quiet hour or two.'

'Oh,' I said. 'I also want to visit the police station here. Talk to some detectives about the reptile fund. Maybe dig deeper into the practice. Work what we call an historic analysis.' I was bluffing my heart out here. 'Go way back in the records. Talk to this Curly guy. It might undermine my authority if you were there overseeing all I did.'

I felt bad for lying, but I'd find a way to make it up to her.

'You've got a deal,' she said. 'But you will behave yourself, won't you?'

'Who, me? I'll stick rigidly to my agenda.'

I comforted myself that it was only a half lie because I didn't tell her what my agenda was.

The mains arrived and didn't disappoint. They were absolutely delicious.

'Norman and I have a friend called Toddy,' I said. 'He was the head cook in Chelmsford and Norman set him up with his own restaurant in London. He'd be proud of this. The best ingredients cooked simply is his motto.'

'Maybe someday I can dine there.'

'To get into the spirit of it, you need to bear in mind that in a previous existence Toddy was the best forger in the land.'

'So how did he get caught?'

'He was so proud of his forged twenty-pound notes that he signed them!'

'What an exciting life you lead. Makes mine seem positively dull even though I work for the police.'

'Nothing wrong with dull, although I would miss the adrenaline burst when you crack a case.'

Coffee arrived and I asked for the bill. I phoned for a cab for Morag.

'This has been a wonderful evening,' Morag said. 'I haven't enjoyed myself this much for a very long time. I can't thank you enough.'

'You don't have to. It's been my pleasure.'

The bill was delivered and the waitress told us that

the cab had come. I stood up and shook her hand. She came closer and kissed me on the cheek. Getting to be a habit with women suddenly, but a good one. All in all, a pretty good day.

It didn't last.

NINE

I ARRIVED AT MID ANGLIA HQ the next morning and went straight up to the canteen and phoned Morag to tell her to join me. I would have preferred a different start to the day. Like sleep, basically.

'Wonderful evening,' she said again.

I acknowledged her thanks, but it came out as a grunt.

'Something up?' she said.

'The guidebooks on The Green Dragon missed out the bit about having a skittle alley. That it ran directly under my bedroom. And that it didn't finish until one in the morning. Then there was the clinking of all the bottles going into the recycling bin. I kept waiting for the brass band to turn up for practice. I didn't get to sleep till three o'clock. The only good thing to come out of it was they have offered me a free meal as recompense.'

'This may be a stupid idea, and if you think so you must tell me, but why don't you stay with me? I've a big house that I rattle around in and, frankly, I could do with some extra money and some company.'

I thought for a moment and considered the idea. Could be convenient—we could talk shop and review each day's work. Ten years older and different circumstances, I would have jumped at the chance of staying with a lovely lady in her mid fifties. I didn't think that she meant for any serious relationship to develop, except platonic maybe.

'That sounds a great idea,' I said.

'I'll send you a text with my address. I can't promise to cook anything like The Green Dragon or your friend Toddy, but you won't go hungry.'

'Think about what you might charge me and double it,' I said.

'It's a deal,' she said. 'Now what are we going to get up to today?'

'Go through some more purchases, see the guy who is head of procurement and the one who sent the phoney invoices, then, for a change, go to see some cops in action.'

'Meet me for lunch and I'll take you to Melchester police station and introduce you. Then it's up to you. I won't stick around—as you said, I might detract from your authority. See you later.'

She went away humming a song. I couldn't tell what it was. I hoped her cooking was better than her humming.

I SPENT A couple of hours going through purchase invoices without finding anything suspicious. May have been bad luck instead of the good fortune of yesterday. As my mind started to atrophy, I searched the contacts file and spoke to the head of procurement. Fixed to see him at two when he had a 'time-window'. Before meeting Morag for lunch, I popped out to the nearest supermarket and bought a bottle of fino sherry, vodka and splashed out on a rare Argentinian Malbec from a famed bodega. I also bought a bouquet of mixed flowers and had them wrapped as a present.

Lunch presented a bit of a problem. Should I go for
something light, assuming Morag would cook a big
meal, or go heavy on the grounds that her cooking
wouldn't be up to much? I selected the former option
and went for a tuna salad—tinned, but of good quality.
I filled Morag in on the fruitless morning and asked her
a few questions about their cloud and the information
it contained. My level four grade gave me access to the
personnel files, except the department was now called
Human Resources to throw me off the scent. Together
we looked at the file of the man who authorized the phoney invoices. It didn't fill my heart with joy.

He was called Ralph Canning and he was thirty years
old. The bad bit—he was married with two children
aged three and five at the last update. He'd been part of
the Metropolitan Police before the amalgamation and
I wondered if the scam was started there or whether it
had been cooked up under what I felt was the laxer regime of Mid Anglia. The children bothered me. What
would happen to them, not to mention his wife, when
he was convicted of fraud? Maybe even sent to prison.
Whatever the outcome, the prosecution would want res-
titution and I doubted if he could afford that. I thought
I had better see him before opening my big mouth and
started what would be unstoppable. I fixed to meet him
in the conversation pit at four.

I put a call in to Norman to tell him where I was
now staying and updating him on the case so far. Anji
had done a good job of searching the company issuing
the phoney invoices. Canning was down as a director.
Pretty much sealed the case. She was working on the
information on Melchester Blue, but that was proving

more difficult. Otherwise a couple of cheques had come in on cases finished and a new inquiry was waiting for an interview over what was the problem and what they wanted from us. Life was going on as normal.

At two o'clock I went down to the third floor and found Terry Sutton, Head of Procurement, standing up at one of the high-table arrangements.

'Shannon,' he said. 'Good to see you, my man. What can I do you for?'

He was around six foot I guessed, from my two-inch height advantage, and very lean. I thought of Julius Caesar again. I didn't know if he was hungry. His hair was the current fashion of short back and sides and he desperately needed style counselling—his striped shirt clashed with his striped trousers.

I decided to fight fire with fire. Move onto his wavelength.

'Just touching base,' I said. 'I'm here at the CC's request to turn over some stones. See what crawls out.'

'You can't fool me,' he said. 'You're on the Stone case, aren't you?'

'I can see nothing gets past you, Tel, but I'm looking at all the systems, too, procurement being one big part of that. Came to see if you were the pearl or the grit in the oyster.'

The beaming smile on his face slid a little.

'I was a Met man before I came here. I couldn't believe what I saw. Things I was buying for ten quid, say, they were paying fourteen for in Essex and sixteen in Suffolk. They had no idea of bulk buying. The three of us together now get hefty discounts. I'm saving the force masses.'

'Does that apply to everything?'

'Pretty much so. Everything goes out to tender, too. That means companies cut their prices even more so that they don't lose the contract. Smart, eh?'

'But aren't you spending more with all the modernization? Take the tablets, for instance?'

'Keep taking the tablets, eh?' He laughed at his own joke even though I suspected he'd used it before on many occasions. 'This is not Apples we're talking about. It's pears. No, only joking.' This guy was cracking me up. I don't know how I restrained myself from doubling over in fits of laughter. 'These are made by the Chinese in some sweat shop.'

'And that doesn't bother you?'

'I'm here to save money, not the world.'

'Compared to laptops, tablets must be costing you much more.'

'Not these ones. Think of the quantity we're buying here. Then think of the quantity that would be bought if all the other forces used them. That's the carrot and that's why the prices are so low. Makes good economic sense at the end of the day.'

'I've heard that there have been teething problems. Tell me about those and how they have affected you.'

'It's true that the technology is a bit flaky and we lose maybe one in four because of some failure or other, but we are sent replacements for the ones that are faulty. Doesn't cost us a penny.'

'I'd like to see the results of all the tenders. See whether white man speaks with forked tongue.'

'Sure. No sweat,' he said, but he didn't sound quite so confident now.

I DROVE TO the police station in Melchester, Morag making zoom zoom noises in the passenger seat. I found a parking space in the middle of two marked cars and we got out. The police station, like so many of Melchester's buildings, had been built in the late Victorian era and could be best described as gothic: the uncharitable would have gone for spooky. Inside, a sergeant in uniform was seated behind the desk. There were several chairs in this area but only two taken. Must be the quiet time of the day before the drinkers hit the pubs and then each other. Morag approached the sergeant and explained our business. He directed us to sit while someone came to look after us. Curly came through the door. He was as bald as his reputation and looked as if he was close to retirement. Morag introduced herself— the CC's PA caused a raised eyebrow—and then myself and my mission. Curly seemed only too glad to help. I wondered if his age meant he got all the boring desk jobs. I don't usually evoke such enthusiasm.

'I'll leave you now,' Morag said, 'and go and get some shopping. I'll be back at a quarter to four so we're not late for our meeting with Canning.'

She left the building and Curly shook my hand. 'Fancy some builders' tea, Mr Shannon?'

'Best offer I've had all day, and please call me Nick.'

We walked along a dark corridor that was crying out for windows to relieve the gloom and stepped into the staff canteen.

'Two teas, love,' he said to the large lady standing behind the counter. She wiped her hands on her apron, hefted a huge teapot and poured a dark brown liquid purporting to be tea into two mugs already containing milk. She passed them to us and Curly put some money on the counter. I added sugar to my tea with a spoon tied to the counter. What a world to live in where you can't trust a copper.

We sat at one of the dozen or so long tables in the room. There were six police officers in uniform and around the same number of CID people in mufti or civilian staff disguised as plain clothes operatives.

Curly was in a uniform that seemed on the small side and I reckoned he had put on weight with the sedentary nature of his work. His nose had been broken at some stage in the past, possibly twice, but he had bright laughing eyes. Jolly was what people would have called him.

'Thanks for seeing me,' I said.

'Could hardly have done otherwise after an order from the CC.'

'I need to go back in your case records comparing how things have changed over the years and people say you're the font of all knowledge. Tell me about the system, Curly.'

'The recent files have been put on the cloud, whatever that is, and I'm working on clearing the backlog of the older ones. So far I've gone back two years. The rest are stored down below in the dungeon that also contains the cells. It's pretty much a thankless task, but I'll stick with it and clear the backlog eventually.'

'How far do your records go back?'

'Twenty years or so. We can't keep them all, but I've done an initial filter and saved those of most interest and those that are open cases.'

'Would you have any objection to me poking around? Looking at a sample of them?'

'I'm proud of my system and would welcome the opportunity to show off. Don't wear a suit, though, Nick, it will be dusty work. I'd wear some old clothes if they'd let me, but that's not the police way. Rules is rules. Always was, always will be.' He gave a laugh. 'Although some find ways to get away with a little bending at times.'

So there are others like Collins around. Unsurprising, given the rising sophistication of the crooks.

Time to switch attention for a moment. The reptile fund would need investigating as the next priority on my ever-growing list.

'At some stage I'll want to speak to someone in CID. Who's got the best arrest record?'

'That would be Harry Saunders. He's an inspector. Ten years' experience of the job and gets results where others fail. Some say he's got the best snouts and gets all the juicy tip offs.'

'Sounds like he's the man to speak to.'

Perfect. I finished my tea and hoped its strength wouldn't have stripped the lining from my stomach.

'Good stuff, eh?' he said.

'Never had anything like it.'

He picked up both mugs and took them back to the counter. The woman gave him a big smile. 'You could learn a lot from this man,' she said.

'That's what I'm hoping,' I replied.

Curly led me down the corridor to a set of concrete stairs. This would be the set that suspects fell down on the way to the cells, if necessary.

We went past six cells with heavy doors, slots at the bottom for sliding in food trays and peep holes fitted at eye level so that they could keep a wary eye on the miscreants. I gave an involuntary shudder. I'd seen enough of cells to last me a lifetime and they didn't agree with me anymore. We entered a room about twenty feet square. In the middle was a small table and two chairs. The chair had a tablet and a thick stack of paper. The walls were lined with steel shelves, each packed with brown paper files. I hoped he had a good system otherwise it would be impossible to find anything.

'Here's the holy bible,' he said, pointing to a red loose-leaf binder on the table next to his tablet. He opened up the binder and riffled through some of the pages. 'Each case has a name, description, date and reference number. The numbers run from top left on the first shelf to the bottom right on the last one. Impressive, huh?'

'Staggering,' I said. 'Is there a time when I can go through these without getting in your way? Lunchtimes, long tea breaks?'

'I have the fry up here at breakfast, go for a pie or pasty at one o'clock and have a cup of tea around three. I like to have a cream cake if there's any left.'

God, the man must have an iron constitution. With a diet like that he deserved to be dead many years ago. Maybe it's something unique for the police. Might as well develop coronary heart disease than getting a knife jabbed in there.

'I'll try to work around that,' I said. ''Cause you as little disruption as possible.'

'Be glad of the company,' he said.

We went back upstairs and I sat to review matters and to wait for Morag. In terms of the reptile fund I would need Arthur's help. I had a plan that would involve a lot of luck and a little acting on Arthur's part, but he had the perfect background.

It seemed that if Curly's system was as good as his word, then the hit-and-run, being an open case, should have a file there somewhere. I phoned Norman and asked him to get Arthur to come here tomorrow or as soon as possible if he couldn't make that. There was still no progress on Melchester Blue and Anji was going to Companies House in person to see what she could sweet talk someone into giving. It didn't sound promising to Norman or to me. I had suspicions that this was a dead end.

Morag phoned me and said that she had bought more than she had anticipated and could I come and help her carry some bags back to the car. She gave me directions to the supermarket and I set off for a ten-minute stroll in the sun. I saw her standing outside with four bags of shopping on the ground. We were just dividing up the bags when Morag's phone went. It was the ringtone of the CC. She listened for a while over the volume of the town traffic. Suddenly, there was a roar behind us and a moped mounted the pavement and the pillion passenger snatched her phone from her hand and then they drove off. I shouted, 'Stop! Thief!' like they did in the old days and set off in pursuit.

There were delivery vehicles parked at the kerbside and the moped couldn't get back on to the road. The rider was forced to keep on the pavement until there was a gap. Pedestrians were jumping out of the way and the bike made slow progress. I was gaining on them.

The passenger turned round to look at me. I got the impression he was sizing up the situation. He took a bottle from the bag on the back of the bike and threw it at me. Liquid spilled out of the open top of the bottle. I dodged to the right and pressed myself hard against the rear of a van. The bottle missed me and smashed on the pavement. Bubbles appeared around the broken bottle. Acid!

It was decision time. Keep in pursuit and hope they didn't have more tricks up their sleeves or stop now and abandon the chase. My mind was made up for me. Finally, there was a gap in the parked vehicles and the moped slowed to steer into it. It bumped down on to the road. And hit a manhole cover. The momentum threw the rider and his passenger forward and they cart-wheeled over the bike to land on the kerbside. I ran towards them and stood above them as they started to pick themselves up.

I grabbed the passenger by the leg of his baggy trousers and pulled him along the ground until he was within reach of my boot. I planted it fully on his chest and looked down at him. He looked small and vulnerable now—just a kid, really—and I had to keep focussed on his throwing the acid.

'You can't fight us both,' the rider shouted.

'I don't have to,' I shouted back. 'One will be enough because he will squeal like a pig.'

The rider screamed, took a length of iron piping from the inside of his hoodie and ran at me. I swept across his right arm and knocked the piping aside. Hit him with a straight right that knocked him back on his feet so that he swayed as if drunk. I grabbed his right arm and twisted it behind his back. The piping dropped to the ground. The man beneath me sensed an opportunity and started to push up against my foot. I kicked him between his legs and he slumped back down and groaned.

I transferred my attention back to the rider and pulled him back toward me. He screamed in pain.

'I can break your arm if you struggle,' I said. 'Believe me, I wouldn't want to do that. I could also hurt you like your partner here. I would quite like to do that. But I won't. It's over. Give up.' He made a move to escape my hold. I broke his arm. Threats hold no power unless you carry through with them. I remembered the acid to justify what I had done. They deserved everything they got.

'We'll take over now from here, sir,' said a breathless policeman, arriving on the scene. 'Grateful for your actions, but there's procedures to be followed.'

Morag and I gave our names to another officer and decided we'd had enough. We walked back to the car and put her bags in the boot along with mine. The incident now behind us, the reaction started. Morag started to shake. I put my arms around her and held her tightly to absorb the shivering.

'Why did they do it?' she said. 'Why the acid? Someone could have been scarred for life.'

'Easy,' I said. 'It's over now. No harm done. Everybody's safe and they won't be pulling a stunt like that for a very long time.'

She broke my hold. Gave a nervous laugh. 'Silly of me,' she said. 'I'm a grown woman. Now how did you get on?'

'A couple of promising leads,' I said. 'Nothing to involve you in at the moment.' I was aware that I was being cryptic, if not downright mendacious, but the less she knew the better. That way she could claim innocence if it was a hit(-and-run)-the-fan job.

We drove back to HQ and went into reception. Canning was already there in the conversation pit. He looked older than his thirty years; his skin was gaunt and had dark circles under his eyes. He seemed like he had the cares of the world on his back and was buckling under the weight. I put my arm around his shoulder.

'Let's go for a walk,' I said, leading him out of the building. Morag tagged along, but stayed a few paces back. There was a bench on a patch of grass. I led Canning to it and looked at Morag.

'If you don't mind?' she said.

I nodded and sat down on the right of Canning, Morag sat on his left.

'You know, don't you?' Canning said.

'I know that you've been putting in phoney invoices for a grand a month. What I don't know are the reasons. Tell me everything and then I can decide what to do.'

'When I moved here I lost my London allowance. That made things pretty tight. Our house is still on the market after eighteen months. Needs a lot of work doing so that might be it or maybe we're asking too much. Income down, overheads the same. Then there was the body blow. My wife was diagnosed with MS, primary, relapsing, remitting. She was a changed woman in the middle of the attack phase. She had to give up work— we'd managed not too badly with some child care to cope with the kids, the younger one especially who hasn't started school yet. Our income virtually halved. Same level of care—Teresa was an invalid and needed a lot of attention. I took out a couple of payday loans at crippling rates of interest and couldn't pay them back. I needed money fast.'

I could see tears forming in Morag's eyes. I had a bit of grit in mine.

'So I started the phoney invoices. I'm in IT and we use a lot of outside consultants. I didn't think there was any chance of being found out. I meant it only as a stop gap—get us through the hard times until our house was sold and we downsized to get some money in the bank.'

'Did you intend to pay it back?' I said.

'Honestly?' he said. 'No, I suppose I didn't think I would need to.'

'That wasn't the answer I wanted to hear.' I looked at Morag. 'What's the CC likely to do when he finds out?'

'Crucify him.'

'Hell! That wasn't the answer I wanted to hear either.' I got up from the bench. 'Give me a minute or two to figure something out.'

I went for a walk, leaving both of them sitting there sad and Canning frightened, I suspected. Technically, it would be an ethical problem if I didn't tell the CC what I had uncovered. Make me an accessory after the fact, too. I looked across at Canning and thought of his wife and kids. What was best for them? I walked back to the bench. Stood there looking down at Canning.

'Here's what I'm going to do. I'm going to see the CC—'

'We're going to see the CC,' Morag interrupted.

'We're going to see the CC. I'm going to try to extract a promise of leniency from him. Then we three meet him in the morning and you make a full confession. You swear that you will pay all the money back just as soon as your house is sold. You also promise never to do anything as stupid as this ever again. Agreed?'

'Agreed,' he said. 'Thank you. Both of you.'

'Morag, tell the CC we want an emergency meeting tonight and then one for the three of us at eight o'clock in the morning before everybody else gets there. I don't want everyone looking into his fishbowl and twigging that something bad is going down. You be there, Ralph, on time and looking contrite. We might just get you out of this hole.'

'Thank you, Shannon, for giving me this chance.'

'Don't let me down. Remember, full confession and plan of action for paying the money back.'

'This is an issue where the Staff Union may help,' said Morag. 'Short-term loan till you're back on your feet. Being a civilian you're not the responsibility of the Federation. The CC's never flavour of the month with the Staff Union.'

I wondered if there was anywhere he was flavour of the month.

'Go home, Ralph, and practise what you are going to say. Now, scoot.' The CC was as resplendent as ever in his uniform. I wondered if he kept it on at home to remind his wife he was the big cheese. Morag and I sat down facing him. I felt like I had been pulled up in front of the headmaster for stealing chocolate from the tuck shop.

'You have a problem, Shannon?'

'I have uncovered a fraud—the first of many,

maybe—but it's a small one, nothing more than a tick on an elephant's hide.'

'And?'

'There are extenuating circumstances. I'd like you to regard the crime with compassion. Let the man off with a slapped wrist—it really is small beer.'

'And if I don't agree?'

'I might not be as closed lipped as I could be with what I find here.'

'And I might remind you that you signed the Official Secrets Act when you took on the contract.'

'If you agree to treat the crime with leniency, the offender is willing to make a full confession.'

'You seem to have got yourself personally involved, Shannon.'

'Me, too, CC,' Morag said. 'There really are mitigating circumstances.'

'You and I have been together a good few years, Morag. Because it's you I'll tell you what I'll do. I'll hear the confession and treat the case on its merits. How's that?'

'We'll be here at eight tomorrow,' I said.

'Looking forward to it. Now leave me to get on in running this force before you tax my patience.'

Meeting adjourned. We trooped out, collected our things—tablets being the most important—and took the escalator down to the ground floor.

'You know him much better than I do,' I said to Morag. 'What will he do?'

'If he says that he will listen to the facts and judge the matter fairly, then that's what he will do.'

'I'd like for there not to be some weasel he'll latch on to.'

'Let's face it, Nick. That's as good as you're going to get.'

I grunted. Good as you're going to get was less than I had hoped, but time would tell. Maybe he wasn't as bad—as unprincipled—as I thought.

'See you soon,' she said. 'Gosh, I hadn't thought of it before. I hope you like cats.'

'This man's best friend,' I said. 'Apart from Norman and Arthur that is, and I reckon Norman has the stealth of a cat about him, and Arthur is cuddly when you get to know him.'

'Then I hope to meet them both.'

'You won't be disappointed.'

'And I hope the CC doesn't disappoint you.'

'Amen to that.'

TEN

MORAG'S HOUSE WAS a large Victorian semi that had a lot of charm—it looked like it had been extended over the years and now had a basement and then three levels above that, the topmost having dormer windows. I parked on the drive next to Morag's car and rang the bell. She had changed from her formal working gear into a knee-length light brown skirt and a yellow T-shirt. She was also wearing an apron, which seemed like an encouraging sign—took her cooking seriously. I gave her the flowers and she seemed genuinely excited. I followed her along a narrow corridor with original features like a ceiling rose, coving and a dado rail into the kitchen. It was light oak with a black granite worktop and a large Aga.

'You really shouldn't have,' she said, taking a large vase from the window ledge and running water into it.

'More supplies, too,' I said, taking the bottles from the bag. 'The sherry should go in the fridge—never drink fino sherry anything but chilled.'

'I look forward to it. We have *coq au vin* tonight—please say you like chicken.'

'I like chicken.'

'You're not just saying that, are you?'

'If this arrangement is going to work, we both have

to say what we feel. Right now I feel like a vodka. I can pour sherry over some ice, if you're as desperate as me.'

'Let me show you to your room and you can freshen up. A drink would be wonderful when you're ready.'

She led me back out into the corridor, opening doors as she went and giving me a house tour. There was a large lounge with a three-piece suite in a rust colour and some occasional tables, a TV and a state-of-the-ark stereo that looked like it had come from a museum and took up more space than the sound it would produce. The next room was the dining room with a table that would seat six comfortably or eight at a push. The remaining space was taken up with an upright piano.

On the first floor there were three bedrooms and a bathroom. The final floor had two bedrooms in the eaves and another bathroom. put my suitcase in the bedroom she had indicated and looked out the window. The view from this far up was stunning: rolling countryside as far as you could see and a sunset that promised a fine day tomorrow.

I freshened up, put on a pair of jeans and a white T-shirt to keep Morag's informality company, grabbed the tablet and my mobile and went back downstairs to the kitchen. Appetizing smells were now in the air.

'It's a fine house,' I said.

'For a family, yes. It's far too large for me. I'll have to downsize at some stage, but I still think of it as our house. I feel like a traitor when think of moving.'

'I'm sure your late husband wouldn't think that way.'

'Maybe,' she said. 'The cats love it, too.'

'Cats are adaptable. Do you know the difference between cats and dogs? Dogs have owners, cats have servants. Cats are self-sufficient creatures. Time to think of yourself.'

'Maybe,' she said again. 'Anyway, glasses are in the cupboard. Time for that drink.'

I took out two small tumblers. I got ice from the freezer, put three large cubes in each glass and retrieved the fino from the fridge. I poured sherry into her glass and a large slug of vodka in mine, which topped up with the purported freshly squeezed orange juice. I passed her the drink and we clinked glasses. The drink felt good and I started to relax.

'Where do you keep the corkscrew?' I asked.

'Second drawer down. You could get some cutlery out while you're in that direction.'

I uncorked a bottle of the Malbec as the first priority and then took two knives and forks and a couple of spoons in case they came in handy. Paper napkins were in a pretty holder on the worktop and I took two of these, too.

'I thought we'd eat in the dining room.'

'Don't go to too much trouble just for me.'

'It doesn't get used often enough these days,' she said. 'I thought we'd just have a green salad. How are you on French dressing? It never turns out right when I try.'

'You've just hit my speciality,' I said. 'Ingredients?'

'Tall cupboard in the far corner. Do say if this is getting too domesticated for you.'

'I enjoy cooking. Arlene and I used to take turns to cook the meals.'

'Arlene is...?' she said, falteringly.

'My late wife, yes.'

'Then let's make dear departed ones a taboo subject while you're here.'

'Seems sensible,' I said, knowing it was too early for that to work for me.

She opened a bag of salad leaves, tipped it in a wooden bowl and set to adding tomatoes, cucumber and spring onions.

Having made the dressing, I asked her whether she wanted it as it was or poured over the salad and tossed. She went for tossed, which would have been my choice. Encouraging.

'I think we're ready to go,' she said. 'If you could take things through to the dining room, I'll bring the plates of chicken.'

I gathered up the cutlery, napkins and salad and went through to the dining room. I set the table and looked at the piano while waiting for Morag to join me. I would have preferred to eat in the kitchen.

Morag entered and laid the plates of *coq au vin* on the table and a basket of fresh baguettes in the middle of us.

'This looks lovely,' I said, suddenly realizing how hungry I was.

'We best get the money sorted out,' she said. 'So as to avoid any embarrassment. I was thinking of a hundred pounds a week.'

'I was thinking of a hundred pounds a day, so we'll go with that. Subject over.'

'But really…' she started to say.

'Subject over,' I said firmly. 'By the way, this is delicious.'

'I'm glad you like it. It was fun cooking for someone rather than just myself. I never do anything elaborate just for me.'

'I understand.'

'Do you mind talking shop?'

'Not at all. Go ahead.'

'Do you think Sam did it?'

'If so, it's one of the most clumsy frauds I've ever seen.'

'Do you think someone is framing her?'

'That's the way it looks to me, although proving that is another matter.'

'Motive?'

'Pure greed—there's a lot of money involved—and malice. It might be easier if she was hated by someone. That would at least give us a start. Any ideas?'

'She wasn't popular with the CC, but outside of that she seemed well liked by the other police officers.'

'When I met her, we tried to think if any one of the criminals she'd sent down might have done it, but it seems like an inside job to me.'

'That would mean someone has managed to upgrade their cloud status to the highest level. Otherwise how could they manipulate the bank accounts and make the transfers.'

'I'd feel more confident of catching whoever it is if we weren't talking about these tablets and the cloud. I don't have much experience of that for one. For two, the guy who spends the money on the tablets admits that the technology is a bit flaky and the failure rate is around one in four.'

I picked up a piece of baguette and tore it up so I

could dunk it in the chicken juices. I wasn't flattering her when I said it was delicious.

'You keep looking at the piano,' she said.

'Was I? I didn't realize.'

'Do you play?'

'I used to, but I haven't played for many years.'

'Why don't you play anymore?' I held up my left hand with its two missing fingers.

'Nonsense,' she said. 'Django Reinhardt only used two fingers of his left hand and was widely regarded as the best jazz guitarist of all time.'

'How do you know that?'

'My husband was a fan of the Quintette of the Hot Club of France. I've got some of their records somewhere. I tell you what. Let's play together after dinner. You play melody with your right hand and I'll play chords with my left.'

'I don't know.'

'Phooey. It will be fun. Might lay a ghost to rest, too. I insist.'

I sipped some of the wine, hoping a short break might change her mind, but there was to be no escape.

'Well? What do you say?'

'Just for you.'

'Splendid!'

We went without the offered fruit or cheese and cleared the plates. Morag rinsed them—belt and braces—and stacked them in the dishwasher. My stomach had butterflies. I was beginning to think let's get this over with and get back to talking shop where I felt comfortable. We went back to the dining room and she dragged one of the chairs over to the piano so that it was alongside and on the left of the stool.

'Sit,' she said. 'What shall we play?'

'Do you know "Summertime", the Gershwin song?'

'*Porgy and Bess*? If you play the melody, I think I can improvise on the chords.'

I sat down on the stool and looked at the keys as if they were some enemy waiting to attack me. The version I most liked was a simple one by the Modern Jazz Quartet in the fifties—I'm hooked on jazz piano, John Lewis in this case, and could bore for England on the subject so I'll spare you the detail. I started to play. It was terrible. Six notes murdered.

'Relax,' Morag said. 'You're far too tense. I can feel it.'

I interlocked my fingers as best as I could and spread them wide. I took in a deep breath and tried the notes again. Better, but not yet good enough. Third time lucky.

Ba bom ba bom ba bom. Summertime and the livin' is easy.

Morag started playing accompaniment. It felt good. I got captured by the music and relaxed to the extent that there were no bum notes anymore. I started singing along. It felt good. A part of my life back where it belonged. We finished. I fought back the tears.

ELEVEN

WE DROVE TO HQ in separate cars so as not to get the gossip-mongers' tongues wagging. Morag and I met outside the CC's office where Ralph Canning was already standing, hopping from foot to foot.

'You know what you've got to say?' I said.

He nodded.

'And the tone you've got to say it in? Penitent?'

He nodded again.

I knocked on the glass door. The CC looked up and barked, 'Enter.'

Not a good sign and we were unlikely to improve his mood.

We trooped in and sat, Canning in the middle of the three chairs, Morag and I on either side.

'Good morning,' I said, trying to take the chill out of the atmosphere. The CC looked at Canning.

'What have you got to say for yourself, Mr...' He looked down at his tablet.

'... Canning?'

'I've been stupid,' Ralph said. 'Very stupid.'

'And?'

Give him a chance, I thought. The poor man's nervous enough as it is without you interrupting and breaking his flow.

'My life is falling apart. I have a wife with MS who

can't work anymore and two kids to support and kids aren't cheap.'

'So you thought you'd raid the piggy bank? Our piggy bank? The piggy bank that I am responsible for? How much, Canning?'

'A thousand a month for sixteen months.'

'So you've been swindling us for sixteen months until Shannon caught you out?'

'It was only supposed to be temporary.' An excusable lie in the circumstance, I reckoned. 'till we sold our house. Then I was going to pay it all back, I swear.'

'Swear as much as you like, Canning, but there's no room in my force for cheats and swindlers. Pack up your things and leave this building. I never want to see you again. Pay every penny back. Now get out of here before you make me retch.'

Bastard! I couldn't believe it. Ralph slumped down in his chair. Morag opened her mouth to speak, but I raised my hand. No sense in her jeopardizing her career. I had nothing to lose.

'You promised to hear the case on its merits,' I said.

'You promised to hear the case on its merits,' he mimicked in the whine of a schoolgirl. 'That's exactly what I have done.'

'But you've heard the mitigating circumstances. He's not a crook, just a silly man who thought he could see a way out of his problems. He'll never do anything like this in the future. If you sack him now, he's never going to trust anyone in authority ever again.'

'If he acts like he has done, why should I worry about him? I'm treating this leniently. I could charge him with theft and then where would he be? And why should you care? You're supposed to be investigating bigger fraud, not just stirring up trouble here. What progress have you made?'

'I've traced the money back to the next stage. I'm on the case. Put pressure on me or treat me in the way that you have treated Canning and I'll stir up a hornet's nest. Get the Federation on your back for standing in the way of justice and maybe go to the media, too, Official Secrets Acts or not.'

'I'm surprised at you, Morag, for getting personally involved in this. Take care. No one is indispensable. Now go, the three of you.'

He stood up from his chair and walked to the door, held it open.

'Go,' he repeated.

There was no point in staying. He was resolute. Nothing I said or did was going to make him listen. I put an arm around Canning and led him outside.

'Get three espressos, take away, and meet me in the pit,' Morag said.

I walked through to the cafeteria, Canning in tow, and bought the three espressos and got some sugar and stirrers. Went downstairs despondently.

Morag was already there. She was carrying a plastic bag and was heading from the direction of the lockers. She pointed to the highest level, which at this time of the day was empty as was the place in general. We sat down and I dished out the coffee. We took the cardboard lids off and she reached into the bag and brought out a three-quarter full bottle of single malt. Sacrilegiously poured a generous measure into each espresso.

'You're full of surprises, Morag. Where did you get this from?'

'I keep this for the CC for when he gets into one of his moods. I thought we all needed a pick-me-up and that this would take the sour tastes from our mouths.'

I added sugar to my coffee and took a sip. Early as it was in the day, it still tasted good.

Canning was staring into his coffee looking stunned.

'He promised,' he said. 'You said he promised, didn't you?'

'And he lied,' I said. 'This is now personal between him and me. I'll make him pay for this if it's the last thing I do. I'm going to bring him down from his ivory tower and send it crashing to the ground. You just watch me.'

'What am I going to do? How am I supposed to pay back the money with no job? How are we going to eat and pay the bills?'

'I'll think of something,' I said. 'Trust me. Finish your coffee and go home. I'll be in touch. Unlike the CC, I keep my promises.'

He downed the rest of his coffee and walked off disconsolately.

'Poor soul,' Morag said. 'I never thought it would come to this.'

'He conned us, the CC, that is.'

'What are you going to do?'

'I've no idea, but I'll do something to restore Ralph's faith in human nature.'

'You better do it quickly. God knows what state he will be in when he tells his wife. Their world is going to fall apart.'

'You best go after him, in case he does anything stupid.'

'I can only spend an hour. David Yates is coming later this morning and I have all the arrangements to make.'

'Why is the Home Secretary coming here?'

'He's always coming. This is his pet project. If the Mid Anglia experiment fails, Yates will have failed.'

'Maybe we can use that to our advantage,' I said.

'In what way?'

'I have no idea, but I'll work on it. You best be off. Do what you can to help Ralph break the news to his wife and get as much help as possible from the Staff Union.'

She got up and left the building. Now I had another item to add to my ever-increasing list. Get even with the CC. Make that two items. Get even with the CC and find Ralph another job. The first could wait a while, the second was the priority. I took the cardboard cups over to a bin and dropped them in. Started thinking what I was going to do today, and right now I hadn't a clue.

ARLENE USED TO accuse me of having a butterfly mind, flitting from one thing to another. I would try to explain that much of what I did was routine—deadly dull routine—and grew tedious after even a short while and that the only cure for this that I had found was to move frequently to something else and then move again and so on. I finally decided to pay the Federation a visit. Get their angle on the missing money. Not that I didn't trust Sam, but two angles are always better than one. I'd then skim through some more purchase invoices to see if anything else popped up. After a couple of hours of that, I planned to spend lunchtime looking at Curly's files and the afternoon on the tendering system.

The Federation's offices were back in Melchester in a modern block where they occupied four rooms on the third floor. I walked up the stairs.

A young girl in her early twenties answered the buzzer. She was wearing a very short flowery skirt on a white background and a pale blue tank top. I wondered how she would get on with Anji. Might dress similarly, depending on what persona Anji was adopting that day, but less feisty by the meek demeanour this girl displayed. She was distinctly nervous.

'Nick Shannon,' I said. 'I phoned earlier.'

'Emily,' she said. 'As I said on the phone, I don't know if I can help you. You should really talk to the chairman, but he's on holiday this week.'

'It's Sam I want to talk about. I expect you knew her better than he did. I'm trying to help her defend her case. Prove that she's innocent. You'd like that, I presume.'

'Of course. Come through. I'll make some coffee.'

'Not for me, thanks. I'm caffeined out already. How long have you known Sam?' I asked.

'Three years now. I was pretty green then. Straight out of college. She helped me a lot to get experience. Didn't seem to mind that I made mistakes as long as I didn't repeat them. She was kind to me.'

'What about the chairman? How did she get on with him?'

'Fine, as far as I know. It's true she wasn't his first choice for the job, but she was elected.'

'What about the bank accounts? Who else has authority? What happens if Sam isn't around and payments need to be made?'

'I have authority up to £5,000 and if it's above that, the chairman has power.'

Sam must have trusted her if she had given her authority for up to five grand. But this was what I wanted to hear. I could eliminate her from the list of subjects, unless she was a whole lot cleverer than I reckoned. Of course, I've been wrong before, but not this time.

I CALLED IN on Curly while I was in Melchester town and told him of my intention to take over the dungeon while he was at lunch. It would only give me an hour for my Secret Squirrelling, but I didn't want him to get a sniff of what I was up to. I doubted whether he would let me take any files away with me so I would have to be discreet about my activity.

I drove back to HQ and up to where the three ladies sat in their reserved positions. I left my laptop distrustingly in the boot until needed it later. Didn't want to appear to be a tablet traitor until absolutely necessary.

They were thrilled to see me and have another outlet for their sweets. I was even offered a barley sugar, something I hadn't seen or heard of since the age of about five. I couldn't resist one for the taste and the trip down memory lane it provided.

I took the pile of today's invoices and settled in for a bit of brain numbing. Every now and again I changed my perspective and looked away from the invoices and around the office. You need a break once in a while or you get sloppy and might miss something. I decided to go down to the pit and await the arrival of the CC's bosom buddy.

The first sign of any action was two guys with earpieces walking through the door. They had obviously opted for off-the-peg suits as the bulge in their jackets screamed that they were armed, but maybe that was the message they wanted to send out. They looked around the pit, didn't see anyone with a T-shirt with *Terrorist* in big letters on the front. One man went back outside and returned a moment later with Yates.

He was a small man, like a normal-sized person shrunken down so that everything was in proportion, a fact that hadn't registered with me from his television appearances and he walked in a very precise way as if treading on rice paper and didn't want to tear it. Unlike the guards, his dark blue suit was made to measure. Wouldn't you guess it?

I remembered reading that he was coming up to sixty and had little time to go if he wanted to reach the pinnacle of Prime Minister, but maybe Home Secretary was the peak of his ambitions. He still had a full head of hair, cut in a conservative style with some grey streaks along the sides and one at the front that gave him the unfortunate appearance of a badger. He had a long nose that was either inherited or Pinocchio syndrome.

The CC came down in person to greet him. Wow!

They stopped to chat to one of the receptionists— no one's too small to warrant my attention, the gesture said, or maybe I'm just being cynical. One of the guards went up in the lift to, presumably, secure the top floor. A moment or two later I could see the other guard talking into his microphone and the lift came back empty.

Yates, the CC and the bodyguard stepped inside and were lost to my view.

Yates only stayed fifteen minutes and left looking decidedly less happy than when he had arrived. He managed a weak smile in case there were any TV cameras present or people taking selfies and, flanked by the bodyguards, left the building. All that palaver for fifteen minutes. Hardly seemed worth it, but, of course, I didn't know what they had spoken about. I wondered if my name had come up as someone who was stirring the muddy pond to see what rose to the surface.

I went back upstairs and worked my way through the balance of the invoices and one more barley sugar. Nothing stood out as being suspicious so I gathered my things, including the untrustworthy tablet, and set off back to Melchester police station. Curly was in pre-lunch mode, sat at the desk with a file open, his tablet ready to take input and licking his lips.

'Steak and kidney pie today,' he said.

'I think I'll pass.' I wanted to be able to move in the afternoon rather than waddle with pie sticking to my ribs.

'Remind me,' he said. 'What exactly are you looking for?'

Damn. It was the question I was hoping he wouldn't ask.

'Anomalies,' I said, hoping that would stop him in his tracks.

'Anomalies?' he repeated, with a question mark hanging.

'Resources,' I said at a second try at getting him to ask no more.

'Resources?' he said. This time the question mark was apparent.

I thought quickly. 'Resources allocated for each type of case.'

'Ah,' he said.

I was winning.

'Cost control,' I said.

This time I had him, surely.

'In what respect?' he said.

Damn again.

'Are sufficient resources being allocated for each type of crime.'

'I see now,' he said.

Thank God for that. I was running out of bluffs.

'You see,' I said. 'We're both on the same side. If you need more help, I'm the guy to get it for you.'

'So how do you go about this?' he asked, just as soon as I had thought I was safe.

'Random choice,' I said.

'Ah,' he said. 'How does that work?'

'I take a random sample of the files working back over time. Look through them and analyse the working methods on each file and see if they come up as sub optimal.'

I liked that. Sub optimal. Had a nice ring to it.

'Well, I'm off to lunch,' he said. Got him. As with most people, I had bored him past his interest level in just a few well-chosen sentences.

I took his master binder that contained the catalogue of cases still to be transferred to the cloud. I looked back through it and found the notation *Shannon, hit-and-run*. I put a dot against it in pencil and then worked forward, putting a dot against every tenth one. That was my random sample in case he wanted to see it.

He was right about the dust and I was wrong to ignore his warning. My prime interest was the hit-and-run and that was a long time ago. The dust level that far back was horrendous. Everything I touched caused some to fall on the floor and the rest to fly into the air. I had a coughing fit as I touched each one.

The file wasn't there, or if it was, it wasn't in the place it should have been. I went back to Curly's magic list and checked in case I had made some mistake. I hadn't. The file number was right. It was now going to be like finding a needle in a haystack.

I started my search by going one to the right and one to the left in the shelves and then repeating the process when I found nothing. It was a long slog, and fruitless.

Curly came back and found me on my knees.

'Not praying are you, Nick?' he said.

'Let's just say I'm thinking about it.'

'Got a problem?'

'I can't find a file.'

'Which one?'

I gave him the reference number. He checked back in his list.

'Should be here,' he said. 'Let me see.'

He joined me and worked his way along the shelf until he came to where it should have been.

'Can't understand it,' he said with a perplexed frown. 'The system's never wrong.'

'Could someone have borrowed it?'

'If they did, then they didn't tell me. I'll have a search for you, Nick. Can't do it right now, but maybe later or even tomorrow depending on whether there's any urgent demand from CID for anything.'

'I'd be grateful,' I said.

'OK then, Nick. Has anyone ever told you that you've got the right name to work in the police force?'

Frequently.

'No, they haven't,' I said. 'Nice one, Curly.'

I didn't like the way things were panning out. No gold. There was an added problem, too. So far I had only referred to the file by reference number. If he checked thoroughly, he'd see the name Shannon there and put two and two together to arrive at the obvious answer. I could claim it was a coincidence, but who was going to swallow that?

'I'll leave it in your capable hands,' I said. I took a card from my wallet and handed it to him. 'Give me a call if you have any success. And maybe if you don't have any success either. These things are good to know.'

'Won't be a black mark, will it, Nick?'

'Not for you, Curly. Maybe someone else if they've borrowed it without your permission.'

'Spoils your analysis, I suppose. One of those anomalies you mentioned?'

'Definitely.'

I collected up my things and prepared to go.

'Sorry if you've wasted your time,' he said.

'Time is never wasted,' I said. 'Only spent as an investment for the future.'

How's that for cryptic?

I DROVE BACK TO HQ, took my laptop out of the boot and went to find a quiet spot. I walked up the stairs, checking on each floor. The third floor was sparsely populated, so I sat myself down, put my tablet to the left of me and fired up the laptop. This was going to be a frustrating exercise. In the real world, which most of us live in, I could have worked with a computer of some sort with an extra screen. That way I could have the tender file open on one screen and the spreadsheet I was concocting on the other screen. I'd even have settled on one computer and split screen, but the tablet was fiddly. The screen was too small so that was having to scroll through every five lines. It was frustratingly slow.

The first column of my spreadsheet was the date the contract was awarded, the next was what for, then, progressing along, amount purchased, price paid, company with the winning tender. I worked back for every tender since Mid Anglia had come into being. I'd do some manipulation tomorrow and find out if there were any patterns and what they told me. For now, it was time to find Morag and head home. I hoped tomorrow would be more productive.

MORAG WAS IN the kitchen when I arrived at her house. I poured us each a drink.

'My God, that's good,' Morag said.

I took a sip of my vodka and orange juice and agreed with her.

'What upset Yates today?' I said. 'He did not look a happy bunny.'

'God knows. Usually the pair of them are as thick as thieves.'

'And that's how the CC jumped up the promotion ladder?'

'I couldn't possibly comment.'

'You don't have to. It's been said by others before.'

'By whom?'

'I couldn't possibly comment.'

'Touché.'

'It doesn't seem right that you come home from work each day and then have to start preparing a meal. We must take advantage of that complimentary meal at The Green Dragon. Maybe tomorrow or the next day. Give you a break.'

'That sounds good, but I enjoy cooking and your company while I'm doing it. It's not a chore with you around.'

'Well, bear it in mind.'

My phone rang. I apologized to Morag and stepped into the lounge to take it. It was Norman.

'Arthur and I are coming up tomorrow. I'll bring Anji, too. It'll be part of her education. Is that OK? You did say it was urgent. I'll get Toddy to do us a hamper.'

'Let me call you back.'

I went back to the kitchen.

'I've got a favour to ask,' I said to Morag. 'Norman and Arthur want to come and bring my PA tomorrow when we've finished work. We could go out to eat, but we don't want to be overheard. Could we have the meeting here? They'll bring food and drink.'

'If you are going to discuss police business here, I need to know what you are talking about. I want to sit in.'

'Let me check.'

I went back to the dining room and rang Norman. He was edgy about Morag sitting in, but I managed to persuade him by saying that she was loyal to her boss despite his faults and that she would be loyal to our friendship.

'Despite your faults,' he said.

'Ha ha!'

I gave him the address and we signed off. I went back into the kitchen and broke the news to Morag.

'You're in,' I said. 'Welcome to the gang.'

'Let's celebrate with another drink then,' she said. 'This is exciting.'

I was beginning to feel that I was a *very* bad influence on her.

TWELVE

Travelling separately again to HQ, Morag and I met up in the cafeteria. Too early for coffee, but it was a good space to spread out. We grabbed a table by the window. It was a fine day with bright sunshine and a cloudless sky—spring had finally arrived. There were daffodils in the grounds of the building and snowdrops in beds near to the benches. It felt good to be alive.

I set up the laptop on the table and brought up the spreadsheets I had created to investigate the tendering system and see if it looked like someone was leaking information to the winning companies.

Buyers love tenders, suppliers hate them—buyers see it purely as an exercise to beat the suppliers down to the absolute minimum price and lowest profit. All tenders—the document sent out to the bidding companies which contains the specification of every last nut and bolt that the supplier must provide or pay a forfeit—include a clause that says that the purchasing company is under no obligation to take the lowest price. No one believes this. It's about the money and nothing else.

Together, Morag and I worked our way through the spreadsheets I had created that analysed the data by winning company, type of purchase, date of tender, size of contract and any other variables that I could think of. Nothing leapt out at me. There seemed to be no pattern worthy of note: no company winning more tenders than would have been their fair share.

'Remind me what we're looking for,' Morag said.

'Any pattern that might throw up a question mark. Why is such and such a company more or less successful in its bids. The most common trick is to be fed confidential information on other bids received that the scamming company can undercut at the last minute. That company then pays a bribe for its information. If that was happening, I would expect to see one company standing out as more successful in the tendering process. Then I would look at who on the inside could be feeding information.'

'And you'd expect that to be Terry Sutton, the head of procurement?'

'Could be anyone, but Sutton would be the prime candidate. He'd be the one most likely to have an opportunity to have a sneaky peek at the other tenders. Looks as though he's clean, though. I can't find any suspicious pattern.'

'Take me through them again,' she said. 'It's possible that a fresh pair of eyes may spot something.'

I gave a shrug. Unlikely, but there was nothing to be lost by humouring her.

'This is the master list of all of the tenders,' I said, showing her the first spreadsheet. 'And this is that list sorted by product or service bought.'

I let her study it for a while and then brought up each of the other sheets in turn.

'How do you know about spreadsheets?' I asked.

'I do the CC's expenses. I have a spreadsheet that he submits for payment and then other sheets that analyse them by category and VAT amount and allocation to budget fields. What about,' she said, 'if you analyse category supplied by date rather than having them as two separate sheets?'

I clicked on the sheet and did another sort as she had suggested.

'Nothing interesting,' I said. 'No one supplier stands out.'

'Exactly,' she said.

'What do you mean?' I asked.

'It's too regular a pattern. Company A then company B and so on.'

I looked again. She was right.

'Oh, hell,' I said. 'It's "Buggins's turn". It's too regular. They're operating a cartel. Instead of competing on price so that the lowest gets the contract, they agree a price that would win the tender and give a proper profit and Company A goes for that and the others bid higher. Next time around it's Company B's turn to win and so on and so on. They've worked out a system that beats the tendering process. You're not getting the best possible price after all. Brilliant work, Morag. I'll make a fraud investigator out of you yet.'

'It's so exciting,' she said. 'A world away from what I normally do. Make your stay here as long as possible. I'm loving every minute of it.'

My phone pinged to tell me that a text had come through. I opened the app. The message was from Curly. Cum c me now. My heart started beating faster. It sounded like he had some important news for me. Let it be that he had found the file.

No such luck.

'You haven't been totally honest with me, Shannon.'

As soon as I stepped through the door of the dungeon I knew something was up. He had a face like thunder with added bolts of lightning. It was obvious I had been rumbled.

'In fact,' Curly said, 'you haven't been honest with me at all. The missing file has your name on it. Shannon. Writ large. No wonder you kept going on about calling you Nick. Do you want to deny it, or shall we move on from there and decide what I'm going to do with you?'

'It's an open case. You said so yourself. That's why the file should be down here. You said open cases are kept for inputting on to the cloud. As long as it's an open case I thought someone should be investigating it.'

'And that someone should be you? What's so important about that case? It's before my time, so enlighten me.'

'My sister was crippled by a hit-and-run driver and her boyfriend was killed. That needs investigating until the culprit is brought to justice.'

'You made me look a fool,' he said. 'Before I realized what was going on, I sent an email to everyone asking if they had the file. Now people will think I'm running errands for you.'

'I didn't mean you any harm or to lose face, but look at it from my point of view. Something isn't right. Why would that file go missing if there wasn't anything suspicious going on? This smells to me like a cover up. What does your copper's nose tell you?'

'It could just be coincidence.'

'Come off it, Curly. That's hardly likely. Someone wants this case buried for good. Aren't you interested in finding out why? And where's your sense of justice?

Isn't that one of the reasons you became a police officer? To put criminals behind bars so they can't hurt anyone.'

'Relax, Nick,' he said. 'I'm playing devil's advocate. You're preaching to the converted. Like you, it didn't take me long to realize it was unlikely that it was a co-incidence. I decided to check on the cloud just to see if someone else had input it while I was on holiday or something.'

'And?'

'It's on the cloud. God knows how. We couldn't find the file because it should have been shredded once it had been input on the cloud.'

'Interesting. Why get rid of the file and put it on the cloud so that it still exists?'

'That occurred to me, too.'

'So are you going to let me have a look at it?'

'It's not as easy as that.'

'Why not?'

'It's marked level 7 only.'

'And what does that mean?'

'The CC's eyes only. The only person who can see the file is the CC. Unless you can steal his tablet and know his code, you can't access it.'

'Curiouser and curiouser.'

'It's a dead end,' he said. 'Something's not right, but we're going nowhere.'

'Hell! I thought we were getting close for a moment.'

'I'll give it some thought, but I can't promise anything.'

'Thanks, Curly. I appreciate it.' A thought struck me. 'What about asking the other officers if they remember the case and any details?'

'Only if the opportunity presents itself and I judge it not a risk to myself. I'm not going out on a limb for you. I'm too close to retirement to lose my pension. If you take my advice, leave well enough alone. Let sleeping dogs lie. Isn't that what they say?'

'Only when the truth could be dangerous to someone.'

'That's as good as it gets from me, Shannon. Now go and do the job you're here for instead of involving me in a wild goose chase that could blow up in my face.'

Mixed metaphors, and their meaning was that this avenue was a cul-de-sac and I didn't know where to turn next. Take Curly's advice, I suppose. Head back to HQ and stir up trouble there instead.

I got into the Beamer and headed for the ring road. At this time of the morning it was quiet. I went up the ramp and on to the dual carriageway. A black car followed me up the slope and settled in behind me. I increased my speed to seventy. The black car matched my speed. It got closer.

I had two options; put my foot down and shake him off or let him pass to annoy someone else. I took the latter course. The black car stuck where it was. I gave a shrug. I was in no hurry and he'd get bored soon with tailgating me.

We were approaching a right-hand curve in the road when the car rammed me from behind. What was going on?

I had to work hard on the steering to get the Beamer to follow the road rather than being pushed over the embankment and down into the surrounding trees. While I was fighting to maintain control, the black car pulled alongside. There were two people in the car, both wearing balaclavas. They side-swiped me, trying to push me off the road and down into the trees. At this speed I would crash into a tree and sustain a lot of injuries, air bags only lessening the impact on me if I was lucky. Not a good scenario. There was nothing for it. I floored the accelerator and the Beamer leapt forward, putting a lot of distance between us. I was doing over a hundred and they were still trying to catch me up and get me again.

There was an exit coming up leading to a roundabout. I increased my speed and, at the very last moment, swung left and down the exit lane. The black car followed. I entered the roundabout, jerked the handbrake up while simultaneously steering hard right. The car jack-knifed ninety degrees and went round the roundabout. The black car couldn't match the manoeuvre: didn't have the power, didn't have the skill. Having gone all the way around the roundabout, I was now behind them. The hunter had become the hunted.

The black car lost it and swung around so that it was now travelling backwards. It sent their car careering on a course to take it into one of the stanchions holding up the road above. There was a terrible collision followed by a deafening bang. Their car caught fire and sat there with flames coming from the engine. There was no movement from the occupants. They were frying in hell. Big price paid. The ultimate price.

I pulled to a halt up the slip road and took out my mobile. I needed a friend to get me out of this mess. I called Morag.

TWO POLICE CARS, a fire engine and an ambulance arrived at the scene. Morag was already there by then.

We walked down the slip road to the roundabout. A police officer motioned us to stay where we were while he blocked off the road to traffic. The fire engine was getting itself organized and, after what seemed like a lifetime, started to pump water on to the burning car. The ambulance waited patiently for what was going to be left of the occupants. There was no hurry.

One of the police officers approached us. He stopped in his tracks—he recognized Morag.

'Ms McClellan, what are you doing here?'

'I'm here to vouch for Mr Shannon. You can trust his word. He's working on a special case for the CC.'

'Car looks a bit of a mess,' he said.

It was an understatement—rear smashed and a big indentation and scrape down the right-hand side.

'You better tell me what happened.'

I took him through the route from the police station and the drive to here and how what was left of the black car had tried to force me off the road.

'And why should he or she do that?' he asked.

'Seems like I may have upset somebody.'

'Big time,' he said.

'I'm working to clear Sam Stone's name. Maybe someone doesn't want that to happen.'

'I liked Sam,' he said, like all the others using the past tense, 'but that doesn't buy you any favours. Come down to the station this afternoon and give us a statement. We'll see where we go from there. I can't promise anything.'

Seemed like the catchphrase of the day.

I LOST THE rest of the afternoon hanging around at the police station to give my statement. Morag sat patiently with me. The time wasn't wasted as I spent a long while on the phone with Anji. I got her to hire me a car, get the Beamer picked up and taken to my local garage and start what would inevitably be the long drawn out procedures with the insurance company.

Curly walked through the station reception area and jolted back when he saw me.

'What have you been up to now, Shannon? Have they found you out at last?'

'Very funny, Curly. Someone tried to kill me, that's all.'

'You're joking, aren't you?'

'I may be a wise guy at times, but that's something I don't joke about. Whoever it was tried to force me off the road—'

'And finished up roasting in hell,' the desk sergeant interrupted.

'You're not supposed to be eavesdropping,' I said.

'It's as boring behind this desk as it is in front. What else am I going to do to stop me dropping off?'

'Roasting in hell?' said Curly. 'What do you mean?'

'The car chasing him hit a stanchion of the road and burst into flames. No way anyone could get out alive,' the desk sergeant said.

'Seems like you're a dangerous man to know,' Curly said.

'Strange,' I said. 'I was thinking the same about you.'

MORAG DROVE US straight to her house after I had given my statement. In an unspoken agreement, we went directly into the kitchen and poured drinks. Large ones.

'Trouble seems to follow you around,' she said after a big sip of her sherry.

'Sometimes it gets ahead of me, too,' I replied.

She nodded wisely.

The doorbell rang before we could get into a philosophical discussion of my magnetic power with the iron of trouble.

Anji walked in first; feisty mode today. Just looking at her told me she'd get everything under control and wouldn't spare anyone that got in her way.

'Hire car is in the driveway,' she said. 'I got the fastest they had, but it won't be a patch on the BMW.'

Norman followed. He seemed to rock back on his heels when he saw Morag. I wondered if that was what they called the thunderbolt.

'Pleased to meet you, dear lady,' he said, shaking Morag's hand. 'So kind of you to welcome us all to your lovely house.'

Morag gave a little whimper.

Arthur gave a polite cough. He had a large wicker hamper in each hand.

'Where shall I put these?' he asked.

'The dining room,' Morag said. 'Please follow me.'

She led the Shannon Investigations party into the dining room where Arthur placed the hampers on the table and Norman opened the first one.

He took out two bottles of red wine and a corkscrew and set about opening the first bottle.

'Didn't go for the Pomerol,' he said. 'Would have got too shaken up on the journey. I went for a modest Malbec instead.'

Good choice. Like he'd been reading my mind.

Anji opened the other hamper and took out five plastic goblets and set them before Norman who filled them lovingly. He passed a glass to each of us, took a sip, beamed with pleasure and started unloading both hampers.

'The best that Toddy can provide,' he said, spreading plates and cutlery around the table.

Many dishes followed. A sumptuous cold buffet stared up at us from the table. There was enough to feed an army, but maybe that was what we now were.

Norman pulled out one of the chairs and gestured to Morag that she should sit down. He tucked the chair in under her and sat down next to her. The rest of us took our seats. Anji started passing dishes around for us to help ourselves to the feast.

Norman looked at me. 'So we're on a pro bono case that may not generate any money and you've pretty much written off the BMW. Not going well at the moment, then?'

'Thanks for your concern,' I said.

'He doesn't mean it,' said Arthur. 'Do you want me to shadow you for a while? Watch your back?'

'Not yet. At least I know to keep a look out for danger from now on.'

'This is only the start, isn't it?' Anji said. 'Does anyone here think that they're going to give up after two of them are dead?'

'It's the *them* that's a problem,' I said. 'Who set up the attack on me?'

'And why?' Arthur said. 'Seems to me you've riled people. Now why would that be? Apart from your annoying habit of acting the wise guy, that is.'

'Two possible reasons,' I said. 'Either someone doesn't want me to prove Sam innocent or it's to do with the hit-and-run. Curly—the policeman who looks after the archives of open cases—sent round an email to see if anyone had the case file. Now everybody knows I'm digging around. Could be someone wants the case buried for good. And me with it.'

'The hit-and-run or a million pound fraud,' said Norman. 'Tough call.'

'These prawns are good,' said Morag. 'And this was done by the forger?'

Norman looked at me with a raised eyebrow.

'I've been filling Morag in on our history,' I said.

'Nothing wrong with that,' he said to my surprise. 'I trust this lovely lady implicitly.' He gave her a smile and touched her hand.

'There is one bit of good news,' I said. 'We do have the money from the phoney invoice scam.'

'How much is that?' said Norman.

'Our ten per cent fee is £1,600.'

'That won't go far,' said Norman.

'Especially as I want to give it away,' I said.

All eyes fell on me.

'Explain,' said Norman. 'Too early for Christmas presents, so you must have a good reason.'

I explained about Canning and his financial problems and the family that depended deeply on him.

'The money will buy him a little time till he sells his house in London.'

'So it's a loan rather than a gift?' Norman said.

I shrugged.

'Is he always like this?' asked Anji, looking at me.

'Unfortunately,' said Norman.

'That's so sweet,' said Morag.

Norman looked at her and paused for breath. 'Give him the money,' he said. 'His need is greater than ours.'

Out of character for Norman and I had a clue how it had come about. Life in the old dog yet.

'I've got a job for you, Arthur,' I said.

'This always spells trouble,' he said to Anji. 'OK, hit me with it.'

'Mid Anglia has a reptile fund in cash for paying informants.'

'And where there's cash…' said Norman.

'There's a fiddle,' I completed.

'So where do I fit in?' said Arthur.

'You're going to become a copper's nark,' I said.

'What! That goes against my deepest principles. Plus, if it gets out, I'll never live it down. I'll be a marked man.'

'Or you could be the hero who brought a bent cop to justice—if he's guilty, that is. Don't worry, no one will find out, and it's in a good cause. You're going to get in touch with a Detective Inspector Harry Saunders and offer him a tip-off about an armed robbery on his patch. It will need to be someone you know from Brixton so that it's plausible. You ask for £500 and see what happens. If what he eventually pays you is less than what goes through the books, then we've got him.'

'Doesn't it bother you,' Morag said, 'that you always have to look on the black side of people? Always having to assume they're on the make and looking out for only themselves?'

'It's part of the job,' Norman said. 'We couldn't operate any other way. You have to get inside the fraud-ster's mind and that means you're wrong a lot of the time and right in a minority of cases. That's the way it works. Always was, always will be.'

'It doesn't mean,' I said, 'that we think everybody is bad—the reverse is generally true—but as the CC would say, you have to hunt for the rotten apple and there usually is at least one in most large organizations.'

'I see what Morag means,' said Arthur. 'I'd never thought of it like that before. It's like we don't trust anybody. Not a great way to go through life.'

'But when we trust someone,' I said, 'we do it with all our hearts. That's why Morag is sitting here. We could easily have met without her—in somewhere less private, granted—but we believe she is worthy of our trust and, thus, we include her to a full extent. If we're wrong, it doesn't mean we'll never trust anyone again, only that we might be more careful next time.'

Arthur dipped a large prawn in the Marie rose sauce and prepared to pop it in his mouth. He paused with it in mid-air. 'I like to think of life as eating a prawn,' he said to our bewilderment. 'Every now and again you get a dodgy one. Doesn't mean you shouldn't ever eat prawns again. You have to trust each one that it won't cause you any harm.'

'Noble thought,' I said. 'But what landed you in prison? Too much trust.'

'Doesn't mean I'll change my view, though.'

'You're always so refreshing to talk to, Arthur,' I said. 'You keep our feet on the ground and our heads from out of the clouds.'

'Can I ask a question?' Anji said.

'Providing it's not asking for a salary rise already or danger money,' Norman said.

'I was going to ask when do I get into the action.'

'You're already in it,' I said. 'Don't worry, I'm sure there will be plenty of action to go round.'

'OK,' she said. 'Just as long as you know I'm up for it.'

'What did you find from a trawl through Sam's documents?'

'She's meticulous. Saved much more paperwork than a normal person would. Goes back five years. She was a wealthy woman then. Lump sum of £50,000 paid in. Insurance company, so I'd assume that was on the death of her husband.'

'Fifty thousand doesn't go far these days,' I said.

'Exactly,' she said. 'It's been dwindling since then. Living beyond her means. But that doesn't make her a spendthrift. Apart from the odd holiday, she's frugal. Just not enough coming in for the day-to-day expenditure. I reckon she's hanging on for retirement—take a lump sum and then a monthly pension and hope it all comes right.'

'Amen,' said Morag.

'Keep digging,' I said to Anji. 'Go through it all one more time to make sure you haven't missed anything. Check on all the fine detail. Go through her credit card bills again and see what it tells you about her. Where she likes to eat, where does she do her shopping. Where she likes to go on holiday. Get inside her mind and tell me what you find.'

Anji nodded.

'Forgive me,' said Morag, 'but you sound like you

think she might be guilty. All this checking and double checking.'

'This is all material that the prosecution can bring up if it suits their case. No harm being pre-warned.'

We carried on eating for a while, talking only of inconsequential things such as the offices and their futuristic concepts of melding work with play and allowing the inner creative to burst through the minds of typical workers. Morag was defensive on the topic, but we could sense her heart wasn't really in it.

After strawberries and cream, Norman turned to Anji. 'Why don't you give Morag a hand with the washing up while us old lags talk of days gone by.'

She stood up, collected some plates and started the clearing up process. When he was sure that Morag was out of earshot, he turned to me.

'Lovely lady,' he said with a twinkle in his eye. 'Is she taken?'

THIRTEEN

I MET CANNING HALFWAY between his home and Melchester. It was partly convenience, cutting down on travel time for each of us and permitting me to devote more of my time to Mid Anglia, and partly because I didn't want to know more about his circumstances than I did already—going to his home wasn't an option. I was involved, but didn't want to be more so. I didn't want to see his ailing wife. I didn't want to see his two children and look in their eyes. I had overstepped my remit in getting Norman's agreement to give him the money from our fee and I didn't want to feel so responsible that I committed us to more. This had to be head over heart.

I also needed to see him alone: what I wanted to ask might not go down well with his wife.

Like spooks, we met in the castle park at Colchester. There was a small café where I could look up at the castle and down through lush lawns to the bowling green. There were a few tables and chairs outside, all unoccupied. A weak sun was shining and the air was cool rather than having a chill about it. Pretty nice day to what we had been having. I chose a table in the sun and which was sheltered by the wall of the café. I bought two cups of tea and some sticky buns.

'How's it going?' I said, although I could tell the answer from his haggard look.

He was wearing a long dark coat over a thick grey jumper. Must have been cold at home for all these layers.

'Not good,' he said. 'The stress only makes my wife's condition worse—they want her to go into hospital for a week to have steroids, but she's worried how the kids will cope. They already sense something is wrong. The sooner we can sell our house and sort out our finances the better. I have to get a job soon—we've no savings to fall back on. Without a reference, I don't know how easy that will be.'

'Tell me more about what you did at Mid Anglia and I might be able to help. All I know is that you said you worked in IT and had something to do with the cloud. Doing what exactly?'

'I handled the system's parameters.'

Well, that told me a lot.

'Pretend you're talking to an idiot,' I said, 'and tell me what that means.'

'The cloud is like a giant computer. All the users are connected to it and every individual wants a swift response to their needs. To do that, someone needs to keep the cloud clutter free. Think about what happens on your computer at home. The more programs you have running, the slower it gets. Now multiply that by a few thousand times for our number of staff and you get an idea of the stresses on the system. Plus, add in that all the storage for all the users is there, too, and each user wants to access their data quickly and easily. Think of it a bit like a Formula 1 car—to keep it at its fastest you have to be constantly monitoring its performance and tweaking all the component parts.'

'So let's take a hypothetical case. Suppose I wanted access to the files of someone else. How would I go about it?'

'I could access up to level 6 with no problem.'

'This is level 7.'

'But only the CC has level 7 access.'

'Well, what a coincidence. So how do I gain access, hypothetically speaking, of course, to the CC's files?'

'It's a two-part authentication system. First, you could only access it from the CC's tablet. Second, you need either his passcode or his fingerprint. Do you have, hypothetically, his passcode?'

I shook my head.

'Then, you would need to kidnap him along with his tablet and hold his finger on the sensor.'

'More drastic than I had in mind. I'm told the tablets are a bit flaky and the technology isn't as good as an iPad. Is there any way I could use that weakness?'

'The fingerprint recognition could be more precise, granted, but unless you have a finger that's ninety per cent similar to the CC's, the recognition would pick up the difference and wouldn't allow you access. You could always chop off his finger.'

'I'm looking for something more subtle than that. Some way where no one could tell that anything had happened. Some way that wouldn't link back to me.'

He sipped his tea and prodded the icing top of the sticky bun. His finger had left a mark.

'That would be good enough to fool the recognition software,' he said.

'I'll bear that in mind,' I said.

It was disheartening news—not only did I have to

steal his tablet, but either get his passcode or his fingerprint, too. I took an envelope out of my pocket and
passed it to him.

'What's this?' he said, opening the envelope and
finding the cheque inside.

'Let's call it a consultancy fee. Something for today
and a down payment for times to come. It's our fee for
finding you out. Seems right you should have it.'

'But I can't accept this.'

'You just have. Spend it wisely till you get another
job and sell the house. It won't go far, but hopefully
will tide you over.'

'I don't know how to thank you.'

'Then don't try. Start sending off CVs as soon as you
get back. Maybe they won't all ask for a reference.' I
stood up and shook his hand. 'I'll be in touch,' I said.

'I owe you,' he said.

'You certainly do. Now get out of here before we
both start crying in our tea.'

FOURTEEN

THE FIRST REVIEW of Sam's case was set for ten o'clock. Morag and I got to the police station early and met with the solicitor, Martin Baker. I had worked with him before on other cases, all on the prosecution side, though, and he was cool and efficient. Because of these virtues, he exuded confidence and that made me and his clients feel better. We all had felt that he was a good man to have on your side. Uncharacteristically for normally sombre solicitors, he was wearing a light grey suit with a pinstriped blue shirt and a red tie. I suspected he was making a sartorial statement to throw the police off guard.

We stood outside and updated him on progress on our investigation, which was little. His advice was to leave the talking to him, unless asked specifically by him for input.

Sam came along in a black suit with a long skirt, her hair tied back and minimal make-up—no-nonsense businesswoman was her style of the day. I introduced her to Martin and told her not to worry. Easier said than done, I thought. We entered the police station and were shown into a large interview room with a one-way mirror. The four of us sat on one side of a rectangular table, awaiting the arrival of our interrogators.

'I know this room well,' said Sam, 'but always on

the other side of the desk. Seems strange.' She gave a shudder.

'There's nothing to worry about,' said Martin. 'This is just a first hearing. It basically just means that the police state their case and we deny everything. It's good for us because if the case seems weak we can apply for the charges to be dropped. I would have done that in any case, but it's all a formality. We're just going through the motions at this stage.'

Two plain-clothes officers entered. One was short and going to fat, the other tall and thin with grey hair. It looked like Central Casting had given them the roles of good cop, bad cop. Introductions were made and the tall one paused with his finger on the button of a digital recording machine.

'Before I start the machine,' he said, 'let me say that this gives me no pleasure, Sam. We've known each other a long while and this is just a job that I've been given to carry out. It's nothing personal.'

'I understand, Joe,' said Sam. 'I would feel the same in your position. Don't worry about it.'

He switched the recorder on and read out the caution, the charges and names of those present.

'Wait a moment,' said Martin. 'I would say on the record that if at any stage I feel there is a conflict of interest, I will ask for the investigation to be carried out by another force.'

The fat one gave a sigh. 'You don't need to throw your weight around,' he said. 'After this preliminary hearing, we'll pass the investigation on to the Fraud Squad.'

And unleash another conflict of interest. Still, we

might be able to play that to our advantage. Choreo-
graph something with Collins. Get the case dismissed
on some technicality.

'Now, can we get started?' Fat Guy said. 'What do
you have to say to the charges?'

'My client has no comment to make. As her repre-
sentative we will be defending the case against her as
a frame up. Someone's stolen the money and pinning
the blame on Ms Stone. It's the crudest attempt at fraud
I have ever seen. No one with any brains would have
moved a small amount of the money into their personal
bank account where it could be so easily identified. And
we can all agree that Sam has brains. What other evidence will you present?'

'Our bank has told us the bulk of the money—the
£1,000,000 less the two lots of £25,000 in Ms Stone's
account—has been paid into the account of a company
called Melchester Blue and from there transferred to
Liechtenstein.'

Martin looked at me and I nodded my agreement
of the facts.

'And from there?' Martin said.

'The trail runs cold.'

'And what link do you have between Melchester Blue
and my client?'

There was silence and Martin nodded at me.

'Melchester Blue,' I said, 'is a recently formed limited company bought off the shelf. Whoever owns it
now has filed no changes to the share capital or directors. Again the trail goes cold, but we're working on it
to prove that Sam has no connection.'

'Although the onus is not on us to disprove a connection,' Martin said, 'it is on you to prove one.'

Fat Guy sighed again and said, addressing Sam, 'How do you explain the two sums of £25,000 that were transferred into your account from Mid Anglia and the Federation?'

'My client has no comment.'

'We have all the proof we need to convict you of fraud,' Joe, the thin guy said. 'You know how the system works, Ms Stone. Admit your guilt and everything goes easier for you, length of prison term most of all.'

'My client has no comment.'

'We have you bang to rights,' Fat Guy said, getting agitated. His face was growing redder with each interruption from Martin. I could see veins starting to throb on his forehead. 'It's a cast-iron case. Admit it.'

'My client has no comment.'

'Are you going to say that to every question I put?' said Fat Guy.

'Definitely,' said Martin.

'Then we might as well stop here,' said Joe. He reached across and switched off the recorder. 'Good luck, Sam,' he said. 'You're going to need it.'

WE SAT IN a coffee bar just up the street—like most high streets there were plenty to choose from.

'What was the point of that?' Sam asked.

'We now know what their case will be based upon,' replied Martin. 'The two smaller amounts will be enough to convict you. We have to defend that line of attack. We only have one chance.'

'Trace the money going through Melchester Blue,'

I said. 'If we can prove someone else benefitted from those amounts, then their case falls apart.'

'Then I'm sunk,' Sam said, staring into the froth of her cappuccino.

'Maybe not,' I said. 'There might be a way to find where the money went from the Liechtenstein account.'

Martin raised an eyebrow. 'Is this legal?'

'Not as such,' I said.

'Then I don't want to know about it. I have three words of advice.'

'And they are?' I asked.

'Don't get caught.'

With those words, he left. Morag and I did our best to cheer Sam up, but she ignored our efforts and demonstrated displacement activity by scooping at the cream in her coffee and rearranging it. I suspected the enormity of the task of proving her innocence had at last sunk in.

'How are you going to trace the Liechtenstein money?' she said.

'Not me. I can't do it, but I know someone who might.'

She managed a half-hearted smile. 'Why the *might*?' she said.

'It relies on what operating system the bank has.'

'It wouldn't involve hacking by any chance?' Morag asked perceptively. 'In which case I'm not sure I want to hear any more, although I would be fascinated to know how you're going to do it.'

'Sounds like a long shot,' Sam said.

'About the same chance as Brian Blessed winning a whispering contest. But it worked once in the past— an insurance company fraud I got involved in while on secondment to the Fraud Squad—and, let's face it, what have we to lose?'

'Only your freedom if you get caught.'

'There is that,' I said.

FIFTEEN

THE RESTAURANT WAS as crowded as on our first visit. We got a special welcome as I said my name and were shown to a table by the window where we could watch the passers-by if conversation faltered. We looked at the menus and ordered drinks. I'd booked cabs as there was little point in limiting our alcoholic intake as the drinks and the meal were on the house. We might as well take full advantage of the situation.

'About this Liechtenstein account,' Morag said.

'I thought you didn't want to know anything about it.'

'I've given up on trying to keep you in check. Every barrier anyone puts in front of you, you seem to find a way round. I might as well know the full story.'

'Let's just say that there is a back door in computers running Unix as their operating systems—and that's the most common operating system that bigger companies use. That's about all I can tell you. But I know someone who has got the key to that back door. I just need to persuade her to open it for me.'

'Past lover? Is that the problem?'

'I wish it was that easy. Let's just say she owes me nothing except trying to frame me for fraud. That's the trump card that I have. Trouble is I don't think she feels that that suit is trumps. It matters little to her, as she has little conscience where I'm concerned. I need to find an edge.'

'I once heard Clint Eastwood use those same words in a movie. It seemed to lead him to kill every person that crossed his path in a different way. Are you going to destroy people? Leave corpses in your wake?'

'Only metaphorically, but I suspect yes. It seems to be part of my DNA, although that's too easy a cliché to use. My philosophy is that everybody should get their just deserts.'

'A noble thought. And yet you let Canning off the hook?'

'He's learnt his lesson. He won't do anything as stupid ever again. He's not a crook, just someone whose circumstances got too much for him. He panicked. Thought he had found an easy way out. Sometimes in life there is no easy way out.'

'Gosh, that's deep. I feel like I should be taking notes and spreading the word. The gospel according to Shannon.'

Our starters arrived, cutting short the philosophical discussions.

'They're here again,' Morag said.

'Who?' I asked.

'The two people from the force. Tapping away at their tablets. We really will be the talk of Mid Anglia now. Two dinners in a week. They'll be starting a collection for wedding presents tomorrow.' She gave a little giggle. 'Norman seemed a charming man.'

I'd heard Norman described in many ways, but charming had never come into it.

'Excuse me,' I said, getting up. I walked over to the

table with the men on tablets. 'Sorry to interrupt,' I said. 'I'm planning to buy a tablet and you seem to be doing well with yours. Is it any good?'

'Best value for money around. OK, it's Chinese, but it does pretty much the same as a tablet three times its price. I could get you one if you like.'

'How much could you get one for? I don't have a big budget.'

'How does £200 sound?'

I screwed my face up.

'Let's say £175,' he said.

'Sounds great,' I said.

'Be here Friday night with cash—no credit cards or cheques. Let's say eight o'clock.'

He shook my hand to seal the deal and I walked back to our table and Morag.

'What was that about?' she asked.

'I think I've just found out why the tablets have such a high failure rate. They're condemning them and selling them on. Get a free replacement from China and no one is any the wiser and no one gets hurt. Except Mid Anglia, that is.'

'How do you know?'

'When was the last time you heard of someone buying something cheap from a man in a pub that wasn't stolen?'

'Your experience is greater than mine, but I take your point. If it's true, then you're a very lucky person.'

'Seven years in prison. Just lost my wife. Yeah, lucky.'

'I'm sorry. I didn't mean to sound insensitive.'

'I'm sorry, too. I didn't mean to jump at you. I just

think I deserve a bit of good luck from time to time. Luck evens out in the final analysis. You just have to ride out a bad spell and surf on the wave of a good one. That's what I'm trying to do and this case is helping. Stops me dwelling on things I can't do anything about.'

'I understand.'

'Tell me, how long did it take for you to get over your husband's death?'

'I'm not sure I really am over it. I still think of the good times we had together and cry when looking at old photos. Seems lonely without him even now.'

'Any advice?'

'Try not to dwell. Build yourself a new life. It won't stop you thinking about her, but you'll have some sort of diversion. Won't stop you getting sad, but it will ease things gradually. Don't moon about things you wish you'd said or done. She would have understood. Keep a little part of your brain dedicated to her, but build replacements. You have good friends. Go to them when you're low. They'll only be pleased that you came for help rather than moping. And one more thing.'

'That is?'

'Get two cats.'

SIXTEEN

I HAD BRIEFED ARTHUR as best I could, given the un-
certainties of the situation. Had I been lucky in my
choice of Saunders and, for that matter, was there any
fraud going down at all? That was the question. This
was the plan.

Arthur would make contact with Saunders and
say he could deliver a juicy bit of information about
a forthcoming armed bank robbery. We had chosen
my nemesis, Freddie Ronson, as the mastermind. He
was a known villain, although less active since I had
blinded him with the two fingers that were subsequently
chopped off in revenge. Everything about the story was
checkable and would seem authentic. Arthur was to ask
for £500 and negotiate from there. He was to insist on
new fifty-pound notes—makes more of a show at the
local pub when buying a round of drinks was the excuse. After all that, we were winging it. Or maybe we
were winging it from the very start.

Now for my role.

'Spot check,' I said to Edward Tennyson, head of
accounts. 'I need to count the cash in the safe and rec-
oncile it to the amounts in and out.'

'By all means,' he said. 'Make yourself at home.'

Was he a cool customer or was he on the straight and
narrow path with no guilty conscience?

I took all the cash out of the safe and counted it. I was surprised at the amount of cash there was—nearly £4,000.

I looked up from the desk at Tennyson. He read my mind.

'Got to be able to cope with all eventualities,' he said. 'The reptile fund often needs cash quickly—too quick even to go to the bank.'

'And how do you control that expenditure?' I said.

'I insist on invoices for the normal petty cash and a signature from the officer requesting payment from the reptile fund. Admittedly it's nowhere near fool proof, but it's the best I can do under the extenuating circumstances.'

'Doesn't it ever give you an uneasy feeling?'

'Always, but, as I said, what other solution is there?'

I shrugged, understanding his predicament, but my empathy was tempered by the lure of cash. There is something about cash that is irresistible to the potential fraudster. Large or small denominations doesn't matter, it's the feeling, or anticipated feeling, of notes in your hand that is somehow tempting. Gives you more of a buzz, makes you feel richer than a number in your bank statement.

I took the opening balance from the spreadsheet, took away the amounts paid out and added the money drawn out. Theoretically, that should equal the amount of cash in the safe. It did, but that wasn't the purpose of the exercise. I took down the serial numbers on the new fifty-pound notes—that was the purpose, that was the sting in the tail of the exercise. Where did they go after Arthur's payment?

I spent the rest of the morning skulking outside Tennyson's office, watching the comings and goings. If the timing was right, Harry Saunders would soon be a customer for the reptile fund. I didn't know what he looked like, but a large man entered and spent just a couple of minutes. He seemed a fair bet. He was tall and broad, not someone I would like to meet on a dark night. He was wearing a black leather jacket, black T-shirt and matching chinos, taking plain clothes to the most noticeable limit. Tennyson came out after the visit and returned five minutes later with a cup of some beverage in a cardboard cup and something in a paper bag.

Arthur phoned mid afternoon. Had the bait been taken?

'Well?' I said.

'Yes, thanks,' he said. 'I had a bit of a cold yesterday, but it's not too bad now.'

'I meant "well, what happened?"'

'Oh, sorry. I met him in a café near the police station. Had a cup of weak tea that wasn't worth the money and a jam doughnut that was. Lots of sugar and didn't spare the jam. Raspberry, it was. Only raspberry should be used for a doughnut. Got to keep up with tradition.'

'Arthur, can you get to the point? What happened with Saunders?'

'The cheapskate only gave me £200. Said there'd be more for me when I told him the exact date and location. Not a man to trust, though. Fancies himself too much. Reckons he's a hard man. I could break him in two pieces with my little finger.'

'You might just get the chance,' I said. 'If he's bent, he won't be a happy bunny. This could get very nasty. If he's on the straight and narrow, he won't be too pleased either, come to think about it.'

'You leave him to me.'

We agreed to meet later and disconnected. I phoned Morag and asked her to meet me. This needed witnesses. I looked at Tennyson's door from my viewpoint and waited. When she arrived we went together, knocked, although it wasn't really necessary given the glass door, and entered.

'Spot check on cash,' I said to him.

'But you only did it a couple of hours ago.'

'That's the idea of spot checks,' I said. 'They can happen at any time.'

I stood there looking down on him. He shook his head, sighed and got up. Unlocked the safe and looked at me.

'Go ahead,' he said, 'although I can't see that this is necessary.'

Morag sat down in one of the chairs. I took the accounts book and the cash from the safe and sat down at the desk beside her. I noticed a new receipt: £500 signed for by Harry Saunders. I counted the cash, again noting down the serial numbers of the fifty-pound notes, and verified that everything balanced. Harry Saunders had pocketed the £300 difference he had made from what he had drawn from the reptile fund and what he had paid Arthur. All I had to do now was prove it. I had to act quickly before he had an opportunity to get rid of the evidence. We left Tennyson and went to the CC's office. Morag gave me a look that said, 'Do you know what you are doing?' I shrugged.

The CC stared up at me through the glass with a look

that sent Beano daggers in my direction. We walked in and I hit him with it.

'You're not going to like this,' I said.

'Strangely, that doesn't surprise me,' he countered.

'You've got a bent officer who is stealing from the reptile fund.'

'That's a big accusation. I hope you can prove this.'

'I can, if you come with me to the station and we search him. And no warnings, please. We have to hit hard and fast.'

'Oh, Shannon.' He sighed—people seemed to do a lot of that when I was around. 'Life was so much more simple before you came. You do realize that I will crucify you if you are wrong?'

'I expected nothing less.'

'Morag, get me my driver. Tell him to meet us downstairs in two minutes. Let's go.'

Morag made a phone call and in a couple of minutes we were standing outside as a white Jaguar pulled up. The CC held the back door open for Morag, then climbed inside. I got in the front. The journey took ten minutes and we entered the station. The officer behind the desk stood up straight and saluted. I resisted the temptation to salute back.

'Where's Harry Saunders?' the CC said.

'On his rest break,' said the desk sergeant. 'You'll find him in the canteen. Do you want me to phone up and get him?'

'No,' said the CC. 'We'll meet him there. What interview rooms are free?'

'Number two.'

'Keep it for me.'

We went up the stairs and the CC told us to wait outside the canteen. He went in and emerged a moment later with Saunders—the man in black. We filed down the stairs and entered the interview room. Saunders sat on one side of the desk with Morag, who sat with pad and pen ready to take notes. The CC and I sat opposite.

'I should give you the opportunity to call a lawyer,' said the CC.

'Whatever you have to say, I don't need a lawyer. I've done nothing.'

'Shannon here has made a serious allegation. He says you're stealing from the reptile fund. What do you say to that?'

'There are ladies present,' he said, 'so all I can say is utter tosh.'

'Empty your pockets,' I said.

He looked at the CC, who nodded.

He took out a pack of cigarettes, a lighter, a number of tissues, neatly folded, and his wallet.

'Put the notes on the table,' I said.

He took out a wad and I saw some fifty-pound notes among them. We had him, I was sure.

'Pass the fifty-pound notes to Morag.'

He took them out of the wallet and passed them over. Morag made a note of the serial numbers. This was the crunch point.

I placed my notepad next to the CC.

'Read out the numbers,' I said to Morag.

Bingo! They matched. But only three of them. The other three were missing. Where had they gone? He had to have spent them already. That must have been quick work.

'I am going to have to suspend you,' the CC said. 'Hand over your warrant card. I need to take the notes as evidence. Do you need a receipt?'

'I don't need anything,' Saunders said, looking threateningly at me, 'I'm innocent.'

'It doesn't look that way,' the CC said. 'With luck, we can clear this up quickly, but it doesn't look good. Get someone from the Federation to advise you.'

'Like, who is that going to be? The rep is suspended, too. I expect they have enough on their plate without bothering with me.'

'I can ask for someone from another force,' the CC said. 'Would you like me to do that?'

'No, sir. You've got this all wrong. Someone's framing me.'

'There's a lot of that going around,' I said.

'You're going to regret this, Shannon,' he said. 'Boy, are you going to regret this.'

'You must like living dangerously. You just made a threat before the Chief Constable,' I said.

'I heard nothing,' said the CC. 'How about you, Morag? Did you hear anything? Before you answer, think of your job and do you still want it.'

The moment of truth. Whose side was she on?

'Yes,' she said, 'I still want my job; no, I didn't hear anything.'

Saunders sat back in his chair and smiled at me. If you could call it a smile. Qualify it by calling it the sort of expression a crocodile has just made before it eats you. Then has crocodile tears over it.

'Looks like our business here is over,' I said and walked out of the room.

I was stranded there. Unless I called a cab—and that would look kind of petty—I had to travel back in the CC's car. I got in the front seat and waited. The driver looked at me and registered my expression.

'Can be a right bastard, can't he?' he said. 'Although I'll deny that I said that to the last breath in my body.'

'Denial seems to be the watchword at the moment,' I said.

'Doesn't make it any easier being in fashion.'

Surprised at his perceptiveness, I looked across at him. 'Why do you put up with it?'

'It's a job,' he said. 'One that's secure and pays pretty well. So I keep my head down and say, "Yes, sir, no, sir, three bags full, sir." Once you've done it for a while, it becomes second nature.'

'And you go home and kick the spouse.'

'The cat, actually.'

That fitted one of my theories.

The CC and Morag appeared and got in the back. Morag avoided my gaze. This was going to get awkward. The arrangement of staying with her had worked well to date and Arthur was due to come tonight to talk through his conversations with Saunders and do some future planning. The word embarrassment was putting it mildly.

I sat back and mentally massaged my bruised ego. Then it came to me.

'Tennyson has got it,' I announced.

'Tennyson has got what?' the CC asked.

'The missing three fifty-pound notes. That's the only explanation. Saunders can't have got rid of them so quickly. All we need do is search Tennyson. It's your duty. You can't shirk it.'

The CC sighed. This was getting annoying. If he did it again, I didn't know whether I could resist the impulse to grab him by the collar and bounce him against the nearest wall.

'You're sure about this?' the CC said. 'This is an extremely serious allegation against a very senior member of staff. I won't be able to protect you if you're wrong.'

Like he had been protecting me up till now?

'Very well,' he said. 'We do it as soon as we arrive back. And, frankly, I can't wait.'

TENNYSON PROTESTED LOUDLY at the request to search him, his belongings and his office. We—I, actually— did it systemically and thoroughly with no stone, or the office equivalent, being left unturned. We found nothing. We even went down and searched his locker. Absolutely zero, zilch, nada—the result was the same in any language. If he had taken the cash—and, frankly, I was beginning to doubt it myself—he couldn't have got rid of it except by tearing the notes up and eating them. Well, I suppose that was a possibility, come to think of it. I realized I was clutching at straws. There was no alternative. Time to keep everyone happy by eating humble pie.

'My apologies, Mr Tennyson. I have misjudged you. I hope you will forgive someone with a vivid imagination and a poor judge of character.'

'Nicely put, Shannon,' he said. 'I'll try not to hold it against you.'

That was big of him. Unless he didn't do it, of course.

The CC left and I followed him out the door. He moved swiftly to his office, shaking his head.

'Nick,' said Morag. 'We need to talk. Let's have a coffee. Please.'

I looked in her eyes and saw the pain going on there.

'Come on then. Your treat.'

'Yours, I'm afraid. I need to add cash to my card.'

A lightning bolt struck me! How could I be such a fool? That's how Tennyson had got rid of the cash. He'd fed it into the machine and credited his card.

'Morag, you're a star,' I shouted. 'Let's go.'

'Where?'

'I don't have a clue. Wherever we can get inside the cash machine. You tell me.'

'I suppose we need to see the person in charge of the company that has the contract for the catering.' She took out her tablet and switched it on. Did some searching and I heard the call ringing through the loudspeaker. Apparently, he was on level three and we rushed down the escalators to meet him.

He was a small man with oversized spectacles, wearing a black suit with a crease on the trousers that you could have sliced bread with.

'How can I help you?' he said when we had tracked him down. 'If indeed I can help you, that is. Always a dilemma, don't you think, in these circumstances?'

I explained who I was and Morag added the CC's imprimatur for my authenticity and my requests to be met.

'I need to see the cash that has been paid into the machine.'

'Certainly,' he said to my relief. 'Anything to help the smooth running of the force. People don't put enough importance to helping others nowadays, don't you think?' I nodded and hoped he would get on with it. 'Although,' he said, 'you won't find much there.'

'Why is that?' I asked.

'It was emptied just after lunch. We try to empty it frequently during the day. Wouldn't want that sort of temptation, and resultant thievery, in a police headquarters. Still, you're welcome to what we have.'

My heart plummeted to floor level. I felt like sighing, but thought it would be hypocritical.

We went through the motions. Went behind the wall in reception to empty the machine and found just a handful of ten-and twenty-pound notes. Tennyson had got away with it. Damn the man!

Worse than that—the run of good luck had been broken.

MORAG FIDDLED AROUND with her coffee, stirring non-existent sugar around in long, slow circles so as to deliberate while not running the risk of slopping the liquid over the edge of the glass.

'I need to explain,' she said.

'You don't need to justify yourself to me,' I replied.

'But I do. We've become friends—good friends—and I wouldn't want anything to jeopardize that relationship. Nick, you have to realize that I am the sole breadwinner in a one-person household. I can't afford to lose this job. It's well paid, carries a good pension and I like what I do—most of the time, that is. I'd find it hard to replicate those points elsewhere. You have to appreciate the power that the CC has. He could block me getting a job anywhere else. I'm trapped, and something had to give. I couldn't go against him. But look on the bright side.'

'And what is that?'

'I was taking notes of everything that was being said.'

'And you would switch sides if it came to the crunch?'

There was a long pause.

'I would,' she finally said, 'but if it goes that far, everyone gets hurt. The CC would have to go, I'd be a whistle-blower who couldn't be trusted and you would have stirred up a hornet's nest. How many clients would you lose because they'd be afraid of what you might uncover?'

'Then this is what we do. Type up your notes and take two copies. Give one to me and keep one for yourself. Keep the original notes and send them with a typed up copy to Martin. Then there's the important last step.'

'And what's that?'

'We will have a very large drink when we get back to your house and forget our temporary differences.'

WE HAD THE DRINK, but not on our own. Norman and Arthur turned up again unexpectedly, although Norman did have the courtesy of phoning a short while beforehand. The hamper was laid out again on the dining room table.

'Surprised to see you, Norman,' I said. 'I thought it was only Arthur who was coming.'

'Didn't want him to be lonely on the journey,' he replied.

'How considerate. Nothing to do with Morag then?'

'I can't deny the lady has a certain appeal, but—as you know full well—with me it's always business first. Where is she, by the way?'

I suppressed a knowing grin. 'In the kitchen making some drinks. Perhaps you'd like to help her.'

He was gone in a flash. Arthur looked at me and smiled. 'Randy old sod,' he said.

SEVENTEEN

I WAS DRIVING ALONG the dual carriageway at a sedate speed—I didn't think the hire car did more than a sedate speed, or maybe it was all relative. Suddenly, blue lights flashed behind me. The unmarked police car settled in the fast lane parallel to me and an officer gestured that I should stop. Hell! What now?

I pulled on to the hard shoulder and got out—that's what the psychologists reckon is the best tactic. Get out of your territory and demean yourself in theirs. Makes them feel better, more secure. The last thing I needed was an insecure cop. Two guys in uniform got out. They were both tall and burly like rugby players and looked like they could hold their own if things got nasty.

'How can I help, officers?' I said.

One of the cops walked behind my car and took a kick with his heavy reinforced steel-toe-capped shoes at my rear light on the driver's side. It shattered.

'Defective light, sir,' he said. 'Tut, tut.'

The other cop handed me a gadget. 'Blow in there, sir,' he said.

I did as asked and handed the machine back to him. Nothing seemed to have changed. He looked at it and pronounced, 'The colour has changed, sir.'

'It looks the same to me,' I countered.

'We're experienced, sir. Trust us,' which was the last

thing I was going to do. He read out the caution. 'I'm charging you with driving over the permitted limit. I'd like you to accompany us to the police station, sir, where we can take matters further.'

'Do I have any option?' I said.

He laughed. 'What do you think?'

'I think that this is a stitch up and that you'll regret it when my lawyer gets started on the charges we'll bring against you.'

'Maybe,' said the cop, 'but that will be a while yet. Time's on our side. And a lot can happen in a short time.'

The other cop got in the hire car and the cop who did the talking ushered me into the back of the police car. At least he didn't handcuff me. He climbed in and we headed back to the police station. I took out my phone and called Martin, said I needed him urgently. He said that he was on his way. Give him an hour and he'd be at the station. A whole lot could happen in an hour. Like me resisting arrest and getting beaten up in the process.

'That's the one phone call you're allowed,' the cop said. 'Put your mobile away now before I have to pull over and take it from you by force.'

Which, I got the impression, he would enjoy.

The dreaded scenario looked like it was starting. I tried to stay calm and keep my anger under control. In a few minutes we were at the station and the cop led me inside by clutching at my elbow and dragging. He stopped at the desk and gave a biased report on what had happened—supposedly, I had used offensive and abusive language, although the difference between the two was lost on me—and the custody sergeant, with a weary expression that signalled that he had seen it all before, booked me in.

'I want a doctor here straight away to take a blood test,' I said.

'All in good time, sir,' the sergeant said. 'All in good time. Now empty your pockets.' He took the contents of my pockets and put them in a plain plastic bag. He turned to the cop who had brought me in. 'Cell number two is free,' he said. 'Follow me.'

We trooped down the stairs, past Curly's room and stood in front of a door so solid it looked like it could survive a nuclear attack. He took a key from a board screwed to the wall and opened the door.

'Let's have your tie, sir,' the custody sergeant said. 'Shoe laces, too.'

At least they weren't going to concoct a convoluted suicide with me hanging from a rope constructed from one tie and two shoe laces.

'Harry Saunders was a friend of mine,' he said. 'Friend of everybody here, too. Think on that, Shannon. Think on that.'

He swung the door open and the hinges squeaked as if they hadn't had much business for a while. I knew what was going to happen. My blood started to run cold. He pushed me through into a tiny cell about eight foot by four. There was a narrow concrete ledge that served as a bed and a bucket, nothing much else. There was no window and the light came from a gloomy bulb within a grid of steel. He pushed me in and slammed the door behind me. The clang started the process that knew I couldn't stop. I was back in Brixton. I shuddered.

My skin prickled and I began to shiver. No matter

that I told myself that the guards wouldn't come to chop
my fingers off, it did no good.

I broke out in a cold sweat. My testicles shrivelled
and tried to climb back to safety inside my body. My
breathing quickened and I knew I was about to have a
panic attack. Short, sharp breaths came and I was taking in far too much oxygen. I sat down on the bed because I realized that at this rate I was going to pass out.
Maybe that would have been the best thing.

Sweat formed on my face and trickled down on to
my chest to join the river that was running from my
armpits. Then I could hold it no longer. I screamed.

I don't know how long I screamed for, but there was
no response from the sergeant. I lay on the floor and
curled up into the foetal position. That's how Martin
found me when he finally arrived.

The moment the door opened, I leapt up and through
the open space—the escape from hell—knocking over
Martin and the custody sergeant as I pushed past them.

'Get a doctor here now,' Martin shouted. 'I want a
full medical examination. What have you been doing
to him?'

'Just our duty, sir,' the custody sergeant said. 'Just
our duty.'

I must have started to recover because the sergeant's
annoying habit of repeating himself got to me. I was
thinking of other things rather than the claustrophobic
space that had imprisoned me. I was ashamed of myself, but knew I couldn't help it. Some people can't cope
with heights, with others it's open spaces, or maybe it's
spiders or rats. We all have our room 101 and they had
just discovered mine. It was going to make for a ner-

vous future, because I knew they would exploit that knowledge at every opportunity.

The sergeant led me upstairs. Martin put his arm around me and guided me up each uncertain step. I remember passing Curly en route. We went into the same interview room and waited for the doctor. While we were waiting, Curly entered with a cup of builder's tea, hot and sweet. I thanked him. He shrugged at me as if to say I didn't deserve that treatment, but he understood where it had been coming from. I was my own worst enemy, he seemed to be saying.

'Take me through everything,' Martin said. 'In your own time.'

I drank some tea, cradling the cup in both my shaky hands. Slowly, I moved from gibbering idiot to a normal sane person again. I relayed the events to Martin and he permeated my story with disbelieving shakes of his head.

'I'll make them pay, Nick, but not for a while. It's their word against yours and they will probably get away with it. But they are on my hit list now. I'll take every opportunity to make them pay, and pay dearly, for what they put you through.'

A doctor arrived, female, with all the looks, charm and bedside manner of Rosa Klebb on a bad day. She jerked me around as she examined me roughly and made me undress to check that there was no hidden bruises or other signs of assault I could claim at a later date. She pronounced me A1 fit and then proceeded to take a blood sample.

'I'll have a sample, too,' said Martin, 'for independent analysis.'

'Don't you trust us?' she said.

'Not one per cent,' he replied.

She took more blood, squirted it into a vial, put it in a clear plastic bag and handed it over. Gold dust. It would prove that I had no alcohol in my system and that would at least get me off one charge.

The doctor left and the sergeant came into the room. 'You're free to go, Mr Shannon,' he said. 'For now, that is.'

'You forget to say "Don't leave the country",' I said.

'That, too,' he replied.

Martin and I exited the station where his car and my slightly damaged hire car sat. Martin turned to me with a serious expression on his face.

'You don't have to say it,' I said.

'Say what?'

'This could just be the beginning.'

He nodded. 'I'll start charges of harassment as a holding position, but you have to be very careful from now on. Try to always have someone with you as a witness. You're a marked man, Nick. Unless we are very careful, and a bit lucky, this could turn very nasty. If I didn't know you would ignore the advice, I'd tell you to quit this case and go somewhere very far away from here. But I don't want to be wasting my breath. This is not a good time to be stubborn.'

'I have an obligation to Collins. I owe him, and, through him, Sam. I can't renege on a deal. That would be without honour and not something I could live with. There's also the fact that this is more than about this fraud case. This is the best chance I'll ever have to find out who was the hit-and-run driver. It's too important to give up now.'

'Like I said, I don't want to waste my breath. Just be very careful from now on.'

'Don't worry, I will. This is a case that's coming to the boil.'

'Just don't get scalded.'

'Who, me?'

EIGHTEEN

I KNOCKED AT the CC's door and entered before he had a chance to keep me out. The carrier bag was swaying as I walked. I put my papers exactly where planned on top of his desk and stood back.

'It's time we smoked the pipe of peace,' I said, taking the bottle from the bag. I followed it with the two glasses which I wiped clean with a tissue. I set them on the desk and poured a generous slug of malt whisky into each. I picked up one tumbler and toasted him.

'We didn't get off to a great start,' I said. 'Maybe we can put things right now.'

'Always willing to give a man a second chance,' he replied. Apart from Canning, that is. The CC had a very selective memory.

'You and I could make a good team,' I said. 'I could help you put things right here. Financially speaking, of course. I leave the due process of the law to you.'

'You haven't made many friends here.'

'It's a cross I always have to bear. Fraud carries a stigma. No one likes to be proved too foolish or too trusting.'

I picked up the tumbler and toasted him again. At last he cracked and took the glass in his right hand, raised it slightly toward me and took a sip.

'Good whisky,' he said. 'Doesn't make you any more likeable, though.'

'And here was I thinking we were building bridges.'

He laughed. 'Take more than one glass of malt to change my mind about you. You're trouble, Shannon. I knew that from the moment I first set eyes on you and, boy, have you proved me right.'

'What are you going to do when the edifice falls down upon your head? Can't imagine the Home Secretary will be too pleased.'

'You leave Yates to me. We understand each other. He's got a vested interest. If I fail, he fails. He won't allow that to happen.' He drained his glass. 'Now get out, Shannon. Wish I could say it was nice talking to you, but I don't like to lie.'

I got up from the chair, put my glass into the bag, followed it with his—which I picked up with two fingers from the inside—and left the bottle on the desk: he was welcome to it. I carefully scooped up my papers from the desk and headed out.

I wondered how long it would take him to realize I had switched tablets.

NINETEEN

'MARTIN TOLD ME what happened,' Norman said when I arrived back at base to catch up with other work.

'So much for client confidentiality.'

'He's worried about you. He said you freaked.'

'He's right,' I said with an edge in my voice. 'And if I'm in the same situation again I will probably freak again. Satisfied?'

'This can't go on, Nick. It's years since you were in prison. We have to get this sorted. It makes you too vulnerable.'

'I could say what has this to do with you.'

'And I'd say that I am a friend. Someone who only has your best interests in mind.'

Undeniable. Don't transfer your own anger and self-reproach to a friend.

'I'm sorry, Norman. I didn't mean to jump down your throat.'

'Martin gave me a number. Someone who he says will be able to help. Unconventional but effective.'

'Are you suggesting what I think you are?'

'Yes. There's no stigma in it. Plenty of people have counselling.'

'A shrink, right? You think I should see a shrink?'

'All I'm asking is you give it a try. I've made an ap-

pointment for you tomorrow morning. Just go along
and see what you think. If it's no good, then fine. We
gave it our best shot.'

'Who knows about this appointment?'

'Just you and me. I haven't discussed it with anyone,
although I think we should tell Arthur. I'm sure he's as
worried as I am. No one else knows. As far as Anji is
concerned, you will be seeing a potential client.'

He was right, of course, although that didn't make it
any easier to admit it. The weakness was now known
and Saunders's friends would do whatever they could
to exploit it. I was a marked man.

AND THAT'S HOW I came to be sitting in Arthur's giant
white van with him at the wheel.

'You really think this is necessary?'

Arthur looked across at me (he had the job of
driver—Norman didn't trust me a hundred per cent to
keep the appointment.)

'You tell me, Nick. Do you think your heart can
cope with any more palpitations every time you enter
a tall building and see a lift? Get out the van, Nick. At
least give it a go. Norman did what he could for you in
Chelmsford, but this is the last stage in the process that
could see you back to normal.'

I looked at him with an eyebrow raised.

'OK, I spoke out of turn there. You'll never be normal, but this would get you a little closer. Look, if you
don't go in there, I'm only going to drive you back home
and make you go for another run with me.'

I was out of there before he said another word.

I APPROACHED THE SMALL, single level building with my
heart racing, even though there clearly wasn't a lift journey ahead.

'I'm here to see Dr Morgan at 10 o'clock,' I mumbled
to the shabby floor of the reception room in case anyone I knew spotted me.

'Name?'

Nice informal welcome! And surely that was obvious from the list of clients in front of her. Or perhaps
this was the first part of the test. Inwardly sighing that
the barrage of questions had already begun, I glumly
replied, 'Shannon. Nick Shannon.'

No flicker of recognition. That was one good thing
at least.

'Take a seat, please, Dr Morgan is nearly ready for
you.'

I took up one of the plastic seats and wondered what
Dr Morgan would be like. A Freudian complete with
long white beard and anxious to analyse my dreams?
Or waiting to delve into my subconscious like a true
Jungian? Whatever, was it too late to flee? Even the
thought of having another punishing run with Arthur
wasn't as scary as this.

'Mr Shannon. Dr Morgan will see you in Room 1
now. It's just down the hall to your right.'

It was too late. More anxious than every time I'd
gotten into a lift, I walked down the corridor. Maybe
this was why therapy was effective. The prospect of it
was so much more intimidating than the thing you actually came in to cure, you immediately felt your fear
was less scary. And what was it that was scaring me?
A fear that through talking I would reveal something

of myself that would destroy my self-belief. I might be able to get in a lift, but I might not get in the building in the first place.

I listened to my heart thumping in my chest as I pushed open the door, only for it to be opened from the other side at the same time. I stumbled forwards, almost head-butting the woman who seemed to be exiting. As I fell forwards, I felt a little flash of jealousy at this person allowed to be leaving and tried to think of a way I'd be able to escape with her. But as I brought my eyes up from the floor, those other thoughts couldn't help but be replaced.

Her face, which was only a few inches from mine for a brief time, had a radiant quality, long lashes on big eyes opened wide in surprise at the close encounter. She pushed back the blonde hair which had fallen across her face as she stood up straight again. It took me a little longer than perhaps necessary to recompose after finding myself so face to face with this striking woman, but I eventually stood up straight and held the door open for her.

'I think we may struggle to make much progress if I leave already, Mr Shannon.'

'Hm?' The power of speech seemed to have fallen out of me as I tipped through the door.

'My name is Dr Morgan, I'll be working with you in our session today.'

Say something, Nick, you're paying to be here and talk after all.

'Of course,' I said in my most professional voice. It even came out in perfect Queen's English to my sur-

prise. 'Erm, sorry about that. I wasn't expecting…er…
you.' Nope, didn't think the accent and tone would last.

She smiled warmly, faint laughter lines appearing at
the sides of her mouth. The effect was even more disarming than the initial door debacle.

'I'm sorry to surprise you, Mr Shannon, Toni the receptionist mentioned you appeared a little nervous, so
I thought I'd come out to collect you.'

Like a child at the dentist. Perhaps that panic I'd experienced in the waiting room had shown on my face.
Good job I wasn't in a profession where I needed to
conceal my emotions. Oh, wait a minute…

She seemed suddenly to be aware that we were con-
ducting our conversation in the doorway so ushered
me inside the small office. The character of this room
especially was completely at odds with the state of the
building on the outside (a rundown demountable, like
I remembered littering our school grounds once the
space inside the main building had been exhausted). It
wasn't spacious by any means, but the unadorned ivory
walls prevented it from feeling claustrophobic: it had a
lightness about it like a cloudless spring morning in the
heart of the countryside. A plush cream sofa was pushed
against the far wall under a window where the majestic
view of the car park was obscured by a lace blind. To
the left of the sofa was a plain wooden chair which had
been pulled away from a desk so it faced the sofa. The
other wall was lined with shelves where books were in-
terspersed with various *objet dwarfs* which appeared to
have been amassed from a different set of exotic foreign
destinations. Most of the books were appropriately titled
therapy and psychology works, but others caught my eye

as they didn't quite fit into the mix. *Winnie-the-Pooh*, the complete Harry Potter series, *Catch-22* and *Fifty Shades of Grey* were a few titles which jumped out.

The set-up of the room was simple and I felt more at home than I'd expected.

'I thought a couch and a large leather armchair were pre-requisites of any therapist's office?'

'Well, as you have already commented, I don't quite fit normal expectations, Mr Shannon.'

I had to put an end to this Mr Shannon business.

'I suspect that I'm going to have to reveal some dark recesses of my mind so I think it's appropriate that you call me Nick.'

'Sure. Please take a seat on the sofa, Nick.'

I sank into the sofa at the end furthest from her desk and chair and looked up sheepishly like a child called into the headmaster's office.

Dr Morgan wasn't sitting on the chair looking back at me though. She was standing at the bookcase looking for something so I couldn't help but notice other aspects of her appearance as she hovered there. Her hair was curled immaculately at the ends and just brushing the shoulders of her navy jacket.

'I understand from my conversation with Martin that the problem seems to be claustrophobia.'

'Not just seems to be,' I said. 'Emphatically is.'

'We'll come to that in due course. First, I need some context. All I know about you at the moment is what I read at the time in the papers and saw on the TV. Please tell me your story, Nick, in your own words.'

'Honestly?'

'There would be no point in anything else.'

So I told her everything. The planned study for a Masters in maths specializing in games theory at Sussex, the fateful night of the hit-and-run, buying the drugs and administering the fatal injection, the look on Susie's eyes as it took effect, the trial, the time in Brixton and the loss of my two fingers, the long spell in Chelmsford, Arthur and Norman acting as mentors and the time and rehabilitation since being set free.

She was a very good listener, only interrupting to clarify a point or to get me to expand. She used a lot of non-verbal prompting, too, using nods of the head or simple phrases such as umm, I see, and such like. She never used closed questions where I could only answer yes or no, but favoured open questions where I had to reveal more about myself. When I looked at my watch, I was surprised to see that an hour and a quarter had gone.

'Let's look at your sister's death,' she said. 'How did you feel about that?'

'Guilty,' I said. 'Guilty, guilty. Guilty that I hadn't insisted that I pick her up from the disco. Guilty that I couldn't protect her. I was her big brother, that's what big brothers are supposed to do. I failed her. I let her down and so I had to kill her.'

'You didn't kill her. You released her from a body that didn't work anymore. You can't beat yourself up about that. You know from the media around your trial that most of the public were behind you. Bear that in mind until we talk again.'

She got up from the chair and extended her hand to me. Helped me rise from the sofa.

'I want to stop there for now. There's some areas I'd like to probe at our next appointment.'

'How long is this going to take?'

'I could say a piece of string, but I won't. I have an idea of what may be happening, but it's too soon to be definite. Martin said you're pretty tied up at the moment, but I'd like you to make this a priority. See my secretary on the way out and tell her this takes precedence. Cancel another appointment if necessary. If the next session goes well, we could be close to a breakthrough.'

'Forgive me, but we haven't talked much about claustrophobia so far.'

'But we've talked about the deeper reasons why it may be happening. We have to address the root cause, only then do we make progress.'

'I would say I know the root cause.'

'Yes, you would and you may well be right, but things can look different from where I'm sitting as opposed to your seat. Give me a little time, Nick. We've made good progress today. In the meantime think back to your time in Chelmsford and how you coped with closed doors then. That could be a good starting point for our next session.'

I shook her hand and wondered just how much of a distraction she might be to some of her male patients. She was certainly having an effect on me. I wanted to please her and so for the trip back to Melchester, I thought back to that tiny cell in Chelmsford that I had shared with Norman and his constant bullying of me in order to distract me from that closed cell door.

TWENTY

It was Friday evening and we were sitting in Toddy's, we being myself, Arthur, Anji, Norman and, at Norman's insistence, Morag. She was to be Norman's guest for the weekend and he was going to show her all the culture that London had to offer, even though what Norman knew of culture could be written on the back of a postage stamp. He had enlisted Anji's support and she had filled his diary with events suitable for creating a good impression.

Morag's inclusion had created a possible slight problem, but not till much later. My main purpose couldn't start till Toddy had finished in the kitchen.

I could see Morag taking in the surroundings and wondered what she would make of it. The décor and fittings had a masculine air about them, but women were generally wooed by the simplicity. The tables were polished beech and unadorned with tablecloths. Placemats of rural scenes á la Constable. The knives were all serrated, built for heavy duty, but would be replaced with suitable alternatives for those having fish.

'This is cosy,' said Morag, won over maybe by the pink napkins, although the place did wrap itself around you with an air of quiet comfort.

Toddy's strength came from quality ingredients not fussed over too much. It had rapidly gained a reputation for those seeking a fine meal without paying the excessive prices of other favoured restaurants. You needed to book at least a fortnight ahead, although that didn't apply to Norman, who, as owner, always had a table kept for his use. We had ordered and sat back sipping our wine, ready to have a catch-up session.

'I don't suppose you had any luck with Melchester Blue?' I said to Anji.

'I tried my best,' she said. 'Went along to Companies House in person. Used all my feminine charms, but no luck. The guy in charge said that if no papers were filed on change of directors or shareholders or registered office, there was nothing he could do. Blind alley, I'm afraid.'

I turned to Arthur, resplendent in a brown leather jacket that made him seem as warm and cuddly as a well-trained bear. 'Any news from the grapevine on whether there's a contract out on me?'

'My sources come from the wrong side of the law,' he said. 'It's the cops you have to worry about.'

'Norman?'

'I don't have anything to work on. Without some numbers to get my teeth into I've got nothing to contribute.'

'I have something to report,' said Morag.

All eyes turned to her.

'The CC's tablet no longer works.'

I was sipping a glass of Norman's pomerol at the time and I choked on it. Arthur had to give me a big slap on the back, although from Arthur any slap was big.

'As I thought,' Morag said. 'Good job he seems to

make it a habit of losing tablets otherwise you would be in the frame, Nick.'

'Where do we go from here?' Arthur asked.

'We've no alternative,' I said, 'but to unleash Mary Jo.'

'Things that bad, are they?' Arthur said.

'Who's Mary Jo?' asked Morag and Anji simultaneously.

'Mary Jo is my late wife's daughter,' I replied. 'We keep Mary Jo in reserve for when there's no other option.'

'Explain,' said Morag.

'Nick and Mary Jo haven't had the best of relationships in the past,' Norman said. 'Took a long while to convince Mary Jo that Nick didn't have an ulterior motive, wasn't simply after Arlene's money.'

'How does she fit in the picture?' said Anji.

'Mary Jo has a penchant for computer whizzes. Attracts them like a magnet. Lovers and husband. She's now an expert on computer systems and how to hack into them. She helped us crack a case in the past—broke into an insurance company's computer and got the vital evidence we needed.'

'So she's going to break into the Mid Anglia system and the Federation one, too,' said Anji.

'It's possible,' I said.

'Why only possible?' Morag asked. 'If she's so good, why not definite?'

'Because it depends on what operating system is being used,' I said. 'We'd need the force to be using a very special system. She can only hack those using UNIX. There's a bug in the system. A password that hardly anyone knows about. It's UUCP. UNIX to UNIX

Communications Protocol. Meant solely for one computer to communicate with another—mainly for updating software. If the banks we need to look at use UNIX, we're in.'

'Can you trust her?' Arthur asked. 'She did try to frame you once. No guarantee she won't pull the same trick twice.'

'I don't think so,' I said. 'The funeral brought us close together. We are friends now, not rivals for Arlene's affection. Or the money.'

Our starters arrived and we changed focus. Arthur, though, gave a grunt that indicated that he wasn't convinced.

'Wow, these mussels,' said Morag. 'How does he get them so good?'

'First of all, only young mussels,' said Norman, 'so they are not chewy. Then he uses a fine white wine—if it's not good enough to drink with pleasure, it's not good enough to cook with—lastly the addition of wild garlic.'

'I'm impressed,' said Morag.

'I was hoping you would be, dear lady,' said Norman.

Arthur and I exchanged glances and suppressed knowing grins.

'How much longer is this job likely to last?' Anji asked. 'I've got two clients lined up when you're finished.'

'I have a feeling that a breakthrough will come soon. We're approaching a critical point. Maybe it's something from Mary Jo. I don't know, but I just have a feeling that it will all slot together soon.'

'The forensic accountant's equivalent of women's intuition,' Morag said.

'Call it what you will,' I said, 'but I can see us making a quantum leap very soon.' If I had to rationalize it, I would've had to explain the contents of the bag at my feet, and the less Morag knew, the better. It would soon be time for Toddy's opinion.

As we finished the meal an hour or so later, a waiter signalled to me that Toddy was free. I picked up the bag and went through to the kitchen. Service was finished and the staff were busy cleaning down ready for tomorrow's lunchtime trade. Toddy was sitting on a high stool drinking a thirst-quenching beer. He was still dressed in his whites, but had taken off his chef's hat to reveal his thinning grey hair.

'What can I do for you, Nick?' he said in a broad Yorkshire accent.

'I need for you to go back to your past profession, if you could call it that.'

'I prefer talent,' he said, 'but go ahead.'

I took the glass out of the bag and set it down on the counter. 'On this glass is a fingerprint. I need you to copy it on to this.' I took out the thin latex glove and passed it to him. 'The copy needs to be on the index finger of the glove.'

'This wouldn't be anything illegal, would it?'

'I suppose that would be a matter of opinion,' I said. 'This fingerprint could help to crack a case I'm on, but, more importantly, could lead me to the hit-and-run driver who crippled my sister.'

'As long as it's in a good cause. It will take a while though.'

'When should I come back?'

'Not that long. It should only take forty-five minutes. Linger over a coffee and a brandy and I'll bring it out to you.'

'I'll let you get on then. Thanks, Toddy.'

'Don't thank me yet. Wait till you see whether it works first.'

'I have faith in you.'

'So you should. How was the meal, by the way?'

'Superb. Norman's lady friend was impressed. You've made a new fan.'

'Always good to keep the boss happy.'

'I would say he's in heaven at the moment.'

I left the kitchen and sat back down at the table.

'Forty-five minutes,' I said to Norman.

'Coffee and digestives, everyone?' he said, summoning a waiter. We settled back in a warm glow and prepared for the finishing touches to a wonderful evening.

Exactly forty-five minutes later, true to his word, Toddy came across to me and handed the bag back. 'Hope it works,' he said.

'Me, too, my friend,' I said. 'Me, too.'

TWENTY-ONE

MORAG HAD GONE to bed and the house was silent. I sat on the bed and got the CC's tablet from my briefcase. I was finding it difficult to stay calm. So many of my thoughts over the years had been building to this moment. I had the destroyer of my sister's life within my grasp. I put on the glove and pressed the button to awaken this sleeping dragon. When the system asked for the code or print, I put my gloved finger on the button and held my breath.

It worked! Toddy's mastery of the art of forging had worked! I was into the cloud with the highest priority. It felt like the world had opened up for me.

I was already familiar with the settings through the use of my own tablet. I entered the filing system that Curly had used to archive the open cases. There was a lot of them. I selected the search function and typed in my surname. It was like stealing sweets from a baby. Up came the file, easily identifiable by the date. I let out the breath I was holding and highlighted the file. It opened up in front of my eyes.

There was a serial number, a title and then the words of the file came up on the screen. My hand was shaking. I scrolled down.

A message popped up: Input file passcode.

What? This shouldn't happen. Or maybe it should.

The CC had built in an extra layer of security. I stared at the screen not knowing what to do. I had no idea what the cloud wanted from me. A name? A number? I was lost. Didn't even know his birthday or the name of his dog. Nothing to go on.

The instruction repeated itself. Had I gone to all this trouble only to fall at an unforeseen hurdle?

I stared at the words on the screen. An enticing promise of what might come. Then suddenly a message said *Timed out*. The words of the screen took on a life of their own. Letters started to rain down from the top to the bottom of the screen. Then they gathered pace, eventually building to a cascade. The file was destroying itself. When the screen was empty, I threw the tablet on to the floor and resisted the temptation to stamp on it and destroy it for ever. Thwarted when the end of the sorry tale was in sight. I had no idea what to do next. Crying would have been the easy option. Fight back, Shannon. Your destiny is to find the truth. There has to be another way. Doesn't there?

TWENTY-TWO

IT SEEMED I WAS friends with Curly again. He had phoned to say that he had located a policeman who was serving at the time of the hit-and-run and might be able to remember something. He had said that I had to be quick as the man was in pretty bad shape with terminal cancer. I lost no time jumping in the hire car and setting off.

The hospital was on the outskirts of Melchester in the opposite direction to Morag's house. Finding it was easy, parking was a nightmare—in an ever-changing world some things are as constant as the Northern Star. I ended up driving back out of the hospital and parking in a side street. I walked to the building and got my bearings. To the left was A & E, dead ahead—not a phrase I should have used—was the main entrance. I walked inside and consulted a large plan of the hospital buildings. I walked up two flights of stairs and pressed a buzzer outside the door of the ward. It was opened automatically, which made the whole point of having a buzzer and a locked door irrelevant, and I stepped inside.

There was a central desk with four doctors and two nurses sitting down and several people standing consulting thick files. One looked up at me and smiled.

'I'm here to see Mr Truscott,' I said.

She frowned. 'You know his condition?' she asked.

'He's very weak so you shouldn't stay long. You mustn't overtire him. We want his last days to be as peaceful as possible.'

'I understand. I'll try and be as brief as I can.'

She led me past the main ward, mostly old people dozing in bed or in heavily padded chairs. None of them looked good, but that was only to be expected in hospital, I guess, but it would have been nice to have seen someone who looked like they were recovering. We went into a side room and there was Truscott with a multitude of wires and drips and other esoteric equipment connected to him and beeping away. His complexion was grey, drained of the colour of life. I was no doctor, but my prognosis was that it was lucky I came today. The nurse left after warning me again not to tire Truscott and I sat myself down in a chair by his bed. He opened his eyes and took a moment to take in his surroundings and me.

'You must be…'

'Shannon,' I said. 'I've come to talk you about your time in the police. When you were a firearms officer.'

He nodded and spoke in stutters. 'Long time ago… I used to be able to shoot the wings off a fly in those days, but maybe that's my memory playing tricks as usual.'

His breathing was raspy and had developed that rattle that comes shortly before death.

'I need you to think back nearly fifteen years. There was a hit-and-run. A boy was killed and a girl was crippled. You were the officer in charge of the case. Do you remember it?'

He gazed up at the ceiling as if the answers were there.

'Hell of a stink that day,' he said.

'What do you mean?'

'Gun went missing.'

'Why did you need a gun?'

'We didn't need the guns for the hit-and-run. We were just finishing a training exercise when the 999 call came through. No time to hand in the guns or take off our body armour. When we checked in afterwards we were short one gun.'

'How many of you were there?' I didn't know where this was leading, but I had a hunch it was important.

'A dozen. Plus Yates. That was the most embarrassing part. Didn't reflect well on us.'

Maybe it wasn't leading anywhere after all. 'Why was Yates there?'

'A routine visit. He was a junior in the Home Office then. Liked to put himself about a bit. Get publicity any way he could. When he heard we had an exercise, he wanted to join in. Couldn't say no, could we? Knitted him out and he played Cowboys and Indians. Had a whale of a time.'

He paused, picked up a beaker of water and took a sip. I could tell this was taking its toll on him. I reverted to the main topic.

'Tell me what happened when you got to the scene.'

'Hell of a mess. The boy was obviously dead, blood and brains splattered everywhere. Enough to turn your stomach, even for us used to it.'

'And the girl?'

'I didn't give her much of a chance. She was like a broken doll, lying there bent and twisted. Breathing, but that was the only sign of life.'

'And what about the scene?'

'Skid marks everywhere. Driver must have lost control and gone all over the place, mounted the kerb and hit the kids.'

'There was a boot print. Special boot, I understand. Special Forces and firearms officers only. Do you remember that?'

'Strange. Small boot. Size seven. Too small for a man. We marked it for a cast so there should be something in the file.'

'The file has been doctored.'

'Someone's protecting the driver then.'

'Looks that way. But at least you've given me something to work on. All I have to do is find out who would wear a small boot. Maybe I can get at the records of the training exercise.'

'Long time ago. Doubt anyone would have kept them.'

'Then I'm at another dead end.'

He looked at me and a spark of recognition came into his dull eyes.

'You're the brother, aren't you? That's why you're here. That's why this is important.'

I nodded. 'I need closure and someone is stopping me getting it.'

'Closure or revenge?'

'Let's just say justice.'

'Well, I hope you get it. Probably too late for me, but let me know if by some miracle I'm still alive.'

'Will do. Good luck.'

'My luck has all but run out. Let me pass the last bit to you.'

'I appreciate the thought. Thanks.'

I stood up and stretched across to shake his hand. It was as cold as ice.

I WALKED BACK to the quiet side street where I had parked the car. The sun was out and it had the warmth I needed after the chill of the handshake. I started to put together a plan of action about how to find out who fitted a size seven boot. I was in my own little world when I heard someone speak my name.

'Well, Shannon, time to put an end to your meddling.'

The speaker was a tall, suited man of light build, his eyes shaded by sunglasses. He was flanked by two other similarly dressed men—one shorter and bulkier, the other tall and wiry. They looked fit and threatening. I couldn't see their eyes, but I guessed there would be trouble written there. I wondered whether I could talk myself out of this rapidly deepening hole. I thought a touch of John Wayne might help.

'Whatever you want, pilgrim,' I said, 'you've got the wrong man. Ride on.'

'No can do, Shannon. You've caused us enough trouble. It has to stop here. We lost two good men because of you.'

'You can't blame me if you employ lousy drivers. And don't forget you started it or whoever you hired did.'

The three men were standing by a people carrier. Wiry Man looked back then gave a nod. The car's engine started up. Boss Man took out a large knife: the other two brought baseball bats from behind their backs.

The show was about to start and seemed like it wouldn't take long to reach the finale. After Arthur's lessons I thought I could handle one of them, but not all three. The odds were stacked against me.

I heard footsteps behind me. Completely surrounded now, it seemed. I looked back to check how many and saw Arthur running towards me.

'Can you handle the tall man,' he said, pointing at the boss of the trio, 'if I take the other two?'

'Be a pleasure,' I said.

MANY MOONS AGO, Arthur had arrived at the small ground floor flat I rented in Archway, carrying a pot of red ink, a ruler and two white tea towels. I had no idea what was happening, but guessed it must have had something to do with the current case I was working on while seconded to the Fraud Squad. It had all started with the murder of a man who was stabbed to death.

'Take off your T-shirt,' he said. 'Let's go into the garden.'

Mystified, I followed his instructions, stripped off and unlocked the door to a small patch of grass that just about qualified as a garden on the agent's particulars.

He took the pot of red ink and poured some on a handkerchief. He wiped the ruler with the handkerchief so that the sides were wet with ink. He passed me a white tea towel.

'Knife attacks are tricky to defend,' he said. 'You can try to ward off the attack with your hands, but that only serves to cut them to shreds. Wrap the tea towel around your left arm.'

OK, keep obeying orders. Maybe it will make some sense in time.

'The tea towel could be anything. A coat would be best, padded one even better. That protects you against the knife. You use your left arm to sweep away the attack, your right to try to go on the offensive. Disarm him the best you can and then it's an equal fight.'

He came at me with the ruler. The move was unexpected and the makeshift weapon raked across my stomach, leaving a thin red line of ink.

'Too slow,' he said. He wiped more ink on the ruler and came at me again, slicing at my right side. The ruler produced another red line from my right shoulder down to my stomach.

'Come on, Nick. Use your left arm. Knock me away.'

He came at me, aiming straight for my navel. I swept my padded arm from left to right, knocking the ruler way from my body.

'That's better.'

While I was congratulating myself he sliced across me again.

'Watch the attacker's eyes,' he said. 'They'll telegraph where he intends to strike the next blow.'

He was nimble for a big man and sprung on to his toes and moved quickly to my right. The padded arm was the wrong side now. The ruler swept across me.

'The eyes, damn it, Nick. Watch the eyes.'

It was a hard thing to do: you naturally want to focus on the knife. Nevertheless, I watched his eyes and there was a noticeable flicker down to my left. I jumped right and swept the knife aside with my left arm.

'Better,' he said, smiling. And like a flash, he cut

me in the left side of my stomach while I had momentarily relaxed.

'If this was real, don't ever relax. You have to finish the job. Sweep with your left arm, use your right hand to chop at the wrist with the knife.'

He went to strike again, his eyes told me my navel was again the target. I moved right, swept with my left arm and chopped down on his wrist.

'Bravo,' he said as the ruler slipped to the floor. 'Now we're getting somewhere.'

He came at me again. And again. And again. For the next hour until I was coated in sweat which trickled down my chest and made the ink all over my body run. When he was satisfied he stepped back and said, 'How about a nice cup of tea? Although that wouldn't happen in real life. You've done well. Won't stop me worrying about you, but at least you can drag out a fight now until help arrives. There's a chance now that even though you haven't completely won the battle, the attacker might think it's a harder job than he thought and give up.'

He shook my hand and, while the tea was brewing, I had a shower. Lots of red going down the plug hole, but at least it was ink rather than blood.

WE BOTH TOOK off our jackets and wound them round the lower part of our left arms.

The three men hesitated, taking in the new scene and the raising of the odds against them. Something clicked with Boss Man.

'You're Dangerous Duggan, aren't you?' he said. 'I remember watching you years ago. You're too old for this. Walk away, old man, and let us do the job we're being paid to do.'

'I could take all three of you,' Arthur said. 'Trouble is Shannon will accuse me of being greedy. I'd never live it down. Come on. Let's get this over with.'

He started to walk forward. I joined him on his right, which put me in line for Boss Man. He smiled as I approached.

Focus on the eyes, Arthur had told me. The movement of the eyes will tell you what direction the attack will come from. That's when Boss Man made his first mistake. He took off his sunglasses and put them in the top pocket of his jacket. I could see his eyes. They were the green of jealousy. There was a flash from them that took in my stomach. He was going to fillet me starting there. I took another step toward him and, as he lunged forward, I swept the knife away with my left arm and sent a straight right to his face. I heard the bone in his nose break.

The dangerous thing about a hit on the nose is that it causes the eyes to fill with tears. I hit him again while he couldn't see. Same punch. Same place. Same effect—except the nose was squashier.

He backed off and reassessed the situation. Wasn't going to be as easy as he thought. He took a pace forward and those green eyes centred on my heart—always tricky for the attacker since you have the ribs in the way and likely to cause the knife to veer off. It meant I had to ward off a higher blow.

I rocked back as he advanced. Took up a Kung Fu stance with left arm raised and parallel to my body. I placed my right hand behind level with my head. As he jabbed with the knife I again swept it aside and chopped down on his right shoulder. He winced and took a step back. His right arm would be feeling numb from the blow. His eyes spun. He didn't know what to do or where to attack next.

I swept forward and chopped down on his right hand on the wrist. He let out a cry of pain and the knife fell away. I kicked it aside into the gutter. I hit him in the stomach with a punch which came with full force and couldn't have been heavier. He buckled. I hit him with an upper cut below his chin and he was forced upward and back. Time for another punch to his unprotected stomach.

He stumbled backwards and took in the scene from his fellow thugs' point of view. Arthur was handling both of them easily.

'Stop playing with your food,' I shouted across to him.

'But it's so much fun,' he said in return. He smacked Bulk across the cheeks and the force sent the man spiralling to his right.

'Car,' Boss Man shouted. 'Get in the car.'

He banged on the roof of the car and it reversed up ready to pull away. He leapt into the front seat and the car was moving while the other two were still running back. They jumped into the back seat and the car sped away. But not before I had taken out my phone from the wrapped-up jacket and took a photo of the number plate.

'Well, Arthur,' I said. 'What are you doing here?'

'I've been following you for days,' he said. 'Norman and I have been worried. Thought I'd keep a watchful eye on you.'

'For which I'm truly grateful. I dread to think what would have happened if you weren't around.'

I gave him a man hug and patted his back.

'Seems like you've made a few enemies while I've been off duty,' he said. 'Not that there's anything unusual about that.'

'Someone wants to take me out of the action—killing me, if necessary. There's more to this fraud case than appears on the surface. Unless it's the hit-and-run, that is.'

'Always so many options with you, Nick,' he said. 'The big question is what do we do now?'

'I'm still not on good terms with Mid Anglia. Don't suppose calling the police will achieve much except facing hours of questioning. Time for a call to Walker, I think.'

I took out my phone and searched through to Walker's number. When she answered, I explained the situation and said, 'Can you trace a car for me?'

'Hit me with it and I'll call you back if I get a result.'

I read over the registration number plate and thanked her in advance. The power of positive thinking, I hoped.

'What are you going to do if I find out the owner?' Walker asked.

'I haven't got a clue,' I replied. 'Let's take it one step at a time.'

'You can't help shaking that tree and seeing what falls down,' she said.

'It's served me well in the past.'

'It's got you in a heap of trouble, too.'

'There is that,' I said. 'Maybe it will be different this time.'

'Maybe, Shannon. Just maybe. But don't come knocking on my door if it all goes wrong.'

'Nice to know I have your support, Walker.'

She hung up. I turned to Arthur. 'Do you think there's a decent pub near here where we could get a drink?'

'I passed one about two miles back. Country pub. Thatched roof. Probably all real ale and sawdust.'

'Right now I'll settle for that. Only one, though. Can't go over the limit in case the cops pick on me again.'

I carefully picked up the knife from the gutter so that I wouldn't mar any fingerprints if it finished up as a police investigation. Not that I had much faith in that the way things were going.

'Lead the way, Arthur. I feel a beer beckoning.'

'Be a crime not to say hello to it.'

'Too much crime going round to ignore it.'

'Indeed.'

He set off up the street and got into a car he must have hired especially for the purpose of spying on me—his white van was too noticeable. I waited for him to pass me and then dropped in behind him. Ten minutes later we were sitting trying to spin out our one drink in a pub that was filling up for the lunchtime trade. As we suspected, there were beams on the ceiling and horse brasses on the walls. On a Twee count it scored around seven—not enough cobwebs letting it down.

I phoned Anji, filled her in on our adventures and asked her to swap my hire car with a different one—probably wouldn't throw any enemies off the scent for long, but it was worth a try. I had another call to make, but I didn't want the conversation to be overheard. That would have to wait till we were outside.

'I think you'd better shadow me from now on,' I said to Arthur. 'Whatever's going down is escalating. I feel that we are close to a breakthrough.'

'It's strange when all the suspects are police officers. Doesn't give you much faith, does it?'

'Blue on blue. I heard that no good ever comes from it. I'm beginning to agree.'

'Amen!'

WHEN I GOT outside I took out my phone. Called Curly to see whether he knew if there would be a list of the people on the training exercise. No such luck. I would have to go the long way round. There seemed to be two avenues. Go through the personnel records and see who had qualified for firearms training or find a list of special boots supplied together with their sizes. Seemed like that might be shorter, but the snag was that it would only tell me about current officers and not those from fifteen years ago. Worth a shot, though.

I drove back to HQ and went to see Milly-Molly-Mandy. Posed the problem to them.

'You could look at the back orders of boots and see what sizes had been sent. After that, someone must have kept a record of who they were given to. Procurement is your best bet.'

'I'm not exactly a favourite with Procurement at the moment. If I check back on the invoices, maybe one of you could pick it up from there if I have any luck.'

'Be glad to,' they said in unison.

'OK then, I'd better get started. Got any barley sugars to keep me going?'

Barley Sugar smiled and handed me the bag. I took two, unwrapped one and popped it in my mouth. This could become a bad habit if I wasn't careful.

I found a spare desk, settled down and logged on to the cloud. Started working my way back through the invoices. I was able to short circuit proceedings by drilling down to a sub section labelled Uniforms. From there it was a slog.

It seemed as if there was a regular monthly order for boots so started with the most recent and then month by month from there. A year back I hit the jackpot. And wished I hadn't. One pair of size seven supplied. I suppose that I should have been alerted to the possibility. Too small for a man, so had to be a woman. But why did it have to be this one? Samantha Stone.

TWENTY-THREE

WALKER RANG AS I was driving back to Melchester. I pulled over and took the call. It wasn't helpful.

'The car was stolen,' she said. 'Taken early this morning from central London. Someone is going to a lot of trouble to take you out of the picture. What have you been up to?'

'Shaking the tree,' I said. 'And the fruit tastes bitter.'

'The car will turn up some time, but I doubt there will be much for forensics. Probably burnt out to get rid of any evidence. You need to watch your back if you want to live to the end of this case.'

'I've got Arthur shadowing me. That ought to be some sort of deterrent.'

'Let's hope so.'

I resumed my journey. I'd thought long and hard how to approach the meeting with Sam and decided I needed back up from the police in case I needed to immediately get some sort of arrest. My relationship with Melchester police wasn't going to help me. There was only one officer I thought I could trust. Curly. He may not have liked my approach, but I thought he might be a kindred spirit. Take this opportunity to close a cold case. I found him in the cafeteria eating a slice of apple pie.

'I've got a favour to ask,' I said.

'Why should I want to do you a favour?'

'Because you can close an open case. Put to bed something that took place many years ago. Chance to do some real police work, too. Get you out of the office for an hour or two. Where's your spirit of adventure?'

'I lost that a long time ago,' he said. 'Buy me another slice of pie while I think about it.'

God! This man could eat for England. I walked over to the serving hatch and asked for a slice of pie.

'For Curly, is it?' the lady asked.

I nodded.

'I'll put extra custard on then. Curly loves my custard.'

I took the plate back and sat down while Curly dug in.

'What do you want then?' Curly asked.

'I need a witness, that's all. Maybe you can do an arrest, too. I'm still working out the details.'

'Seems to be a habit with you. Only just short of a headless chicken some would say.'

'We'll see about that, if you deign to come along. We're going to see Sam.'

'That's different then. I'd like to see if there's anything I can do for her. She's a good friend.'

'Then gird your loins, Curly, and off we go.'

He scraped the last of the custard from the plate and stood up.

'One condition, though,' he said.

'And that is?'

'I do the driving. I want to get there in one piece and your current record doesn't go in your favour.'

'Done,' I said. 'Let's go.'

Curly's car was a ten-year-old hatchback that looked like the contents of a sweetshop's rubbish bin. There were wrappers in every available storage box and after they had been filled, the floor had been used. I swept a collection off my seat and sat down. He turned the key in the ignition and coaxed the engine into life. I hoped it was going to get us to Sam's house. We pulled out of the car park and slowly on to the road. He was a careful driver, if you regard keeping ten miles per hour below the speed limit as careful. A few drivers frustrated by his sedate progress honked him and he kept going in his own time.

Finally, we reached our destination and parked behind Sam's car. I rang the bell and waited. Sam opened the door and raised her eyebrows in surprise.

'Nick, nice to see you. Have you managed to prove my innocence?'

'The wheels are in motion,' I said. 'Can we come in?' She registered Curly for the first time. 'What are you doing here?' she said to him.

'To be honest,' he said, 'I haven't got a clue.'

She stood aside to let us in and opened the first door on the left.

'You make yourselves comfortable while I put the kettle on.'

'We're fine,' I said, wanting to get down to the business in hand.

'Tea would be nice,' Curly said, ignoring the glance I sent him. 'Milk and three sugars. Two things you learn quickly when you join the force,' he said to me. 'Never pass up on the offer of a cuppa and never pass a loo without using it.'

'Thanks, Curly,' I said. 'I'll bear that in mind if I ever want a change of career.'

We went into the lounge and I had my first chance to

look around for any additional clues as to Sam's personality. It was tidy—why not when you have time on your hands? There was a three-piece suite in faded green leather and an occasional table to the right of the chair. It faced the television which was the focal point of the room. As I said, why not when you have nothing better to do? There was a print of a Constable scene—Flatford Mill—on the wall above a fireplace with a dated gas fire. The whole room needed loving.

'Here you go, Curly,' Sam said on entering the room. She placed a mug of tea on the table next to him and sat down on the sofa. She tucked her legs under her. 'What can I do for you, Nick?'

'I want to take you back. Many years. There was a drill as an exercise in storming a house where there were hostages inside. Everyone involved has special firearms training. You're all kitted up—Kevlar vests and so on—and everyone carried a gun.'

'I get the picture,' she said. 'If you were a firearms officer there were regular drills on different scenarios. Go on.'

'The drill was a success. The adrenaline is flowing. Someone suggests a drink and everyone agrees it's a good idea to wind down. One officer has too much to drink. The others try to persuade that officer to get a cab. Doesn't listen. Gets in the car to drive home. Drives too fast—spurred on by the alcohol is my guess. Loses control. Ploughs into a boy and a girl. The boy's killed outright, the girl mangled to hell. The driver gets out and walks over to the couple. Leaves a boot print. Gets back in the car and drives off without calling for an ambulance—after all, an ambulance could have done something for the girl.'

'Is there a point to this story?' Sam asked.

I nodded my head. 'The boot print was sized seven. Your size. I think you were that driver. You are ultimately responsible for the death of my sister.'

'Your logic is impeccable. Fits all the evidence. Just one problem.'

She got up and walked across to a bookcase. She took out a photo album. Found the page she was looking for. Presented it to me.

'The only problem with your theory is this.' She pointed to a photo of her riding a donkey, the sun shining above her. 'I was on holiday in Spain at the time of the hit-and-run. See the photo has a date printed on it—so you don't forget the day when it was taken. If you check the leave records—if they still exist, that would bear me out—you'll find I was nowhere near the site of the hit-and-run.'

Curly looked across at me. 'Not your day, is it, Mr Shannon?'

Damn. Another dead end. The solution snatched away from me after I had fleetingly thought I had the answer after all those years.

'I'm dreadfully sorry, Sam. I got carried away. It all seemed to fit so neatly.'

'It's no sweat. We all jump to conclusions at times. I've done it myself. Think we've finished the jigsaw and then find out there's a piece missing. Nothing fits after all.'

I felt a fool and a traitor. I should have trusted her— she was my client and I should have been on her side.

Instead, I'd rushed to judgement. Big mistake. But mistakes are there to be learnt from. Try not to repeat that mistake, Shannon, I chided myself.

'Is there more tea in that pot?' Curly asked, bringing us back to normality.

Sam laughed. 'For you, Curly, I'll make a fresh one.'

As Sam left the room, Curly turned to me. 'What are you going to do now?' he asked.

'I guess it's a case of back to the drawing board, except I'm not sure where the drawing board is.'

'Things haven't been going too well for you, have they?'

'You don't know the half of it,' I said. 'Only this morning three thugs tried to beat me up. I don't suppose, speaking on behalf of the Mid Anglia force, you would know anything about that?'

He shook his head. 'You made a big mistake with what you did to Harry Saunders. The force has closed ranks against you. If I were you I'd think about getting out of Melchester as soon as possible.'

'I owe it to Sam even more now to prove her innocence. Maybe that would blow away the bad odour surrounding me.'

'Wouldn't do any harm,' he said. 'You know what you need, Nick? You need to eat more fish. Fish is good for the brain. A big plate of fish and chips. Worth a try.'

'Thanks, Curly. I'll bear that in mind.'

Sam came back into the room and placed Curly's second cup of tea on the table.

He sipped it. 'You make a lovely cuppa, Sam. Might have missed your vocation.'

'Maybe they'll give me a job in the prison kitchen.'

'I haven't given up hope yet on proving your innocence. I'm about to unleash my secret weapon.'

'And what's that?'

'Best if you don't know. Just trust me.'

'I'm sure everything will work out fine. I have great faith in you.'

'Well, if Curly has finished his tea, we ought to be going. You've been too kind. I hope the next time we meet I will have good news for you.'

'So we're going then?' Curly said with a disappointed tone that indicated he was hoping for a few cucumber sandwiches and some sort of cake to accompany the cups of tea.

Sam came over and kissed me on the cheek.

'Don't think any more of today. I'm sure it will pan out fine in the end.'

Curly finished his last mouthful of tea and got up from the chair. We made our exit, Curly licking his lips and me with my tail between my legs. If that wasn't bad enough, I still had to endure Curly's driving back to Melchester. When would this run of bad luck end?

TWENTY-FOUR

I WAS BACK for my second session with Dr Morgan. The dentist analogy was still accurate. I was nervous, which was stupid. She was such a cool, collected person and there was no pain involved—physical at least. She had a calming presence and I was starting to relax already. I took my place on the sofa and she pulled up a chair for herself, sat down, crossed her legs and balanced a clipboard on her lap.

'I want to start with some cognitive behavioural therapy…'

'Which is?'

'It's centred around coping strategies. They may be able to help reduce the symptoms until we find the root cause and try to eliminate it.'

'And I need this?'

'Nick, what do you say to your clients when they ask for reasons why you're doing something?'

'Ah. "I'm the expert, trust me".'

'Exactly.'

'OK, point taken.'

'I also want to try some hypnosis.'

'Oh,' I said, trying to keep the nervousness out of my voice.

'Don't worry. It's only light, like dozing off in an

armchair in front of the TV. Be reassured you won't wake up thinking you're a duck and going quack.'

'Then bring it on, Doctor.'

'I'd like you to make yourself comfortable on the sofa and shut your eyes. Breathe deeply.'

I did what she said and waited for the ordeal to start. Why an ordeal? Because it was bound to discover my deepest thoughts and reveal areas of my personality that I thought might be best hidden. All the mistakes of the past revealed. I was about to disarm myself. Show my weaknesses. Make myself vulnerable.

'I'd like you to think back to Brixton. To the day when you were about to be moved to Chelmsford. The warders have come into your cell. They have arranged it so that you are alone. What's going through your mind?'

'It was all so deliberate. They'd planned it all beforehand. I knew something bad was going to happen—they were too edgy—the only question was what. I thought at first they might just beat me up. I could have coped with that, although I would have not trusted anyone in authority again. But it was the look on their faces that told me it would be something really bad. Something that I would not recover from. They looked apologetic, like they were only obeying orders—which I suppose was the case, except they would be taking a big pay off in return. One of them even said, "Nothing personal".' I shook my head and laughed. 'As if that was going to make it any better... Look, Doctor, I don't think I can do this.'

'You're doing fine. Trust me. This is important. Go on.'

'One of them opens the door a crack and looks to see if anyone is coming. That the coast is clear. He nods at the other one who takes my hand. Forces my fingers open. Takes hold of the index and middle finger on my left hand. The other warder swings the door back and waits. My fingers are pushed into the steel frame of the door. It's slammed shut. I passed out. The next thing I know is that I'm lying there in a pool of blood.'

I shivered.

'You're now at Chelmsford. You're put in a cell with Norman. How do you react?'

'I couldn't stop looking at the door as if it's all going to happen again. I can't do anything—not lie down or even sit on the chair at the little table. I'm perspiring. I kept looking at Norman pleadingly as if he could open the cell door by magic.'

'And what does Norman do to calm you down?'

'He occupies my mind. He had a plan. Bullies me into thinking about maths. "What's one and one?" he says. I say two and he laughs. "Wrong!" I say three, thinking that he's talking about synergy, the whole bigger than the parts. "Wrong," he says again. I give up. Shout at him. Ask for the answer, all the time staring at the door. "Whatever you want it to be," he says with a smile. And so it went on. Every time I looked at the door he asked me another question. Always an answer I wasn't expecting. He made me work at the maths, the accountancy, so I'd have something to do in the future that didn't need two fully functioning hands. And so my life changed again.'

'We're going to go back further now,' she said, her voice quieter, soothing. 'To that other time your life changes.' There's a sing-song quality to her voice now. 'It's the day of the disco. Your sister is getting ready to go out. Tell me about it. Time to tell me all about it, Nick.'

And that was the last thing I remember her saying. Her voice seemed to tail off. I was aware I was talking, digging deep in my memory for the hard facts and the even harder emotions, but not knowing if I was making any sense.

'I'd like you to open your eyes now, Nick,' she said, her voice increasing in volume. 'How do you feel?'

'Quack,' I said.

She shook her head and tried to keep a straight face.

'God, you're incorrigible, Nick,' she said, laughing. 'What am I going to do with you?'

'Anything but give up. We've come this far so we might as well see it through to the end, if there is an end.'

'I want one more session. I think I'm close to the answer. I said that CBT was partly about coping strategies. I've a present for you.'

She got up from the chair and went across to her desk, opened a drawer and took out a small box. Handed it across to me.

'I'd like you to try this when you feel that you are losing it.' I opened the box. Inside was something I would never have expected. A harmonica!

'There's a book to go with it,' she said, fishing around in the desk drawer again. 'Take some time to practise it. Learn a song or two. You play the piano, so a harmonica shouldn't be too difficult to pick up. When you think you can't take anymore, play a song. Any song. Doesn't matter. Let the song flood out and through you.'

'And this will help?'

'Got to be worth a try.'

My attitude to life summed up in a few words.

WHEN I GOT back to the office, Mary Jo was being en-
tertained by Anji in the lounge area overlooking the
river. She had come to go through Arlene's things and
see what she wanted to take and what could be given
to a charity. She was sipping water from a plastic bottle as if she didn't trust our English water. I suppose
I shouldn't have been surprised—Mary Jo had a poor
record on trust.

'I'm all set to go,' Mary Jo said. 'Thought I'd hang
on and say goodbye.'

'I appreciate that. Have you got everything you
want?'

'I've taken all the jewellery,' she said. 'Technically
half of it is yours'—the will had split everything 50:50
between us—'but what would you do with it? I'll wear
some of it, get some value from it.'

'It's not a problem,' I said. 'I'd only get sad when I
looked at it.'

She nodded and gave me a smile. A smile from Mary
Jo was a rare gesture. Time to catch her in a good mood.

'I need a favour,' I said.

'Oh,' she said. The smile vanished. 'Am I going to
like this?'

'It's something only you can do.'

'Is this legal?'

'Not exactly.'

'That means no.'

'I'm stuck on the money trail of a million-pound fraud,' I said. I need you to try your special skills.'

'I take it you want me to hack into a bank.'

'Could be more than that,' I said. 'I have a feeling the trail is going to get complex.'

'And why should I do this? I'm a mother now. I have a kid. I have a doting husband. I don't want anything to affect my family and my life.'

'We haven't got on well in the past,' I said. 'This would seal the truce between us. It's what Arlene would have wanted.'

'You play dirty, Nick.'

'It's been said before.'

'OK, I'll do it, but I have some conditions. One, I do it from here, in case anyone tries a trace. Two, I use your computer, same reason. Three, if this goes belly up, I deny everything and you take the can. I was never even here. Four, I go by half seven—I have a dinner date.'

'Can't you cancel it?'

'I don't break promises, and Cherry wouldn't like it.'

'You're having dinner with Walker? I can't believe it.'

'We got talking at the funeral. We have a lot in common. We have an affinity for each other. Better than eating alone in a foreign country, too.'

'This is not exactly Iraq.'

'Do you want me to do this favour or not?'

'I can beg, if you like. Yes, I want you to and I'll be in your debt.'

'If I call, you come. Agreed?'

'Agreed,' I said. 'Let's get started.'

'Coffee,' she said. 'Lots of it. Now clear your desk and let me use your computer.'

I went into my office and cleared my desk. Turned on the computer and input the password to wake it up. Took the details of the first bank account from my notes. Then went back into the lounge and started making coffee. Carried the cups back to where she now sat at my desk. She seemed engrossed in what she was doing.

'If you do the hacking, I've got a file of all the employees. As soon as we get a match on an account we can stop.'

I told her the name of the first bank and about Melchester Blue.

She started tapping away. I took the CC's tablet from my briefcase and called up the HR file of employees. Waited for her to give me a name.

'We start at the British bank. Melchester Blue. I can see it. From there it goes to a bank in Liechtenstein.' She broke off and took a sip of coffee while the computer did wondrous things. 'Still called Melchester Blue,' she said. 'Account only lasts one day and the money is on the move again. Bahamas this time. Still Melchester Blue. Wait, it's transferred within the bank. I got a name.'

My adrenaline kicked in. 'What is it?' I asked.

She told me. There was no need to check the HR records. I knew the name all too well.

This was going to create a hell of a stink.

TWENTY-FIVE

MORAG HAD BOOKED a conference room to give us some semblance of privacy. Someone in the catering department had laid on an insulated jug of coffee, one of tea, milk, sugar, and bottles of still and sparkling water and a plate of chocolate digestives as if it was an ordinary everyday meeting. The CC was already there sitting at the head of a table for six, looking at his watch when the three of us entered. Collins went to sit to his right, Walker to his left and I took the confrontational seat opposite him. I poured myself a black coffee and added sugar slowly to build the tension. Boy, was I going to enjoy this.

'I hope this is important,' the CC said, 'because I have a million other things on which I could be spending my time.'

'I think you'll find it's important,' I said. 'Can I get anyone anything?' I added.

'Skip the niceties, Shannon,' he said. 'Let's get started.'

Walker—relishing what was to come—asked for a cup of tea which I poured slowly. She smiled at me and gave me a wink. For once she and I were on the same wavelength. It felt good.

'Found the money at last, have you, Shannon?' the CC said.

'I've found the culprit, too. But first, over to you, Superintendent.'

Collins, with much *Schadenfreude*, read the caution and that we were charging him with embezzlement and that anything he would say would be twisted and turned to get a conviction. Only joking. What fun I was having.

Henderson, no longer the CC in my book, looked appalled. The colour drained from his face.

'Are you mad?' he said.

'You wish,' I said.

He shook his head and stared at me.

'What is this? I don't know what you're talking about.'

'Methinks he doth protest too much,' said Walker.

'Don't get clever with me,' he said. 'You've got it all wrong. Stone took the money. There's fifty grand in her bank to prove it. This is stitch up.'

'The best piece of advice on a fraud case is follow the money,' I said. 'So that's what I've done.'

'I don't have time for this,' said Walker, paradoxically sipping her tea slowly. Somehow the instruction seemed more commanding coming from her. 'Get on with it, Shannon.'

'Indulge me,' I said. I slid my notebook across the table to Henderson. 'This is where we start. You've been very clever, but not clever enough.'

'I don't know what you mean.'

'Come on,' Collins said impatiently. 'The game's up. We have you bang to rights, and other such phrases that you've heard countless times before. We know what you did and how you did it. And the worst thing was trying to frame Sam. A good copper with a fine record. How dirty can you get?'

'I repeat myself,' the CC said, getting tetchy. 'I've done nothing. I don't know what you are talking about.'

I turned to Walker who, because of Collins's past involvement with Sam, was technically the officer in charge of the case. 'Do you want to tell him or shall I?'

'Be my guest,' she said. 'You broke the case, after all. But try not to gloat too much. It doesn't become you.'

'To find the culprit you have to follow the money. You thought you had been pretty clever, putting the two lots of twenty-five grand in Sam's account. You used your level 7 authority to take the money from the force account and to hack into the Federation account—the treasurer helped you is my guess. He was an old friend and probably owed you a big favour. Or was it blackmail? Proof of that is academic, though, seeing as we can prove you stole the money from the force.'

'You're barking mad,' the CC said. 'You're making all this up to get Stone off the hook. Where is your proof for this tale of fiction?'

'The money. Follow the money. The bulk of what you stole goes into the account of Melchester Blue. Page one in my notebook. Look at it carefully because it's not there for long. No returns filed, so that is a dead end. But turn the page, you then use a Liechtenstein account. Should be impossible to track. Except we've got an expert. The money moves from there, next page, to the Bahamas. And from there, turn the page, what account does it go to? To that of a Mr Michael Henderson? That's where you slipped up. You underestimated me, and for that you'll pay. Don't feel bad about that, you're not alone in that—it's a cross I have to bear for being a smartarse at times. None of that matters now. We have all the evidence we need.'

'But I don't know anything about Melchester Blue and money going all over the place. Someone's framing me, that's what is going on here. You've got it all wrong.'

I looked at Walker and she nodded. 'Let's not make a scene,' she said. 'Let's walk calmly past the staff and don't look back until we get outside. We're taking you to our HQ—we'll spare you the humiliation of your own police station, for now at least.'

'I don't know what you mean. This is a frame up. You've got it all wrong.'

'Nice try,' I said. 'But that's where the money leads us. I admit I'm surprised at you, though. Cushy job, big pension to come. You could have sat back and had a comfortable retirement without looking over your shoulder all the time listening for that knock on the door to bring you back down to earth with a bump. Trying to pin the blame on Sam was a big mistake—so clumsy. You might have got away with it otherwise. I suppose you couldn't resist it. Pin the blame on someone who you hated for one reason or another. Maybe you'll tell me the full story someday.'

Walker, patience exhausted, stood up and Collins followed suit.

'We'll take it from here,' he said. 'I don't know how I can ever thank you enough.'

'I'll think of a way,' I said. 'Or does that make us quits? Wipe the slate clean?'

'No, I owe you big time and so does Sam. Will you tell her the good news or shall I?'

'It started with you so that's the way it should end. I'll see her another time.'

One case closed. Just the hit-and-run to go. But first we had a celebration meal to attend. A chance to let our hair down and enjoy our success.

TWENTY-SIX

CANNING LIVED IN A terraced house in a leafy suburb of what would soon be a property hotspot. There was a *Sold* sign outside. Probably would have been better to hold out for the boom, but needs must. He came to the door looking a mess. He was unshaven, his hair was tousled and his eyes were flecked with red. He looked like he hadn't slept for days.

'Thanks for coming,' he said. 'It sounded urgent on the phone. Are they going to prosecute me after all?'

'Aren't you going to let me in? Maybe we can talk over a coffee.'

'Sorry,' he said. 'Where are my manners?'

He led me through to a small sitting room where a thin woman sat in one of those chairs that helped you get up. It was too big for the room. I should have thought about that when I'd ordered it. Maybe they would be able to accommodate it better when they moved.

'This is Sylvia,' he said. 'The kids are at school and nursery so we can talk in peace. I'll make some coffee.'

'As strong as you can make it would be good,' I said.

'I remember,' he said. 'You're the fussy one—sorry, I meant you're an espresso man. I can't rival that, I'm afraid. Would you like a cup, love?'

'Tea, please,' she said. 'If it's not too much trouble.'

'And when would you be too much trouble?' he said.

'Pretty much all of the time at the moment.'

'I doubt that,' I said. 'Anything would be a pleasure for you.'

'Not true, but I'll accept the compliment.'

Canning left the room, leaving the two of us together. I took the opportunity to study her more deeply. I put her age at early thirties—far too young for this sort of life. Seemed cruel, but that can be the way of the world. I'd do what I could and leave them to find the best solution that existed. Give them a fresh start, too.

She had chestnut hair, already with a few specks of grey—seemed like the last few months must have taken its toll. Her eyes were deep brown and would have given her a warm smile, if she ever had something to smile about.

'How are things?' I asked, not expecting a good answer, but it was important to know.

'We cope,' she said. 'That's all that we can do. My neurologist says that the attacks come and go. Maybe I'm near to a spell of remission. When the sale of the house goes through and the pressure's off, that might help. I'm due to start a course of immunosuppressants, too. That's supposed to make the attacks less frequent and less severe.'

'How's Ralph coping?'

'He's a treasure, but worried not just on account of me, but by not having a job. He says that not getting a reference won't make it easy. But what am I thinking? Wittering on about myself when I should be thanking you for the chair.'

'The least I could do.'

Canning came back in and placed a tray on a side

table and handed round the drinks. I took a sip. It was terrible. If this was the strongest he could do, then I hated to know what a normal cup was like.

'I've got some good news,' I said.

'Any good news would be welcome, won't it, darling?' Canning addressed his wife.

'Think positive, Ralph,' I chided. 'The house is sold and that's one big thing you don't need to worry about. Now let's talk jobs. Do you want your old one back?'

'If it was possible, I'd jump at the chance. The CC wouldn't allow it, though.'

'No one need to concern themselves with the CC anymore.'

He looked at me with a puzzled expression. 'How can that be?'

'The CC and Mid Anglia are no longer an item.'

'But I was fired. How could I get my old job back?'

'You weren't fired,' I said. 'You've been on compassionate leave.'

'That's impossible.'

'Just call it my good deed for the day.'

'But my file will have the CC's notes—the missing money.'

'Don't keep saying *but*, Ralph. Trust me.'

'You said that once before and look where it got me.'

'Fact one,' I said. 'You have your old job back. Fact two, the CC recommended you for a salary rise.'

'But—sorry—there's the money I stole. What about that?'

'You never stole any money. You were working for me under cover on a test of the system—see how robust it was. Don't go overboard, though, it still needs paying back. We've bankrolled you till then.'

'None of this is possible.'

'Not unless someone had the CC's tablet and did a bit of massaging of the files.'

'You found a way!' he said. 'You found a way round the system.'

'With a little help from my friends. You're in the clear, Ralph. No more worries. Just one thing.'

'And that is?'

'Get a decent coffee machine for the next time I call. No wonder Sylvia went for tea.'

She pressed a button on the chair. The seat rose and she stood upright. Came over, unsteadily, to where I sat and wrapped her arms around me. 'How can we ever thank you?'

'If ever I need a computer man, I'll come knocking at your door.'

'But why are you doing this?' Canning said.

'Because I don't like to see good people crushed down by circumstances. And because I'm a softie. You look after this lady, Ralph. The kids, too. Play happy families. Oh, and one last thing.'

'What's that?' he said, waiting for the catch.

'Don't ever do anything so stupid ever again.'

TWENTY-SEVEN

'HOW'S THE HARMONICA GOING?' Dr Morgan asked when I had settled myself on the sofa.

'I can play any of a dozen nursery rhymes, but there's not much street cred in that. I'm currently working on "St. Louis Blues".'

'Tried playing in any confined places yet?'

'Let's just say I'm building up to that.'

'These sessions only work if we're completely honest with each other. Let's try that again. Tried playing in any confined places yet?'

'I'm not confident enough at the moment.'

'Promise me you will try that when you leave today.'

'Promise made.'

'OK, let's see where you are and why. Heard of Post-Traumatic Stress Disorder?'

'What soldiers often get after times of deep emotion, maybe when a friend was killed?'

'Not just soldiers, but ordinary people as well. People who have been through traumatic events and, mistakenly, think they are at fault. The cognitive behaviour therapy is part of a programme that helps you see that you are not to blame. Nick, you've had not one but two traumatic events—three if we include the recent death of your wife: the killing of your sister and the chopping off of your fingers. It's no surprise that you are mixed up.'

'So what do we do? I don't think that playing "St. Louis Blues" on the harmonica is going to be enough to turn my life around, nice tune though it is.'

'There are medications you can have for symptoms like depression, but you don't seem to have any problems like that. Through our previous two sessions, we know that closing you in triggers your trauma. That is a big thing to have done. From here we can have more CBT—more talking about your feelings and how to change them.'

'And will that work?'

'It will help, but I see a major problem.'

'Hit me with it.'

'It's your sister's death. It's a metaphor for why you feel as you do. It's a door you can't close because the hit-and-run driver has never been found. Whilst that situation persists, so will the symptoms. You feel responsible for her death—things that you could have done that would have changed the future. We have to persuade your deep inner thoughts to the contrary in order to expunge that blame.'

'So are you saying that while the killer is free, my trauma will carry on as ever? That there is nothing I can do as long as that case remains open?'

'We can continue with talking therapies like the CBT. There's also something called psychodynamic therapy which will focus on talking about your feelings as an abstract and trying to delink with the traumatic event. There's also techniques like exposure therapy, desensitization and flooding that can work on your memories.'

'And how long does all this take?'

'Typically, three to six months—one or two years if you have other problems in conjunction, like the depression we talked about earlier, and sometimes even longer.'

I slumped back in the sofa.

'I can sense,' she said, 'that you are disappointed, dejected even.'

'That's what we pay you for. Wouldn't be any good in your job unless you can tell what your patients are thinking. It all seems too long and that unless the driver is caught there might be no solution. It's all wrapped up together. I've been trying for fifteen years to find the driver and keep hitting a dead end.'

'In our CBT sessions, we'll address your feelings of guilt about her death, but I'm not sure how much that will help. I'm sorry, Nick, but can't lie to you that it is an easy task.'

'Hard to find much that's positive about the future.'

'Don't give up hope. Together we'll keep trying. Who knows, they might find some magic bullet in the form of a new medication or psychological therapy.'

'And the chances of that? Remember what you said—these sessions only work if we are truthful to each other.'

'The chances are slim.'

TWENTY-EIGHT

THIS TIME TODDY'S was the venue for celebration rather than planning. Everyone was in triumph mode. Norman's table had been enlarged to cope with the seven of us, five from the last time we were here, plus Collins and Walker. I couldn't have better companions. Everyone had entered the spirit of the celebration. A champagne cork popped and our glasses were filled by one waiter while another opened a second bottle.

'A toast to everybody,' I said, raising the champagne glass. 'A job well done.'

'I don't want to pop anyone's balloon,' said Walker, placing her hand on mine, 'but you do realize that none of the evidence will be admissible in court? Hacking into computers is the wrong side of the law.'

'But it got Sam off the hook,' said Collins 'and that was the main goal. Finished Henderson's career, too. Be a lot glad of that.'

'Where does it leave Mid Anglia, though?' Morag said.

'A force too big to fail, Henderson told me once,' I said. 'Yates is a slippery customer. He'll find a way out of it. Hush it all up would be my guess. The CC will take early retirement—some health problem or to spend more time with his family—and they'll replace him with some clone. Your job, Morag, and everybody else's, will be safe.'

'Morag's going to take some time off while things quieten down,' announced Norman. 'She deserves a break after all the excitement. We're off on a Caribbean cruise.'

'Good for you,' Arthur said. 'Maybe she'll make an honest man of you. If that's possible, that is.'

'I'll do my best,' said Morag. 'Although I imagine it will be a hard journey.'

'Of Himalayan proportions,' I said.

'Thanks for the character reference,' grunted Norman.

'I'm taking a break, too,' said Walker. 'Haven't decided where yet. Need to get my head round a few things.'

'I shall miss you,' I said.

'Will you?' she said. 'We'll see.'

'Time for me to hang up my gun,' Collins said. 'I'm getting too old for all of this. I've decided to retire.'

'This is sudden,' Walker said, astonished. 'What tipped you over the edge, for something must have done. You never mentioned anything.'

'I thought now that Sam's off the hook we might be able to spend more time together. Maybe rekindle the flames from times gone by. I'll recommend you for promotion, Cherry. You'll be far better than me at running the show. I'm a fish out of water. Now I feel like a dinosaur, too.'

'You and Sam,' I said. 'Two good coppers battling the system. Good luck to you.'

'I'm feeling a bit left out of this,' said Arthur.

'Well, don't look at me,' said Anji.

'I like my women compliant,' he said.

'As I said, don't look at me.'

He placed his bear-like paw of a hand on hers and she smiled.

'Wow, what a job,' she said, shaking her head in disbelief.

'And a permanent one, too, if you want it,' I said. 'Your probationary period is over. Want to stay?'

'You bet.'

'Then welcome to the team,' I said. 'And I think that should apply to Mary Jo, too. We'll make her an honorary member. Without her we couldn't have done it.'

'Almost perfect,' said Arthur. 'Never did find the hit-and-run driver.'

'I'm still working on that,' I said. 'I've got the beginnings of an idea, but it might be best to keep it to myself for the moment.'

Food started to arrive and we focused on eating for a while. Such a lovely atmosphere—good food, good wine and good friends. I was truly a lucky man.

When the meal was over, Toddy came out of the kitchen and over to our table. He was wearing his chef's whites and a pair of white clogs. He had taken his hat off and swept his thinning hair off his face.

'How was it, ladies and gentlemen? Up to our usual impeccable standard?'

'It was delicious,' Anji said.

The rest of us gave our agreement.

'Who had the salmon?' Toddy asked.

'That was me,' said Morag.

'What did you think of the smoking over Earl Grey tea?'

'So subtle. A masterpiece.'

'And the pork belly?'

'That was me,' said Arthur. 'I'd say unctuous if I knew what it meant.'

Toddy smiled. 'What are we celebrating tonight? It is a celebration, isn't it?'

'The cracking of a near impossible case. One that you played a big role in.'

'Ah, the fingerprint, I take it.'

'Impressive work. And you were exactly right on the timing—forty-five minutes to the last second.'

'Well, when you've done one it makes it easy to tell how long the second one will take.'

I was thrust back in my chair as the importance of his words struck me. It wasn't a pretty thought. 'What do you mean when you've done one? When was this?'

'A month or so back. Same fingerprint, too.'

'Oh, hell,' I said. 'We've been had. Led up the garden path. Everything falls into place now. What have we done?'

'You tell us,' Norman said.

'We've done what somebody wanted us to do all along and now we have to put things right.'

TWENTY-NINE

'COME TO GLOAT, SHANNON?' Henderson said.

'I've come to throw you a lifeline.'

'Then you'd better come in because I need all the help I can get right now.'

I had got his address from Morag, but hadn't phoned ahead—he would have only said no. His house was what an estate agent would have called a Palladian mansion, complete with columns either side of a porch. To me, it was just a four-bedroom detached although larger than average. It backed on to a golf course so that must have bumped up the price by a lot. It said successful executive. Which was true no more.

He opened the door fully and gestured for me to come in. He was wearing a pink polo shirt with a pair of dark blue slacks. Either dressed for the golf course or his wife chose his outfits. Without the uniform with its pips on his shoulder he was diminished. I hoped he wouldn't put up a fight.

'I wondered how long it would take you to call. You've always been a man with a hidden agenda. Now it's time for you to reveal it, although it's not hard to guess.'

He led me into a living room which had a strong feminine touch—I didn't think there was much of him in it. Maybe he had to boss and bully at work because he was under the cosh at home. It was a large room with pink flowered curtains, complete with sashes, over large picture windows on three sides. Three sofas in complementary colours in an autumn leaves print and scatter cushions stood artfully arranged around a large fireplace. Always good to have a focal point. I had to remember that and not get dragged off course. He sat down at a sofa to the right of the fireplace and I took a seat opposite.

'I won't offer you coffee,' he said.

'As you wish. I wouldn't have accepted it anyway.'

'Frightened what I might put in it?'

'Believe me, fright isn't the emotion I'm feeling right now.'

'Go ahead. Make your pitch. I'm all ears.'

He was more relaxed than I had expected. Something up his sleeve, no doubt.

'At the moment, you're finished. Disgraced, facing prison'—which was a lie given that our evidence was inadmissible, but he didn't know that—'and no pension to fall back on. Your colleagues and friends will hate you—stealing from the Federation was theft of their money. How low can you get? And you realize that if you go to prison you will be lucky to come out alive. Believe me, I've been there. It's a hard life and a dangerous one, too. Plenty of men who would love to get their own back on the police. You'll be the prime target. Death might well be the easiest option. Right now, Walker is putting together the case against you and looking to see what other charges she can bring. I want answers and if I don't get them, I will leave you to rot.'

'I have friends in high places,' he said.

'They will all have deserted you, and that includes your bosom buddy Yates. I'm the only friend you've got now, so you need to make the most of me.'

'But I didn't steal the money. It's a frame up. Like I've told you all along, I'm innocent.'

'I don't care. It's irrelevant. The case against you is strong. You're going down for a long time. Unless you cooperate.'

He took a moment to think about what I'd said. Time to sweeten the pill.

'I can prove your innocence. If you tell me what you know.'

'It's your sister, isn't it? You want vengeance. I'm the only person who can give it to you. You need me as much as I need you.'

'You took the file, didn't you? OK, the computer file has gone, but...'

'So it was you. I thought it was just me being careless with the tablet. Makes sense now. Did you like the security? Probably not, or you wouldn't be here. I can't claim any credit—my son rigged it up. Isn't it galling that a twelve-year-old child can outfox both of us?'

Focus, Shannon. Don't get diverted into blind alleys.

'As I was saying. You're too smart a man not to have kept the original. I want it or to know what it contains. Give me justice.'

'Justice! Huh! Do you think that the police are all about justice? There wouldn't be so many crooks at large if that were the case.'

'I know that the hit-and-run driver left a boot print at the scene. I need to know who made it. It's all about the print. Time to fess up, as our American cousins would say.'

'I want full proof of my innocence and all the charges dropped. I also want to continue in my role as CC.'

'Trust me,' I said. 'I'll be true to my word. I'll put everything right. Give me a name, Henderson.'

'You're not going to like it,' he said, barely suppressing a smile. 'Oh, how you're not going to like it.'

'Give.'

'It was a day I'll never forget. It was supposed to be a full test of our rapid response firearms officers. Everyone kitted up, including handguns. We were using an abandoned farmhouse. The exercise was how to storm it and gain entry without peril to those being held inside. The test was a success. Proved we could cope with situations like that. Everyone was on a high, so when we had finished, we had a drink or two. Or three or four. Spirits were high, spirits were downed. Then it all went wrong. One of the people had too much to drink, insisted on driving home and lost it. Ploughed into your sister and her boyfriend. The rest you know.'

'Who was it?'

'It was a day when we had a visit from a junior minister in the Home Office. He wanted to be involved, play Cowboys and Indians, so we kitted him out—the works, uniform, Kevlar vest and gun. It was outside of procedures, but we needed the man's influence. He was a rising star. We wanted to hitch our wagon to it.'

'But the boot. The print was size seven. It was Sam's boot.'

'It was the only pair we could find small enough.

Small man, small feet. She was on holiday and her locker was open. We took them without a second thought.'

I started to realize where he was heading. He was right—I didn't like it.

'It was Yates, wasn't it?' I said.

'You've got it on the button, Shannon.'

'That explains your meteoric rise. You cover for Yates and he keeps putting you forward for promotion. Pulls a few strings behind the scene. One hand washes the other.'

'Now what are you going to do?'

'Give me the file—I know you must have it somewhere, otherwise Yates would have done something to keep you quiet forever. You still have a hold on him, don't you?'

He nodded and let the smile he had been suppressing spread across his face.

'I'm going to bring him down,' I said. 'I need the file.'

He got up and left the room without speaking. Maybe he was going to make that coffee after all. Equivalent of a pipe of peace. No chance.

He came back with a large manila envelope and put it on the sofa next to him.

'There's one other thing you need to know. There was a terrible stink after the exercise.'

'Presumably you lost someone's uniform as well as Sam's boots.'

'Yates wanted them as a souvenir. Maybe his girl-friend or wife liked men in uniform, I don't know. Wouldn't be the first time. But that wasn't all. He kept the gun, too. Whatever you decide to do, you need to watch your back.'

'I don't care. I'm going to take him down. The bigger they come…'

'I admire your tenacity, but I don't think that will be enough.'

'I'll find a way. I've waited too many years for this to let a murderer and the man that condemned my sister to an early grave get away with it. I promised her justice and that's what I'll give her.'

'Don't forget your side of the bargain. Prove my innocence—I'll keep the file till you do.'

'Don't worry. I'll put everything right. Everyone will get their just deserts.' It was a weasel, but he didn't seem to notice. 'One last thing, out of interest. What was there between you and Sam? Why the hatred?'

He laughed. 'For such an intelligent man, you can be very naïve at times. We were lovers.'

He looked at me and shook his head as if anyone could be so stupid.

'It was good for a while, but I was never going to leave my wife and marry her. She was too much of a rough diamond. I needed someone with more finesse, someone who wouldn't hold me back.'

'Hell hath no fury, eh?'

'On the button, Shannon. Now I think our business is over. Get out of my house and get me my job back.'

I was pleased to go. I had a lot of thinking to do.

THIRTY

Sam opened the door and took a pace back when she saw Walker at my side.

'I didn't expect you,' she said to Walker. 'Is this wise? Have you closed the case?'

'In a manner of speaking, yes.'

'Well, come in. Chris is already here.'

We walked through to the lounge and Collins stood up as we entered. His copper's instinct told him something was wrong.

'Is this about the other night?' he said. 'Putting everything right?'

I nodded.

'This meeting is off the record,' I said. 'If anyone asks, it never took place.'

'What's all this about?' said Collins.

'It will all soon be clear. Bear with me.'

We all sat down in an informal circle and I took a deep breath. 'Most of it I know, the rest is based on assumptions, but pretty good ones, I suspect. It all started a few months ago, I would guess. Just before you changed banks. That's when you had the germ of an idea, Sam. Then you had to do your research. The first thing you do is awaken your relationship with Chris.'

Collins looked at me with an expression that was a

mixture of worry and bewilderment. The next bit would be hard for him.

'You meet with Chris. Old time's sake would probably be the excuse. You pump him. You pump him dry. You need to find out what the procedures are. What happens when a fraud takes place. Who's the best forensic accountant around? Modesty forbids.

'You get Chris talking. Glass of wine or a scotch to lubricate him, I don't know, but whatever you used does the trick. You get him to talk about the cases we had worked on together. One in particular grabs your interest. The insurance case. The case where Mary Jo hacked into a UNIX computer system. Your mouth must have been watering.'

Collins opened his mouth and I raised my hand to silence him.

'So now you know that the trick—the hack—only works with a UNIX system. The idea blossoms. You visit banks on the pretext of getting a better deal and for added security. You get full details of the systems. Luck is on your side. The bank that Mid Anglia uses is UNIX. You switch banks for the Federation and move on to the next stage. How am I doing so far, Sam?'

'I don't know what you are talking about. None of this makes sense.'

'It soon will. The sting can't be too easy. It has to look like a frame—and a very clumsy one. That's where the Mid Anglia account comes into play. You have to steal from both the Federation account and the Mid Anglia account. Although you would be a suspect for the theft from the Federation, how could you have stolen from the force? I'll come on to that in a moment.

'To muddy the waters, to make it look an even more clumsy frame up, you put the two lots of twenty-five grand into your account and the rest into the account of a company called Melchester Blue. The stage is set. When the frauds are revealed, you call on Chris. Who is best for your defence? Who will follow the same trail as before? It worked for the insurance scam, so I would go about the same procedures.'

'I don't like the way this is heading,' said Collins, rising from his seat.

'I realize this must be hard, Chris, but hear me out.'

'Trust him,' said Walker.

Collins looked at me like I was mad. Like I must have some ulterior motive. The truth was going to hurt—big time.

'Where were we? Ah, yes. Laying down a trail for the unsuspecting Shannon. Let's take a step back. You have to steal from Mid Anglia, too, to provide you with a back-up plan if I'm unsuccessful following the money trail. So how do you do that? Answer—the same way that I did. Switch tablets—it didn't register at the time when Morag said the CC had a bad record with tablets. You were the reason for that record. Now comes a big mistake. One of your criminal contacts knows a forger. You entrust the job of making the fingerprint to him without asking who he would use. Enter Toddy. The best there is. If it hadn't have been for Toddy being so precise with how long it would take to forge the fingerprint, it wouldn't have registered with me.'

'I don't have to sit here listening to your fairy tale,' Sam said.

'But you do,' I said, 'or we can't put everything right

and that's what I have to do for Chris. If he wasn't involved, I'd throw you to the lions.'

Sam sat back in her seat and crossed her arms defensively.

'So you lay down the trail for me. The risk is that I might follow it to the end and see your involvement. So you set up the CC to take the rap. Settles an old score, too. I entrust the task of following the trail to Mary Jo and we have the personnel records file for comparison. After much hacking she comes up with a name that's on the list. Henderson. Bingo. We have our thief. We stop there when we should have carried on. The heat's off Sam Stone. All she needs to do now is get the hell out of it and enjoy her ill-gotten gains. I don't know if you intended to pick up your relationship with Chris or whether he was just being used like all of us. For his sake, let's give you the benefit of the doubt.'

'So where do we go from here?' Walker said.

'Are you going to arrest Sam?' Collins said. 'Is that Shannon's idea of putting everything right?'

'Relax,' said Walker. 'None of the evidence we have will stand up in court. It's all inadmissible. Shannon has an idea. Typical romantic stuff from him.' She looked at me and I took my cue.

'While Mary Jo went a step further on the money trail, she also followed my instructions. The £950,000 has been transferred back to the Federation and to Mid Anglia. Same thing for the two smaller amounts in your personal account. The money is back where it belongs.'

'But you can't do that!' said Sam, seeing her comfortable future disappear before her eyes.

'Oh, but we have,' I said. 'And nothing you can do about it. You're in the same position as you started.'

'Are you going to let her go?' Collins said to Walker.

'If she follows instructions, yes. You are going to resign from your job at the Federation with immediate effect. Take an early pension. Not, I lay everything in front of the CC and let him deal with you as he will, which won't be pretty, I suspect. No pension. Permanent stain on your character. All those people who thought of you as a good copper will have to rethink their view about you. And that includes Chris. You won't have a friend in the world.'

'I take it all of this is true, Sam?' he said.

She slumped back in the chair and nodded.

'And me?' he said. 'How do I stand?'

'You're as bad a romantic as Shannon,' Sam said. 'Do you want to hear it from me? You stand nowhere, Chris. It was all a pipe dream for you. I didn't steal all that money just to share it with you and provide you with a cushy future.'

'You bitch,' he said. 'You've been using me all along. I had hopes for us. We could have been happy together. Money isn't important compared to you and me.'

'If you are not going to charge me, get out of my house.'

'Not yet,' I said. I opened my briefcase and took out a sheet of paper. 'This is your resignation letter. Sign it, please, and then we'll go.'

She snatched the letter from my hand, grabbed the pen I was holding, scrawled her name and flung it back at me.

Collins got up and, shoulders slumped, walked out the door. We followed him. There was nothing more to do.

THIRTY-ONE

IT WAS MY first full day back in the office. My time at Mid Anglia was over. Everything I needed to do now could be done from here. I arrived early and Anji was already there. Team bonus mark.

'I've booked appointments for tomorrow onward—they're in your diary—I thought you might need a day to catch up.'

'Good thinking. I'm going to put a load on you today, so drop everything else. This is a critical time for me. Excuse me if I seem distracted or sharp with you.'

'Most bosses wouldn't bother to apologize in advance. I'm here for anything you need. Willing and, hopefully, able.'

I took the miniature recording machine I had used with Henderson and passed it to her. 'Can you do a transcript of this and make twenty copies. I'd also like you to arrange a press conference for four o' clock. Get in touch with the home affairs editors and chief crime reporters of every major newspaper and TV station to come here, plus anyone that only you, as a young lady, would know from what I would call the fringe media and you would call social or whatever. Say it's about someone at the highest level of government. And get Arthur here an hour earlier; this could get unruly. You best get lots of copies of our brochure to give out, too.

We might as well try to have them get the facts right on us and spell our names correctly.'

'This is the end, isn't it?' she said. 'Something very big is going to happen.'

'It will all become clear when you transcribe the recording. We're going to bring someone big down to earth with an almighty bump.'

'I won't let you down. Oh, and by the way, a man phoned and said for you to call this number.' She handed me a slip of paper. 'Said it was very important. Wouldn't leave his name.'

I went through to the office and started to catch up on my messages and look ahead to what Anji had booked for me. After about an hour went to make some coffee, one for me and one for Anji—she had enough to do without mollycoddling me. Norman came downstairs when he smelt the coffee and I made him one, too. We sat down and stared at the river.

'How did the meeting with Henderson go?' he asked.

'He squealed like a pig.'

'They usually do when there's nowhere left to go.'

'It was Yates,' I said. 'I've called a press conference for four.'

'Probably best that I'm not around then,' he said. 'Nothing like having an embezzler present that gets a journalist's creative juices flowing. Could deflect them from putting the emphasis on the main story. I'll wait in here just in case you need me. Should be good for business.'

'How's that?'

'All the media exposure. Says to clients that we don't

take prisoners, too, no matter how important someone is. I'll be in here if you need me.'

I took my coffee through to my office and looked at the piece of paper Anji had given me. It was a central London number that I didn't recognize. Not an existing client. Someone new with a problem. I dialled the number and when it picked up, someone at the other end said, 'Wait.' I hung on for five minutes and nothing else happened. Maybe it wasn't so important after all. I gathered up the files on my desk and took them through the connecting door to the sitting area. I didn't want anything on show, especially client names, that would interest a reporter.

I made another coffee and sat down opposite Norman.

'It won't help,' Norman said. 'Won't help your edginess. Coffee's a stimulant. Let me add a slug of brandy to it. That would help calm you down.'

'Thanks for the offer, but I need the adrenaline to flow.'

'Remember, I'm here if you need me.'

Another team bonus mark.

I stood for a while in silence and looked out at the river. The boat from Greenwich was passing by and the light of the sun flashed on the waves it created. At any other time the scene would have been idyllic, but it hardly registered today when I was so deep in thought. I wished I'd called for the press conference to be earlier, but that might not have given enough time to get everyone here. I walked back into my office and started moving furniture against the walls to create a bigger space.

It would have to be standing room only, but I doubted they would care when they heard the story.

The door opened.

In walked David Montgomery Yates. He had a gun in his hand.

'Move into the centre of the room. I don't know how good a shot I am and I don't want to miss.'

'What is it with you? Do you think you're immortal? There's a name for that, Yates. It's called hubris and it's always followed by nemesis. You can't just walk in here and shoot me and expect to get away with it.'

'Oh, yes, I can,' he said, sounding like a pantomime villain. He must have thought so, too, for he gave a little laugh. He was raving mad and a mad man is dangerous. The bullet from the gun was seeming inevitable.

'You called me earlier,' he said. 'Invited me here— thanks for the phone call by the way. The records will prove that part of the story.'

I saw his point. He had set me up and must have had a good plan for what to do next.

'You might as well put up your hands,' he said. 'Isn't that what I am supposed to say?'

'If you're going to kill me in any event, it hardly matters. That is what you intend to do, isn't it? Having come this far, you can't afford to let me live.'

'Allow me to crow a bit first,' he said. 'I'm surprised you eventually discovered the truth, but Henderson always did have a loose mouth when he was in trouble. God, but you're stubborn, Shannon. Why couldn't you let sleeping dogs lie? It's years ago, man. I arrange two attempts on your life—my contacts include low lives as well as the high up—and still you carry on. Didn't it occur to you that after a car chase and a knife attack, someone was taking all this very seriously? Anyone else would have given up by now.'

'Do you think that I went through having to help my sister commit suicide and then spend seven years in prison just to give up? You made me stubborn, Yates. I won't stop until I get justice.'

'That's why I have to stop you.'

'So what's the story you've cooked up?'

'You invite me here to talk about Mid Anglia. Big secrets that you will only tell me in person. Doesn't seem any threat so I've left my guards outside. You tell me some cock and bull story about a hit-and-run and then produce a gun. I try reasoning with you, but it doesn't work. I jump you. We struggle. The gun goes off and the unfortunate Shannon is dead. How does that sound?'

'Full of holes, but doubtless you'll lie your way out of them.'

'So the time has finally come.' He raised the gun.

The connecting door opened.

'Despite what I said, do you want more coffee?' Norman asked.

Yates fired at him. I heard a cry from behind me and a bump as Norman fell to the floor.

I leapt at Yates. Grabbed the hand holding his gun. We struggled. That part of his plan was now true. The gun was between us, his finger still on the trigger. I heard a shot. Felt warm sticky blood run over my hand and smelt the iron in it. The bastard had got me after all. I drew back from him.

Without my support, he crumpled. Slid to the floor. It had been his blood on my fingers.

The door burst open. His two guards ran in, covering each other. 'Don't move,' they shouted.

I looked behind at Norman. He was lying motionless on the floor.

'Call an ambulance,' I shouted. 'Call the police.'

'We are the police, Special Branch,' they said.

'So it's all right for me to get up off the floor then,' said Norman. 'Bloody lousy shot. He couldn't have hit that Thames ferry, let alone me.'

'You bloody fraud,' I said. 'You were playing dead.'

'But isn't fraud what we're all about? What would you have done without me? Tried to jump him and got yourself killed before you made it across the room? Bloody good job I was here.'

'If you don't mind,' said one of the bodyguards while the other was talking into what looked like a cotton bud close to his mouth, 'but we have a situation here. You, Skinny,'—Norman protested—'put your hands above your head. You, Lanky, step away from Yates and face the wall.'

Having finished on the phone, that police officer went over and looked at Yates. He turned to his comrade and shook his head. 'Better do CPR just in case. Don't want to get hung out to dry for not following procedures.'

He started pommelling Yates on the chest in a rhythm with his counting. It was a forlorn enterprise. Yates had finally gone to meet his maker. I didn't fancy his chances with St Peter.

Anji entered the room. 'What's going on?'

'I've just survived a shooting,' said Norman. 'And we're likely to be tied up for a few hours.'

She looked at the body on the floor and shivered.

'Ever handled a press conference before?' I said.

'No,' she replied, 'and I don't intend to start now. I'll give Walker a ring. It's right up her street. She'll love the publicity.'

'And if, while I'm gone, you can't handle…'

'Jesus,' she said, putting her hands on her hips. 'One of my bosses has just been shot at and the other has just killed the Home Secretary. What else is there left I can't handle?'

'Fair point,' I said.

One of the officers patted me down while his colleague kept pounding on Yates's chest. He found nothing more incriminating than a barley sugar. He looked at me pleadingly.

'Go ahead,' I said.

He took it, unwrapped it and popped it in his mouth. 'Bad taste in my mouth,' he said.

'You and me both, brother,' I said. 'You and me both.'

A screaming siren from the street told me that back up had arrived—the ambulance had won the race with extra police. There was that same brief inspection of the body and shake of the head. One of the paramedics put a contraption on Yates's chest and gave him an electric shock. Three times he tried, three times he got no reaction. They loaded him on a stretcher and finally took Yates out of my life.

When they were taking me, handcuffed, to the police station, all I could think of was that he had got away lightly. No demeaning trial, no long stint in jail. No having to spend all of it in solitary confinement for fear of what the other inmates would do. Eventually they would have got him. In the end he'd got an easy death. Justice, I supposed, but less than I hoped for.

They put me, and my trusty harmonica, in a cell while they decided who was the most senior police-man to carry out the interrogation. I didn't freak in the cell, just played, so I suppose that meant I was cured. I waited for Martin to come and help sort out the mess. Meanwhile, it never struck me that I had killed a man. Maybe it had been his finger that pulled the trigger. Maybe it was just poetic justice in the end. All I felt was a sense of relief. A long-held mission accomplished. It was a sort of emptiness I felt. Something that had been a part of me for so many years had gone.

After a while they took me to an interview room. Martin was there already. He slid a copy of the *Evening Standard* across the table to me.

'Congratulations,' he said. 'You've made the front page.'

They fired questions at me. Martin took control. Told me to say nothing and he fielded the questions. No comment was said throughout. Eventually, they left me alone with him.

'It could be worse,' he said, 'but not much. It would help if your fingerprints aren't on the gun.'

'I don't have an idea on that. It was all over so quickly. Nothing registered.'

'At least there will be evidence that he shot at Nor-man. That was a stroke of luck.'

'Norman always comes out smelling of roses. He'll have fixed up an exclusive deal with someone already.'

'They're in a panic,' Martin said. 'The Home Sec-retary is dead and they don't know whether to believe your side of the story or not. Anji has given them a copy of the transcript with Henderson. That helps, but it also gives you a motive for killing him. The media circus has started, but no one is baying for your blood. If anything, you're a bit of a hero. I'll play on that and see if we can get a movement going. The man who shot a killer. Wrongs righted. All that jazz. I'll apply for bail—you're no danger to anyone, after all—but can't guarantee anything. They might want to make an example of you—can't be seen as too lenient in the circumstances. You may need to spend a day or two here while I work on things. Can you manage that?'

'I can endure,' I said. 'You just concentrate on what you need to do and don't worry about me.'

'I'll try to get Walker and Collins involved. Get them to verify your story and speak up for you. Make it a blue on blue. Can't hurt, although nothing good ever comes of it.'

'Let's hope this is a first time,' I said.

He nodded. 'I'll leave you for a while. Come back to see you later. If you start losing it, call for me and I'll come straight here.'

He shook my hand and left the interview room. I picked up the paper and started to read the story in detail. To be fair, they weren't too negative. There was a lot of coverage of Yates being the man standing up for justice while, if my story was to be believed, he was a hypocrite and a cold-blooded killer. There was a fair degree of confusion repeating my story of all those years ago—I was a killer, too. The paper trod a fine path between condemning me and treating me as a hero and the man who in the past had opened up the debate on euthanasia. It was out of my hands now.

They interrogated me two more times and then got what little I told them—as cleared with Martin—down on paper as a statement for me to sign.

'Well,' I said, 'what now?'

'You're lucky,' the woman currently interrogating me said. 'The only fingerprints on the gun were those of Yates. Your story seems to hold. Your solicitor is making an almighty fuss and Walker vouches for you, although added you were always attracting trouble and could be a pain in the arse at times.'

'Good to have friends,' I said, 'although I was hoping for a slightly less truthful character reference. What about Collins?'

'No one seems to be able to find him. Gone AWOL.'

Didn't sound good. Sam's duplicity had been a big shock to him. All his plans dashed. He was going to take a while to get over it, if ever.

Then came the good news.

'We can't hold you any longer with no evidence, especially with the media storm that's going around. You're free to go. My advice at this stage is normally don't do it again, but that doesn't seem to be a possibility.'

I walked out of the police station a free man. In every sense.

THIRTY-TWO

'I THOUGHT YOU'D BE wearing your normal smug expression,' Walker said.

'I'm trying to de-smug from now on. Only seems to get me in worse trouble.'

We were sitting in the empty lounge bar at the first pub that was open.

'After what I had to do to Chris?'

'Omelettes and eggs, Shannon. Omelettes and eggs.'

'You think I let her off easy, don't you, but what else could I have done? I gave her the option of building that relationship with Chris, but I guess we both knew how it would play out.'

'She was a user. Maybe that was the real reason she didn't get promotion above the rank of inspector. Nothing to do with the feud with Henderson after all.'

'Still doesn't make me feel any better.'

'You'll get over it. Same as Chris will. He's a survivor. I suppose that his retirement is out of the window and my promotion, too.'

'You're taking this better than I thought.'

'Sometimes there are things more important in life than climbing the greasy pole and hitting your head on the glass ceiling.'

'Wow! Did you have a bad dream or something last night?'

'No. A good one.'

I downed my drink, looked at her and shook my head. 'You will never stop surprising me.'

'Nor you me.'

'Might be a good basis for lowering our defences and getting to know each other better.'

'Maybe.'

Sometimes in life you have to risk failure if you want to succeed enough. Key question: was this one of those times?

THIRTY-THREE

THE NEXT WEEK bore out Norman's view that the publicity would be good for business. We had enquiries coming at us from everywhere. It looked like that if this kept up we might have to go for more staff, but that might have meant me distancing myself from the sharp end, so I parked that idea.

We started on a case of money laundering and put the others in some sort of order of priority. I said to Norman that this was what could happen when you do something pro bono. He nodded his head sagely and told me not to do it again.

Collins came round—Walker was on holiday and he was in the thick of it. He had reverted to type. His hair was unruly, his suit creased, his white shirt looked like it was overdue for washing.

'I don't know whether to thank you or not, Shannon.' He was back to calling me Shannon again, too.

I got from the bottom drawer of my filing cabinet a bottle of finest malt that a grateful client had given me and poured us both a generous measure. He drank his in one go and banged the glass on the table as an order for a refill. I topped up his glass.

'Don't think too badly of yourself,' I said. 'We all get taken in some time. It's how you cope that is important.'

'No fool like an old fool,' he mused.

'If it's any consolation, Sam took us all in.'

'It's not,' he said.

'Came so very close to getting away with it, too.'

'It never occurred to me that she had another side to her. I suppose I'm lucky to be out of it. She would have dumped me when she thought she was totally in the clear. Headed off to the Costa del Crime or wherever and never looked back at the casualties end route.'

He looked so tired, so scrawny, so pathetic.

'When did you last eat?' I said.

'God knows. Doesn't seem important somehow.'

'I'll buy you lunch at Toddy's. A rare steak and a glass of decent red will make you feel better.'

He shook his head.

'I don't take no for an answer,' I said.

'Tell me something I don't know.'

I asked Anji to get us a taxi and warned her that I could be a while. She nodded understandingly. Said she could hold the fort, she was well used to it by now.

Half an hour later, Collins was eating like a trencherman and savouring the Malbec rather than glugging it down. His rehabilitation had begun.

When I arrived back, Anji had a message from Mary Jo. She was calling in the favour. Reminded me of the promise to come when she called. She'd booked me a flight to New York the next day and a hotel—no way was she having me stay with her. I was to meet her in Central Park, like two spooks putting a clandestine world to rights. I got Norman to cover for me and started to pack a bag, which was difficult because I didn't know for how long I'd be staying or what the weather was like in New York at this time of year. I couldn't complain at

Mary Jo issuing orders—we'd never have cracked the case without her, although maybe there wouldn't have been a case without her and her hacking skills, and Collins's loose mouth, of course.

I HAD ONE more appointment to keep before jetting off. The lovely Dr Morgan.

It was a warm day and she was wearing a long cotton dress with a zebra print. Not exactly a classic shrink outfit. Did this mark some change in our relationship?

She was as cool as the previous times I'd seen her. I relaxed quickly and easily and settled back on the sofa.

'Who's been a busy boy then?' she said.

'You've read the reports?'

'And seen the television coverage. One can hardly breathe without seeing your face or bumping into someone who wants to discuss it. You're the talk of the town. How has it been for you?'

'A media circus with me playing the ringmaster.'

'Any regrets?'

'Only that it should have happened a lot earlier.'

'Do we have closure?'

'Yes. It's an episode of my life that won't haunt me anymore.'

'Good. We are making progress.'

'Where do we go from here? Keep playing the harmonica?'

'Can't do any harm.'

'More sessions?' I asked.

'I'm reluctant to have too many more sessions. There's a risk you might get dependent. You're so close to getting over the PTSD, I want you to achieve it on your own. I could book you in for more sessions, but we might just be prolonging the recovery phase.'

'You'll never get rich that way.'

'I wouldn't be doing this job if I wanted to get rich. I do it to help people. But we're supposed to be talking about you, not me.'

'I thought you were supposed to be unconventional.'

'You're enjoying this, aren't you?'

'Just a bit of fun. I can't help it. Just the way I am. But, seriously, I'm grateful for what you've done. I feel so much better to know what the problems are. Only the lift to crack now and I suppose that has to be down to me.'

She nodded. She knew she had done her job.

'One last question.'

'And that is?'

'Can I shake your hand and kiss you on the cheek?'

'It would be my pleasure.'

And so we parted.

A DAY LATER and I was ready to go. The cab was waiting outside to take me to Heathrow. I said my goodbyes to Norman, who grinned, and Anji, who kissed me on the cheek and wished me good luck. Somewhat strangely, Arthur was there, too, who insisted on shaking my hand.

Was there something they knew and I didn't? But then again that wouldn't be unusual.

Here we go. Onwards and upwards.

THIRTY-FOUR

A CAB FROM THE airport took me to the hotel Mary Jo had booked. The room was sanitized and standard against any design feature that might have given it an individual touch. Apart from the connecting door to the adjoining room, I could have been back in Melchester where the adventure started. Wouldn't it be ironic if it ended with a hotel, too?

I took a cold shower to wake me up. I was already suffering the effects of jet lag. Since Mary Jo and I were due to meet in Central Park, I didn't figure the suit was necessary. I put on a pair of blue jeans and a dark blue T-shirt that had Bob Dylan on the front in all his glory. I topped this off with a black leather bomber jacket and thought that would cover the immediate tests that Mary Jo might have in store for me.

I walked over to Central Park in the serene spring sunshine. Serene but for the yellow cab horn blasts, vocal pedestrians shouting into mobile phones and musically challenged buskers that orchestrated their exultations into the afternoon.

Having orientated myself in the city, I managed to find the right area of the park and approach from the right direction with only minor help from my mobile phone's GPS.

However, when I saw the scene in front of me I assumed I'd managed to mislay my sense of direction once again.

DCI Cherry Walker was sitting on the grass, legs curled to one side of her body, like a mermaid perched on a rock. She didn't need to be singing a siren song to lure me in, though. She'd been doing that subconsciously for many a year and now I was ready to surrender, although hopefully not to a rocky ending.

It was disorientating, to say the least, to see her so out of context. I probably would have gawped less if I'd seen a gorilla enjoying a sunny picnic in Central Park instead. Nevertheless, there was no mistaking her, sitting there opposite Mary Jo, on a chequered picnic blanket. She was sipping a red cup of what, from the bottle in the shade, I could only assume was American fizz, but it could have been a crystal flute judging by the delicate sips she took every so often.

Aware that I'd been standing there for at least a minute, by all appearances gawking at two random women in the park, I looked surreptitiously around (yup, a couple of pushchair-wielding mums considering me warily) and added myself into the scene in front of me.

I looked at her, the calculated look that it had taken me years to perfect, the look that was imperceptible to the naked eye, but masked powerful thoughts and feelings.

'Shannon, what are you looking at me like that for?' Damn!

Women really do seem to have evolved very quickly to be able to see imperceptible things.

A little laugh. 'I don't believe I was looking at anything, Cherry. Walker. I mean Walker.'

'You know, it amazes me that a person like you can be so terrible at lying.'

'I think I've progressed past lying. Now I just like to think of it as acting. It's integral to my job. And to my survival most days.'

I was still looking at her. The realization wouldn't pass and it wouldn't let me drag my telling eyes off her! Why have men evolved so slowly that they haven't developed the ability to look away from women when it would give the game away?

I switched my glance to Mary Jo, but, to my surprise, I saw a shining smile directed back at me. After many, many years of seeing no such facial expression from this person, I understood that she knew. In fact, I wondered if she'd known longer than I had.

'I really get the feeling I'm missing something here, folks. Care to let me in on the joke?'

Mary Jo giggled (again a previously unheard of sound effect). 'I'm going to take a little walk, falafel calls.'

'Wait,' I said. 'Before you go, do you mind telling me what's going on?'

'I'm just acting as a catalyst. Someone who can unlock the chemistry between you two. To anyone outside, the feelings are easy to understand. Whenever the two of you are together the atmosphere is electric. I'm just giving it a gentle nudge.'

'Nick, is there something wrong?' said Walker. I noted the use of my first name and took it as a good sign. 'Sit down and have a glass of Californian fizz.'

She poured the wine into a beaker that matched her

own. Handed it to me. I took a sip. Mary Jo had some-how managed to keep it cool. The local fizz was good.

'What are we supposed to do?' I asked.

'Bit too early to ride off together into the sunset, but that's the general idea. I have to say something to you. This cannot ever be repeated. For the first time I'm going to be completely open with you.'

'You have my promise on confidentiality.'

'Come closer,' she said. 'I want to feel you support-ing me. Whatever I say.'

I moved closer to her and put my arm around her. She leant back into me, facing the front so that I couldn't see her face.

'I'm tired, Nick. Tired of climbing the greasy pole by standing on peoples' backs. Tired of a job where we don't ever seem to make progress against the bad guys—it's like that snake thing where you chop off one head and two more grow from the wound. I'm tired of going home each night to an empty flat and eating on my own. And, finally, I'm tired of life—there has to be something more. Doesn't there?'

'We could fix the job. We need to expand. Someone like you would bring all the expertise and experience we need. Do you want to join us?'

'Oh, Nick. For someone so intelligent, you can be so dumb at times. It's not about the job—well only partly. I love you, Nick. Have done for years now. But I couldn't take you away from Arlene. I'd like to start a new life with you.' She moved away from me and turned round to look me in the eye. 'There. I've said it. You can start laughing now.'

'Let's look at this rationally. Do a cost-benefit analysis—pros on the left, cons on the right. So—'

'Shannon!'

'Only joking.'

She smiled back at me, not bashfully, but triumphantly, this as much a victory for her as it was for me. Unknowingly, over the past few months we'd both been shaping the same story between us, and we both seemed relieved it had finally come to fruition.

Mary Jo returned, brandishing three falafel sticks and a knowing smile. She made her excuses and left us alone.

We quickly stood in order to retreat from the growing pigeon unrest and walked off into the afternoon sun hand in hand, and falafel in hand.

'I'm in room 401,' I said. 'I'm guessing you're in 402.'

'How did you know that?'

'Because Mary Jo thinks of everything.'

THIRTY-FIVE

I HAD DECIDED to give Mid Anglia one final visit to catch up on Morag's news on the Caribbean cruise and complete the formalities. I entered the building and stood stock still. The conversation pit was empty, a sight I had never seen before. Where was striding ahead with a beacon into the future workplace? I passed my card across the sensor. Nothing happened. I guessed the reason. Whoever was in charge had cancelled my privileges. Fast worker. I called Morag and asked for her help. She appeared a few minutes later looking flustered.

'Sorry about this, but the whole place is in chaos.'

I kissed her on the cheek and said, 'What has happened to the pit?'

'It's to be converted to meeting rooms. Till then an edict has been issued suspending its use. Things have changed since you were last here. New broom. New regime. Out with old. Zero tolerance. Come on, let's have a coffee and I'll tell you all about it.'

She led me to the escalators—I'll have to brave a lift at some point—and we entered the cafeteria. Another difference—fewer people sitting there chatting and making out it's a working meeting. Still did espresso, though.

We took our coffees to a window table and Morag scooped up the froth as displacement activity while she gathered her thoughts.

'I suspect a lot of people here will be thinking better the devil you know. I've still got my job, but the spec has changed somewhat. Nothing must get in the way of work. Productivity is the god. Everyone is required to list out each morning the tasks that must be completed that day. The new CC does a walk round and inspects a random sample to check. He does the same thing at close of play—although I suppose you can't use the term play any more—and checks on tasks completed. We have gone from passive to proactive.'

'Not a bad thing in itself,' I said.

'It's like being back at school. I keep thinking he'll assign blackboard monitors.'

'Is he likely to give me any trouble?'

'He's giving everyone else trouble. I can't see him making an exception for you.'

'Got any weak spots?'

'Not that anyone has spotted so far. Plays everything by the book. Covers his back that way.'

'How has your job changed?'

'I'm just a cog in the machine. Henderson may have been hard work, but at least he made me feel like an adult. There's no room for personalities with this man.' She paused. 'You know Norman has offered me a job?'

'I didn't, but it meets with my approval. We need more staff and, if you joined, I could develop Anji. With training, she could be good in the field. Surely the distance would be a problem?'

'He's also asked me to move in with him.'

'Wow! Fast worker. What's your answer?'

'I've agreed to give it a trial. Take a sabbatical. Move in with him, rent my house out. What do you think?'

'At the risk of getting into minutiae, what about the cats?'

'Cats are never minutiae. He's said I can bring them along.'

'Be good to have cats around again. The last two didn't fare well—as part of your induction I'll tell you about the Old brook case.'

'And so?'

'You'll fit in great. Welcome aboard.' I shook her hand to seal the deal. 'The cruise must have gone well.'

'Norman is a real gentleman. A perfect escort for what was a wonderful experience. I haven't enjoyed myself so much for many a long time. I've lots of pictures. I'll show them to you when we have time.' She drank the last of her coffee. 'We need to get you to the CC or you'll be late, and that would get you off on the wrong foot.'

'Lead me to him.'

IT WAS THE same office, but transformed. The place had a lived-in look. This was a workspace, not an area to sit and preen. There was a laptop on the desk—was this the end of tablets?—and two trays marked *In* and *Out*. In between was the current file he was working on. It was another cog in the machine. He would have made a great Victorian mill owner. I half expected to hear a whip crack.

He was sitting behind the desk looking intimidating. It was the same black uniform, but a different sort of man. He stood as I entered. He was tall—although all policemen had to be tall in those days—and looked bruised and battered. This was a man who had moved up the ranks the hard way and woe betide anyone who got in his way. He had at least one break of his skew-whiff nose and a scar below his eye on the left cheek. Knife, I reckoned. I shook his hand and sat in the seat opposite his desk, once he had sat down himself.

'Morag said something about formalities,' he said.

'Just making sure you were happy,' I said.

'Of course. You found the culprit and paid us back half a million. What is there not to be happy about?'

I took the document from my jacket pocket and passed it across the desk.

'This is the contract your predecessor agreed to.'

'Late-lamented predecessor I expect some are saying,' he said with a wisp of a grin so small as to be missed unless concentrating.

He looked at the document and then up to me.

'This gives you ten per cent of any fraud found and of any money recovered.'

'So that means £50,000 for the embezzlement. I don't intend to charge for the reptile fund scam, selling the tablets or the cost of collusion on the tenders. Seemed small beer by comparison. I don't intend to charge the Federation, either. Don't like taking money from the little people. The people who are forgotten about too often in these types of crime.'

'But £50,000,' he said.

'And I expect you're happy at being reimbursed for the fraud.'

'Of course. But I'm not sure I can pay that large a sum.'

'You don't have to,' I said.

'That's OK then,' he said, a look of relief wafting across his face.

'You've paid it already. When we transferred the

money back to your account, we took our fee at the same time. So nothing for you to worry about. We were sure that a man so upright like yourself—and one who is a stickler for following the rules—wouldn't renege on a deal. Henderson did that once. I had no respect for him after that.'

He was silent for a moment, mulling over his next move.

'And, of course, you would not like the negative publicity if it was known you'd gone back on a deal.'

'Ah, but you've signed the Official Secrets Act.'

'Quite right, but I couldn't stop some unscrupulous person leaking it to the media.'

'You play dirty, Shannon.'

'You wouldn't be the first person to say that and won't be the last. But I play by the rules. My handshake is worth a ream of legal documents.'

'Morag said that I would understand where you were coming from. That you were a man of honour. You know, I can't help but liking you, Shannon. You've brought down one CC; I don't intend to be the next one. You know they've charged Henderson with accessory after the fact for murder?'

'I would have hoped for nothing less. For covering up a crime and denying justice for all that time, he deserves everything he gets.'

'So you can play hard as well as soft—protecting the little people? I suppose I shouldn't ask how you got the money back.'

'You suppose right.' Time to change the subject. 'What are your chances of turning this place around?'

'I'll do it in time, but I'm not sure how much time the powers that be will give me. As always, they want

instant results. I can easily get rid of the pit and the putting green, but to change a culture takes longer. Too
long? Who knows?'

'Once you've sorted out the reptile fund you don't
need to worry about the accounts function. Milly-
Molly-Mandy are doing a great job. No obvious weaknesses there.'

'Milly-Molly-Mandy?'

'The three ladies who work there. You should get to
know them. They stick to the systems, but it was the
systems that were wrong. However, if you want some
help, we'll happily come in and do whatever you need
to tighten up.'

'For a lot less than £50,000, I hope?'

'Daily rate plus expenses. We don't take advantage
of clients in need. And, as you've seen, we agree everything in advance.'

'If you want a testimonial, you can count on me.'

'And vice versa. I think you can pull off this job.
Might be a long journey, but each journey starts with
small steps.'

'If I ever need a philosopher, I know where to come.'

'One thing you can do for me. Make it clear to the
troops that I'm not a target.'

'Will do.'

We shook hands and I left him to cleanse the Augean stables.

ON DEPARTING I forced myself to take the lift. There
was just one other person in there with me—a tall man
with cropped hair who might be a plain-clothes cop.

He smiled as I got in—if he was a cop, it looked like I had been forgiven.

The lift doors closed and it started to move. So far so good. Then it happened. Between the fourth and third floor it juddered to a halt. The man looked at me and I shrugged my shoulders. He pressed a warning button and we waited for something to happen. Nothing did. I took out my harmonica.

Three hours later the lift began to move and stopped on the third floor. The doors opened and the man ran out clutching his ears.

'If I ever hear "St. Louis Blues" again, I think I'll disembowel myself.'

How ungrateful can you get? Still, it worked for me. OK, there were a few bum notes in the first hour, but I was faultless during the last two. You can't please all of the people all of the time. Shouldn't stop you trying though.

EPILOGUE

IT SEEMED FITTING that everything should end as it began. On the way home I stopped at the same petrol station as on my first trip back. bought some flowers and headed back the slow way to Docklands. Stopped at the same spot as before. Got out and placed the flowers at the bottom of an oak tree.

'Well, sis,' I said. 'We did it and the driver is now roasting in hell. I think it is a door in our lives that can now be closed for good and we can move on to new chapters. See you in heaven, if I'm good enough. Maybe there are a few people who will put in a good word for me, but you can never tell what the future holds for you.'

* * * * *